STRANGE NEW WORLD
STRANGE NEW WORLD
STRANGE NEW WORLD

STRANGE NEW WORLD
STRANGE NEW WORLD
STRANGE NEW WORLD
STRANGE NEW WORLD

RACHEL VINCENT

DELACORTE PRESS

Visit us on the Web! GetUnderlined.com

Educators and librarians, for a variety of teaching tools, visit us at
RHTeachersLibrarians.com

Library of Congress Cataloging-in-Publication Data
Name: Vincent, Rachel, author.
Title: Strange new world / Rachel Vincent.
Description: First edition. | New York : Delacorte Press, [2018] | Sequel to: Brave new girl. | Summary: Dahlia thinks all of her clones have been destroyed, but then discovers that one still exists—Waverly Whitmore, who is teenage royalty, a media sensation with millions of fans—who has no idea that she is a clone.
Identifiers: LCCN 2017043433 | ISBN 978-0-399-55249-6 (hc) |
ISBN 978-0-399-55251-9 (ebook)
Subjects: | CYAC: Cloning—Fiction. | Genetic engineering—Fiction. |
Science fiction.
Classification: LCC PZ7.V7448 Sv 2018 | DDC [Fic]—dc23

The text of this book is set in 11.5-point Electra LH.

Printed in the United States of America
10 9 8 7 6 5 4 3 2 1
First Edition

To my husband,
whose dedication to my career has let me live my dream.
I want the same thing for you.

AT ONE POINT OR another, most parents declare their daughter to be the most beautiful girl in the world. When I was four, I learned how to use the wall screen to search for my name, which was when I discovered that my parents might actually have been right. People loved them. People loved me.

Other girls wanted to *be* me.

I didn't figure out that most kids don't see their picture on national news feeds and gossip sites until I was six or seven. That was around the time I discovered that photographers didn't follow most families when they went out for dinner or to the theater. That most kids didn't have a full-time security detail.

When I was nine, my father gave me a beta version of the e-glass technology my parents' company had invented. I was the third person in the world to own one.

The dress I wore to my twelfth birthday party sold out within minutes of the footage airing. The next day, half the girls in my class were wearing it.

I never bought off the rack again.

The year I turned fourteen, Network 4 offered me my own show. Twelve episodes per season, and cameras would follow me around for one week every month. The demand, they said, was huge. If I gave people a window into my life, they might stop trying to tear down my walls.

They didn't mention that the ratings would make the network a fortune.

The day we started filming, I had a brand-new wardrobe, each piece designed specifically for me. I had a hair and makeup crew to create a signature look, using products from my debut cosmetics line. I felt like a princess. Like the most beautiful girl in the world. I thought I was special. Unique.

I've never been more wrong about anything in my life.

ONE

WAVERLY

With my foot tapping an impatient rhythm on the floor, I poke the air in the direction of the transparent screen covering the far wall of my bedroom. A clock appears in the center. It's 12:08 a.m. Seren Locke's birthday party has just ended, and my friends will be posting about it on their way home.

I flop back onto my bed. I'm not going to look. Only a loser would obsess over a party she missed.

For two whole minutes, I stare at the ceiling of my room. Then, with a groan, I give in and poke one of the icons on the screen. A long stream of messages covers my wall. To the left of each message is a photo of the person who posted it. Some of the messages are pictures. Others are short video clips, playing silently because I've disabled the sound; I don't want to hear about all the fun my friends had without me.

My bedroom door slides open with a whisper, startling

me, and I swipe my hand at the screen, closing the message stream. The e-glass fogs over, then becomes transparent again, showing the wall behind it, which is painted in subtle stripes of ivory and honey milk. Or, as my fiancé describes the colors, white and a little less white.

"Knock, knock," my father says from the doorway, though the door is open. I've set it to let him in but to keep my mother out. Of course, she can override the settings, but the fact that I want to keep her out is enough to make my point.

My dad doesn't say anything, but he saw my screen. He knows I was secretly stalking my friends. "What, no camera crew today?" He glances around my room in mock disbelief as he steps inside, carrying a covered tray.

"What would be the point?" I get up, and the pink-and-white comforter smooths itself out, leaving a flawless, wrinkle-free finish. "Why would the world want to see me sitting here staring at the wall?"

He smiles as he sets the tray on my dresser. "The world wants to see everything 'the people's princess' does."

I shrug. I have fun playing princess on camera, but my father knows me like my followers and cyberstalkers never will.

"You know, we have servants to do that." I lift my chin at the tray.

"I am aware. But when your daughter already has everything, sometimes the only thing left to give her is a personal touch."

"That is so cheesy." I roll my eyes, but I can't hide my smile.

"Actually, it's chocolaty." He pulls the lid from the tray,

revealing two steaming mugs of something divinely sweet-smelling. "Organic Swiss cocoa."

"*Mom's* cocoa?"

He nods. "First shipment of the season."

Okay, yes, it's just hot chocolate. Except that the cocoa beans this chocolate comes from are organically harvested from a farm overseas. Grown in actual dirt and watered by hand. Harvested by hand. Dried and processed by hand. Packaged by hand.

All that specialized labor makes the cocoa insanely expensive.

My mother has a cup with breakfast every morning.

"And . . ." My father lifts a smaller dome lid from an opaque glass bowl at the back of the tray. "Hand-cut chocolate-hazelnut marshmallows."

"Does Mom know you dug into her stash?" I take a mug and use a tiny pair of tongs to drop two large, fluffy marshmallows into it. A glance at the thermostat on the side of the mug tells me it's set to keep the contents at perfect sipping temperature.

"We're celebrating. Let me worry about your mother." My dad picks up his own mug, then settles into my desk chair as I sit on the edge of my bed. "I assume you've seen the ratings?"

"The second they were posted." I consider a modest shrug, but modesty isn't really my thing. So I give him a huge grin. "Highest viewership of a reality show ever recorded. The proposal episode broke the record."

"My daughter, the most famous person in the world." He

takes a sip. "So why aren't you swinging from the chandelier?"

I give him a look. He knows exactly why I'm sulking. How ridiculous is it that I am the single most valuable asset on network and I'm *grounded*?

"Waverly, are you really going to let one missed party overshadow the good news? Why wouldn't she let you go, anyway?"

I tuck my legs beneath me on the bed and blow into my mug. "I honestly have no idea." My father arches one brow at me, but I talk over his skepticism. "No, really. She just said I couldn't go. No reason. She won't even talk about it."

"That's strange."

Normally, my mother is logical to a fault, but . . . "It's like she has something against Seren. She grounded me last year on his birthday too." I pluck a marshmallow from my cocoa and bite into it, frowning as I chew. "And she dragged us all on vacation during Sofia's birthday party this year, remember? Maybe it's not just Seren she doesn't like, but the whole Locke family. . . ."

"I think you're reading a little too much into it," my dad says.

"Or maybe it's Seren and Sofia's mother. The Administrator could creep anyone out." I take the first sip from my mug. The cocoa is decadently sweet and creamy. The kind of thing I should be enjoying on camera.

"So why is missing this party such a tragedy, anyway? There's still a cyber-blackout at Lakeview, right?"

6

My silent sip tells him more than actually answering would.

"Ah. That's it," he says. "What happens in Lakeview stays in Lakeview, right? Because of the blackout."

There are only two parties a year in Lakeview—Seren's birthday party and Sofia's birthday party—and because the Lakeview compound is a digital dark zone, you can do whatever you want without worrying about video showing up online. While you're there, it's like you don't really exist, except to the other people at the party. It's liberating, in an oddly low-tech way.

At least, that's what I've heard.

"Waverly, we can cancel the show if you're feeling overexposed," my father says, his brows lowered in concern. "I said from the beginning, as soon as it stops being fun—"

"No! I love the show." Even though it means the entire world sees everything that happens in my life. My mom actually got hate mail for grounding me from Seren's party, which feels a little bit like a victory. "Besides, the ink ceremony is tomorrow, and our design is going to make history. The ratings are going to be even higher than they were for the proposal."

I smile just thinking about that episode. Hennessy put so much work into keeping his proposal a secret from me. Into truly surprising me. And for those few minutes, it had felt like we were the only two people in the world, in spite of the cameras. He'd reserved the entire National Garden, and while I'd stood there, surrounded by a thousand tulips—my signature flower—he'd dropped to one knee with a tulip in his hand, and—

I blink, shaking off the memory, and find my father watching me, the ghost of a smile haunting his mouth.

"Speaking of which . . . ," I say before he can get all emotional and remind me that we can still delay the wedding by a couple of years. "I've decided on a dress. I haven't even shown Mom yet." With my mug in one hand, I swipe in the direction of my screen and it lights up, showing every app I left running when I turned it off. I gesture toward the one in the top right corner, and it zooms into the center of the wall, showing a two-foot-tall interactive image of my wedding dress.

"One hundred percent," I command as I stand and set my mug on my nightstand. Fabric rustles behind me as my comforter smooths itself out again, and as the dress on the screen grows to its full size, I shrug out of the robe I'm wearing over a black leotard designed to work with the app.

"Dressing room." I step in front of the glass, and the image on-screen turns the reflection of my bedroom into an old-fashioned dressing room, with the last few ensembles I bought hanging on hooks on the walls, waiting to be tried on. In the center of the screen, my dress rotates until I'm looking at the back. I hold my hands up, and the dress rises, then falls over my reflection.

On-screen, I'm wearing my wedding dress.

"Oh . . ." My father stands and steps forward until his

image is in the dressing room with me. It's strange to see him here. I shop for clothes with my mom all the time, but rarely with my dad. The look on his face is exactly what I was hoping for. "You look *beautiful*, sweetheart."

But he hasn't seen anything yet.

"Hair," I command. "Final selection." The image on-screen blurs for an instant, then comes back into focus. My hair is now swept up into a cluster of dark, glossy curls, dusted with highly reflective glitter. I turn, and my reflection on the screen turns to show him the back of my updo.

"Makeup," I say as I face the mirror again. "Semifinal selection, 'Morning Dew.'"

My face blurs on the screen, then refocuses with one of my favorite looks in place—a natural-but-better look with rosy cheeks, nude lipstick, subtle contouring, and a slightly more dramatic eye, to draw people's focus where I want it: to my best feature.

"Very elegant," my father says. That's one of only three or four phrases he has to describe any look I show him, but he means it. I can see that in his eyes.

"Thanks." I swipe my hand across the screen and the app minimizes; then the screen fogs over and returns to its translucent sleep-state. "We've gotten a lot of requests for a glimpse of the dress, but I decided to keep it secret." I shrug into my robe again and reclaim my cocoa. "It'll play better on the show if everyone's anticipating the reveal."

"Well, I think anything you choose would look wonderful

on you, but that is truly stunning, Waverly." He frowns. "I won't tell your mother I've seen it, but you should show her soon, or you'll hurt her feelings."

"I would have shown her tonight if she hadn't grounded me."

A beep echoes from my father's pocket, and I swallow a lump of disappointment when he stands. "Work calls," he says, pulling his tablet out to glance at the new message. It looks backward to me, seen through the reverse side of the transparent device, and I don't bother trying to read it. Most of his work stuff is superdull.

"Thanks for the cocoa." I lift my mug in a gesture of appreciation as he heads for the hall.

"I can't believe my baby's about to get married," he says as the door opens. "You know, we could put this off for a couple more years. You *just* turned eighteen."

But I don't want to wait. I can't *afford* to wait. "You heard the doctor."

"I did. And I understand. I just want you to be happy. Good night, sweetheart." But his happy/supportive expression slips into concern a second before the door slides closed.

Alone again, I swipe at the screen to wake up the glass. "Send someone to remove this tray."

"Command received," a sexy male voice responds. "A server will come for it immediately."

I open my public message feed again. Normally after a party, it would be filled with video clips and pics showing my friends dancing, eating, and generally looking gorgeous and glamorous, but thanks to the cyber-ban from Lakeview, all I get are text messages spoken into their tablets and pics and vids taken in their cars on the way home.

Before I open the messages, I disable the activity notification so no one will know I'm low-key obsessed with a party I didn't get to attend. As far as they're all concerned, I'm much too busy planning the wedding of the century to bother.

I poke the first post. It's from a very gossipy classmate.

Surprise of the night! Waverly Whitmore shows up!
Rumor has it she was wearing a *borrowed* dress,
but she *owned* the look tonight!

Wait, what?

Frowning, I poke message after message, watching videos of groups of my friends pouring champagne in the backs of their cars while they discuss the party on their way home. They rate the menu and the guest list. They dish about some scandalous invasion of the event by Lakeview soldiers searching for a fugitive—*what?*—and there's an entire text thread dedicated to couples who turned the dance floor into a make-out session.

But then there it is again. Another mention of me being at the party.

It's a joke. It has to be. My friends are pranking me because I missed the best party of the year. But it's not funny.

Irritated, I close the public stream and check my private messages. While I'm reading, a clone comes into my room and removes the tray and used dishes so quietly I hardly even realize she's there. I glance at the name embroidered on her uniform, but the only part that registers is the number twenty at the end. The names don't matter and the faces are interchangeable, because all our servants are from the same batch, which matured two years ago.

Clones don't make eye contact, and they rarely speak. Hennessy thinks it's something to do with the cloning process. That replicating a genome somehow damages it, creating servants who are people, obviously, yet *lesser*, mentally and physically, than the rest of us. They're incapable of complex thought or activities, other than the tasks they've been trained to do through years and years of repetition on the Lakeview compound.

As the servant leaves with the tray, a message appears on the screen from the network that airs my show. I open it, and an image takes over half of the glass. It's the new ad for the season finale—the wedding episode. Hennessy and me, looking hot as hell, his arms wrapped around me, this smoldering look in his eyes that millions of girls wish he would turn on them.

But he's all mine.

The ad flashes, "Don't miss the wedding of the century— a Network 4 exclusive! Lady Waverly Whitmore + Sir Hennessy Chapman Forever!"

I squeal with delight and swipe the screen off. Then I change into my new pajamas and grab my tablet on the way out of my room, tapping through the menu as I head down the hall to show my mother the ad.

She's not in her room. She's not in her office. But then I hear her voice and feel a draft from downstairs. The front door is wide open.

"Waverly Whitmore!" my mother snaps. "Get out of the car!"

Huh?

I jog down the stairs, clutching the glass tablet, but I forget all about my mother when I look past her to see Hennessy getting out of a long black car. "Look! They've got it loaded already!" I hold up the tablet to show him the image. "Have you seen it yet? It'll be on every billboard in the city by tomorrow night."

But then my focus settles on the girl standing next to him, and my arm falls limp at my side. My jaw drops. "What the *hell* is going on?"

The girl standing next to my fiancé? She's wearing my face.

TWO

DAHLIA

Seeing Waverly shouldn't shock me. I grew up surrounded by girls who look exactly like me, and she's just another identical. Except that everyone here believes Waverly is an individual, and if she's Waverly Whitmore, I can't possibly be.

I was only able to escape Lakeview by pretending to be Waverly. But being seen with her has blown my cover.

Run.

Every muscle in my body demands that I flee, even though I'm still wearing Margo's flouncy dress and stiltlike heels.

I glance at Trigger 17 and the tension in his frame tells me he's thinking the same thing. But then he gives a small shake of his head, and I follow his gaze to the edge of the broad, tiered lawn sloping up like the mountain this town is built on. The yard is completely enclosed by a ten-foot brick wall. The gate has closed behind us.

Even if none of that were true . . . we've already been seen.

"Mom?" Waverly says, and my focus is drawn to my clone again. I can't look away. She had Poppy's smile, but now she's wearing Iris's scowl, her eyes wide with confusion, like Violet's used to get when she didn't understand something.

Somehow, she looks like most of my friends, yet like none of them.

Waverly is all that remains of five thousand girls cloned from the same genome. *My* genome. And until seconds ago, she had no idea any of the rest of us existed.

Based on her stunned expression, I suspect she still hasn't fully grasped the truth.

"I . . . I . . . ," Hennessy stammers, glancing from Waverly to me, then back.

"Mom!" my clone shouts at the tall, elegant woman still staring at me with shock shining in an oddly familiar set of brown eyes. This is Waverly's mother. Or rather, *my* mother. Though the concept of a genetic ancestor still feels so absurd that I can hardly believe she exists. That she developed Waverly *inside her body* rather than plucking her from an incubator like a normal nanny does.

But the mother of an individual isn't the same thing as a nanny. Right? I'm not sure what a mother does when she's done being a human incubator.

This mother looks like Waverly. Like me. Yet not *just* like us.

Finally, the mother blinks. Her eyes gain a hard focus.

Then she marches past me, the ends of her silky pink robe fluttering, and peers into the car we've just gotten out of.

Hennessy's sister is still asleep in the backseat. Waverly's mother closes the door softly, then leans down and speaks to the driver through the front window. "Take Margo home. Make no stops. Then come straight back here. Do you understand?"

The driver nods. The car rolls around the circular drive, following the metallic cruise strip built into the pavement. The gate opens and the car pulls onto the street, and for just a second, I consider grabbing Trigger's hand and running after it. But the gate is already closing. We won't make it.

Even if we could, where would we go?

I *do not* understand this city, where some people are individuals born from other humans and some are clones with faces familiar to me from Lakeview—the city Trigger and I have just fled for our lives.

"Inside. All of you." Waverly's mother waves an arm at the open front door of her house. "Let's get this sorted out in private."

Waverly's frown deepens. "What . . . ? Who . . . ?"

"Now!"

My clone and Hennessy head inside, confusion written all over their faces. I glance at Trigger 17. I have no idea what to do, and for the first time since I met him, he doesn't seem to either.

"Let's go." Waverly's mother looks like she wants to push

us inside, but she hovers several feet away, as if she's afraid to get too close. "I can't have you standing out here where anyone could see you."

I don't know who could possibly see us behind a ten-foot brick wall. But Trigger and I are wanted by the Administrator and the city of Lakeview, and there's nowhere to run. And now that the initial shock of seeing Waverly has worn off, I realize I'm covered in goose bumps beneath Margo's dress. And my teeth are chattering. It's *cold* in Mountainside.

Trigger shrugs. He's willing to follow my lead, but I can tell from the way his right hand hovers near the pocket of his uniform that he's armed and he won't hesitate to defend us if we're threatened.

He follows me up the curving steps through a tall, arched set of double doors into a two-story, marble-floored foyer, where Hennessy and Waverly are waiting. Waverly's gaze is glued to my face, shock and anger warring for control of her features.

A shiver travels down my spine. If I were a seedling in her garden, I think she would rip me out by my roots.

A loud beeping skewers my brain as we step over the threshold. A red light flashes around the perimeter of the foyer, but before I can process the oddly ornate decor, the beeping fades and a disembodied voice announces, "Weapon detected. Please disarm and place your weapon on the floor. Weapon detected. Please—"

"Disregard," the mother says. The red light fades and

the voice goes silent. The mother turns to Trigger. "You're armed?"

"At all times," he tells her.

"Remove your weapon and set it on the floor or I'll lock down the house, call in security, and have you arrested."

I can't resist a small, proud smile. She clearly has no idea that Trigger has taken down at least a dozen of the Administrator's guards tonight, all fully grown, highly trained soldiers. "He's Special—"

"It's just a blade." Trigger removes a small folding knife from his pocket and makes a show of dropping it on the floor.

"Weapons scan, reassess," the mother says, evidently to the room in general. Or to the house. Her focus rises toward the ceiling as she waits for a response, and I follow her gaze, taking in the large oval foyer.

Overhead hangs a huge chandelier with dozens of bulbs shaped like candles. My borrowed shoes feel slick against a floor so highly polished that I can see my reflection in it.

"No further weapons detected," the voice announces. "Shall I send security to collect the knife?"

"No need," Waverly's mother says. "Disregard."

The voice goes silent again, and the mother bends to pick up the folded knife. She examines it for a moment, then slides it into the pocket of her silky robe.

Trigger's expression is inscrutable.

"Who are you?" Waverly demands. Her gaze slides to Trigger. "Who is he?"

"He showed up at the party with her. I thought he was

your new security," Hennessy whispers to her. "And I thought *she* was *you.*"

"Wait for me in the study," the mother orders in a tone that would make the Administrator proud.

Opposite the front door, a mirror-image set of staircases curves toward the second floor from opposite sides of the foyer. Beneath the second-floor balcony and between the sets of stairs, a broad hallway leads to the rest of the first floor. Waverly and Hennessy head down that hallway, glancing back several times as if they're reluctant to let us out of their sight.

As they turn left through the first doorway, Waverly's voice echoes toward us. She's questioning Hennessy about me. But if he has any answers, he's not giving them.

Hennessy has been stunned silent.

"Down the hall, first door on the right," Waverly's mother orders us, but I wait for her to take the lead, because the hallway beneath the dual staircases looks like the throat of a great beast, and I already feel like I'm being swallowed alive by this house, and this family, and this whole strange city.

Trigger and I follow her through the arched doorway, an architectural echo of the front door, then to the right into a room dominated by a cluster of couches arranged to face a single empty wall.

Across the hall, in a room lined with shelves, Waverly stops interrogating Hennessy as her gaze finds mine, and for a moment we stare at each other from ten feet—and a lifetime—apart.

"I'll be with you in just a moment," her mother tells me

from the hallway. Then she swipes one hand at the door and it closes between us, cutting Trigger and me off from the rest of the house and its occupants.

"That's your long-lost clone?" Trigger says, and I realize I haven't had a chance to explain to him about Waverly and Hennessy.

"Yes." I step up to the closed door, but it doesn't open. "And that's her mother. There's also a father, according to Hennessy. He and Margo have parents too—the *same* parents. They, and everyone else at Seren's party, were conceived and birthed the *archaic* way." A messy and inefficient process that hasn't been used in centuries. At least in Lakeview.

I press both palms against the door, but it doesn't move. There's no knob. No handle. Has the mother locked us in, or am I simply absurdly inept with this technology?

"How is this possible?" Trigger runs one hand through his dark hair. "There *are* no more individuals. There haven't been in centuries. Except the Administrator." Whose genome was retired when she ascended to the highest position in Lakeview.

"She lied to us." I turn away from the inoperable door, my thoughts swimming in and out of focus.

None of this makes sense. Individuals with parents. Family units living in houses instead of dormitories. Clones cleaning the streets of Mountainside in the middle of the night while families sleep peacefully in their homes.

"Trigger, this is . . . huge." I can't come up with anything better to express the scale of our ignorance. "Waverly and her friends are allowed to travel to other cities. To talk to anyone they want. To wear clothes as unique as they are. If Mountainside is like this, other cities could be." My head is spinning. "I think the Administrator lied about *everything.*"

Trigger nods slowly. He's looking at the floor, but his eyes are unfocused, as if he's seeing something else entirely. Something much bigger than this room. "Dahlia, did you notice the clones are all from Lakeview?"

"Yes." I think back to the clones we saw cleaning the streets of Mountainside on our way to Waverly's house. Most of them looked at least vaguely familiar. "They're from previous classes." Identicals who graduated years ago and should be working for the glory of Lakeview.

Except that there *is* no Lakeview, beyond the training grounds. When we fled the city, we saw field after empty field. Not the adult identicals I'd expected, living the lives we've been imagining.

"It was *all* a lie." Stunned, I sink onto the nearest couch. "Lakeview is an anomaly. Everywhere else, I think . . ." I spread my arms to take in the room around us. The house. All of Mountainside. "I think everywhere else, it's like *this.*"

"Why?" Trigger asks. "Why would they design and clone us and tell us that's the way the whole world works if that's not true?"

"Because they don't want to clean their own streets?" I guess.

"What?" But he no longer seems interested in the answer to his question. He's frowning at the far wall now, as if it puzzles him. And it does look a little odd. It's the only one with nothing hanging on it. And it's kind of . . . shiny.

"They don't work for the glory of Mountainside here," I say, thinking aloud as I join him in front of the wall. "They want *us* to clean their streets and wash their windows. I think that's why the Administrator—"

Trigger waves his arm in a broad motion, and the entire undecorated wall fogs over like a bathroom mirror during a shower. Then it becomes a giant tablet.

I stare in astonishment as a series of icons appears on the wall, each as big as my head.

"It's e-glass," Trigger says. "Special Forces was taught infiltration techniques on something similar a few months ago." His frown deepens. "It's a much more advanced system than Lakeview uses, and at the time, I wondered why we weren't using it."

"Lakeview doesn't need that much security," I whisper as the truth becomes clear. "The Administrator wasn't trying to keep anyone out. She was only trying to keep us in." Which must have been pretty easy, considering we didn't even know the rest of the world existed.

I sink onto the couch again. This new understanding is like a weight on my chest, threatening to crush me. "We have to tell them." I look up at him as he turns to meet my gaze. "We can't just run off into the wild, Trigger. We have to go back and tell everyone what the Administrator is doing. About the lies she's telling. The lies they're *living*."

For a second, he looks like he'll argue. Fear flickers behind his dark eyes, and the emotion looks strange there. I've never seen him scared. Not when we were arrested. Not when we were being hunted. Not even when we fled Lakeview, chased by soldiers with their lights flashing and sirens wailing.

"Dahlia, if we get caught, they'll kill you."

The same is true for him, but a soldier expects to die in battle. He's afraid for *me*.

I'm afraid for me too. But I'm also afraid for everyone still living in Lakeview, in ignorance of their true fate. Their true purpose.

"I'm going back," I tell him. "I'm going to find a way to show them what's really happening. That'll be easier with your help, but I understand if you don't want to come."

"Of course I'll come." Trigger steps closer with a smile that makes me feel warm and a bit unsteady on the inside. "They put your genome into production for the wrong bureau, Dahlia. You were never meant to be a gardener." He kisses me, and that warmth explodes inside me, awakening a now-familiar ache to touch him. "You were always a fighter."

"Well, I'm an inexperienced one," I say, indulging in one more second of this contact. "So how do we start? We need to get out of this room, I assume. . . ."

"Yes. But not until we know a little more about the city we're escaping." He turns back to the e-glass. "This system

23

uses voice control and facial recognition, as well as a series of gesture-based commands. And it's connected to everything in this house. Cameras, including infrared. Audio feeds. Security systems." He pokes a finger in the air, in the direction of one of the icons, and it swells to take up the center of the screen.

We both grew up reading academic texts and doing assignments on tablets in class, but this e-glass looks way too big for that. "What is it for?"

"It's for *everything*." Trigger sounds impressed as he pokes and scrolls his way through menus and options I don't recognize. "This thing controls lights, thermostats, door locks, window tinting, refrigerator and pantry inventory, cameras, alarms, weapons detection, motion detectors. But there are apps here I've never seen before. And look at this." He points at a graph I can't make heads or tails of. "The signal strength coming from this system is *immense*. I bet it can reach *well* past the Mountainside city limits."

"And you said it controls the doors? Because there's no handle on this thing."

"Yes, but it looks like we've been specifically denied access to the doors. They're probably the only thing Waverly's mother thought we'd know how to work." Trigger turns to me, his hand still raised to control the screen. "Dahlia, this might take a while. If we don't get out of here before she comes back, they don't need to know I'm Special Forces. Or that I know how to work their system. The less they know about our capabilities, the better."

Waverly wasn't raised as an identical and didn't seem pleased to find out I exist. And her mother's insistence that no one should see us sends chills up my spine. As if Trigger and I are some dirty little secret that must be kept from the world.

"I wish I could hear what's going on in there," I say as I turn back to the closed door.

"Um . . . just a minute." Trigger gestures at the screen, and another box opens in the top left corner. He clears his throat and raises his voice. "Display rooms occupied by three or more people."

"One result," says the disembodied voice we heard in the foyer, and the box on-screen becomes a grid of four camera feeds, each showing the room across the hall from a different angle.

"Primary feed," Trigger orders. The grid becomes a single view, showing Waverly, her mother, and Hennessy seated on couches in the room across the hall.

"Audio. Enhanced. Filter out background noise and maximize voices."

"—is this possible?" Waverly demands on-screen, and I sit back on the couch, fascinated, spreading the bulky skirt of my borrowed dress around my knees. "Does she have a bar code?"

"I don't know," Hennessy says, and I finger the jeweled cuff hiding the code on my wrist. "I didn't see one, but if she's a clone . . ." He shrugs.

"How could she be?" Waverly turns to her mother. "Are you sure she's not my twin?"

The mother huffs. "I think I would remember giving birth to *two* children."

"If she's a clone, then there are more of her," Waverly says from the corner of the e-glass while Trigger continues to poke and swipe his way through menus, pausing occasionally to speak an order to the screen. "How did this happen? How many of her are there? How close are they to being *put into service?*"

"I don't know," the mother says. "I'll put in a call to the Administrator."

"No!" Waverly squeals. "We're not going to *advertise* this!"

"There's no way to find out how this happened without talking to the Administrator." The mother sounds exhausted, but her image on-screen sits up straight, as if indignation is the source of the steel in her spine.

"Besides, she probably already knows," Hennessy says. "How could she not notice that an entire batch of her clones looks just like her daughter's best friend?"

The Administrator's daughter—Sofia—is Waverly's best friend?

"No," the mother insists. "If she knew, she would have said something. She would have used this for a better rate on DigiCore's tech, if for nothing else." The mother's brows dip into a scowl. "Maybe that *is* what she's doing—trying to extort lower prices for Lakeview's tablets and security systems by threatening to humiliate my daughter."

"It'll work!" Waverly moans. "If we don't give her what

she wants, there'll be *hundreds* of mass-produced servants all over the world with my face on them. Maybe thousands! 'Buy a Waverly Whitmore clone to clean your toilet!' I'll be an international joke!"

I turn to Trigger, frowning. "They think the Administrator cloned Waverly to embarrass them?" That's all I understand of a conversation filled with terms I've never heard. Like *extort*. And *prices*.

"That doesn't sound very likely," Hennessy says. "Unless she's been planning this for more than eighteen years. That's one hell of a long game."

"Well, what else could it be?" Waverly demands. "Why else would she risk prison by cloning me without permission?"

I turn to Trigger, and surprise echoes in my voice. "They don't know anything about Wexler 42. And they still think I'm *her* clone." Somehow, despite their advanced tech and limitless communication privileges, Waverly, Hennessy, and the mother seem to have *no idea* how she and I came to be in the world.

THREE

DAHLIA

The door slides open to reveal Waverly's mother standing in the hallway. Trigger and I are seated several inches apart. Not touching. The screen has gone transparent again, showing only the undecorated wall behind it. For all she knows, we understand nothing of her world, its strange, terrifying customs, or its advanced tech.

"Would you both please join us across the hall?" Her words form a question, yet she's clearly issuing a command.

My pulse pounding, Trigger and I follow her into a high-ceilinged room bordered by shelves made of dark stained wood. Lined up on every inch of every shelf are actual books, presumably printed on paper—the kind I've seen only in pictures from history lessons. The kind no one in Lakeside has held or used in centuries. I didn't know such relics still existed.

This room is like a slice of history. I want to touch the shelves. I want to open the books. A million questions rattle around in my head about this room and this place, but I don't even know if I'm allowed to voice them.

In Lakeview, I was only allowed to speak freely with fellow members of the Workforce Bureau, but Mountainside doesn't seem to have bureaus. I don't understand the rules here. Everything seems extravagant, inefficient, and inconsistent. Before I can work up the courage to start asking questions, the mother waves her hand at the door and it closes.

Waverly sits on an overstuffed sofa in the center of the room. She's clearly trying not to look at me, as if the sight of her own face on someone else's body offends her, yet her gaze keeps sliding my way.

Hennessy stands apart from us both, his brow furrowed, alternately studying Waverly and me. He blinks and rubs his forehead, as if he expects his double vision to clear and our two images to merge back into one. As if that's the only thing that would make sense to him.

"Have a seat." The mother glances at the name embroidered on Trigger's uniform. "Trigger 17." Then she turns to me, effectively dismissing him. "I am Lorna Whitmore." The pause after her proclamation says that her name should mean something to me. And suddenly it does.

Whitmore. Her second name matches Waverly's. It's a *family* name. A surname, according to my history text. Yet another custom that isn't quite as obsolete as I was taught.

29

But I don't think that's the kind of recognition she was expecting.

"And you are?" Lorna Whitmore continues.

"I am Dahlia 16." My voice feels very small in this room full of old things and strange people.

"It speaks!" Waverly's sarcasm sounds like Iris 16's, and my heart aches at the thought of my lost sisters.

"I told you," Hennessy says. "She wouldn't have been able to fool everyone at Seren's party if she were a normal clone."

If I were a normal clone, I wouldn't have kissed Trigger or been arrested. My anomalous behavior wouldn't have gotten my 4,999 identicals euthanized.

"And who is he?" Waverly glances at the name embroidered on Trigger's uniform. "I mean, who is he to you?"

I don't have a word for what Trigger means to me. He is like the dawn, lighting up the world so I can see it clearly after a lifetime of darkness. He's like an open flame, beautiful to look at but scorching to touch. He's like a bite of cake, delicious, but so rich I dare not eat my fill.

He is everything good that has ever happened to me. But surely that's not what she's asking.

Waverly's gaze narrows on my expression. "Oh my God, the clone has a boyfriend. Aren't you guys supposed to be, like, sexless?"

I frown, trying to puzzle through her odd words. At my side, Trigger has become a tightly wound coil of tension held in check by the same self-discipline that keeps his jaw locked when he would clearly like to speak.

"Wait, sixteen?" Hennessy looks confused.

"I'll be promoted to Dahlia 17 next month." Well, I would have, if I hadn't been forced to flee the city of Lakeview for my own safety.

Hennessy frowns at Waverly. "Dahlia's more than a year younger than you. How can she be your clone?"

"She isn't." Trigger stares boldly at all three of them, throwing Wexler 42's confession at them like a bucket of cold water. "Waverly was cloned from Dahlia's genome."

Waverly glares at us both. "*Obviously* that's not true. But if anyone heard you say that . . ." She turns to her mother, suddenly terrified. "What if there'd been a camera crew here tonight?"

Camera crew?

"It's true." I turn to the mother as another piece of this mental puzzle snaps into place in my head. "You hired Wexler 42, didn't you? He would have been Wexler 24 or 25 when you met him."

Comprehension breaks over Lorna's expression like a wave crashing over the lakeshore. She stares at me with a fresh blend of horror and fascination as she begins to understand the part she played in this, many years ago.

My clone stares at us both in utter confusion.

"You know Wexler?" Lorna pulls a small, impossibly thin sheet of glass from the pocket of her robe. Her thumb brushes it, and icons appear on the side facing her, visible to me in reverse from the other side. It's a tablet made of e-glass.

"We met him," Trigger answers. "Right before he got us captured, as a distraction so he could escape into the wild."

Lorna's frown deepens. "He's gone?"

I sit on the sofa opposite them and Trigger stands to my right, alert, like the soldier he was trained to be. Having him close—even in his formal stance—makes me feel a little less like this place is going to swallow me whole.

"Who's Wexler?" Waverly's gaze flickers from her mother to me, to Trigger, then back.

Lorna stares at me as if she's still puzzling through my existence. She has my eyes. Or, rather, I have *her* eyes. The genetic connection between us is obvious, even if I don't quite understand it.

Is she my mother too, even though I was created in a lab and incubated in a machine? Until yesterday, did she have five thousand daughters?

"*Dahlia?*" Waverly demands. "Who's Wexler?"

"He's a genetic engineer. Your mother hired him to design a genome years ago. At least, that's what I thought he was saying." But in a city where people are born rather than incubated, Lorna Whitmore would have had no use for a genome—a genetic blueprint. I turn to her. "You actually wanted a baby, didn't you?"

"An embryo," she says. "He was supposed to send me an embryo, and he did."

32

"Well, before he sent it, he cloned it," I explain. "The work he did for your secret project left him with too little time to develop an outstanding order for the Workforce Bureau, so he made efficient use of the labor he'd already done."

"He cloned me?" Waverly grips the arm of the sofa so tightly that her knuckles turn white. "He put me into production as a common *servant*?"

"No. He cloned *me*," I repeat. "But then he accidentally sent the wrong embryo to your mother. I was supposed to grow up here." In this strange building built to house only a few people—a family. "And you were supposed to be trained as a hydroponic gardener, in the Workforce Academy."

"That *can't* be true." Waverly springs up from the couch and begins to angrily pace the length of the room. "There is *no way*—"

"Waverly . . . ," Lorna begins.

My last remaining identical stops pacing and pins me with a furious, incredulous glare. "I can't be a clone. Clones aren't . . . They can't . . ."

I wait for her to finish, but her thoughts fade into a stunned silence. Into some new awareness that seems to leave her lost.

I know that feeling.

Then Waverly shakes off confusion and seizes anger, wielding it like a weapon. "This is *your* fault!" She turns on her mother, rage flashing in the same eyes I've seen in the mirror every day of my life. "You sent my DNA to a clone factory! What did you *think* they were going to do with it?"

"Sit." Lorna points at the couch.

"I have every right to—"

"*Sit.*"

Waverly drops onto the cushion farthest from me, her knees tucked up to her chest, her horrified expression trained on me. "So," she snaps. "How many of 'me' are there in this Workforce Academy?"

"None." My voice cracks on the word. "There were five thousand girls who looked just like you until about twelve hours ago. But now there's only me."

"Five thousand!" She turns to her mother, eyes wide and panicked. "This can't be real! How could we not know there are five thousand girls walking around with my—" Then her gaze finds me again, and the rest of my answer seems to sink in. "Wait. What happened twelve hours ago?"

"The rest of your genome was recalled," Trigger tells her, and the word hits me like a physical blow.

"Recalled?"

"Euthanized." He lays a comforting hand on my shoulder as I hold back tears with sheer will. "All 4,999 of Dahlia's identicals—her sisters—were put to death, because of two abnormalities found in her DNA."

"Management thought they were flaws, but Wexler said my genome is perfect," I explain. "He said the clones were altered from the prototype—me—to fit the requirements of Lakeview's order for five thousand trade laborers."

Waverly's brow furrows. "What requirements?"

"He escaped into the wild before I could ask anything else. All I know is that the differences between you and me are obvious in a genetic comparison. And they're enough to get us hunted down by every soldier in Lakeview."

"You're the fugitives," Hennessy blurts out. "The ones the soldiers were looking for at the party. I thought . . ." He turns to Waverly. "I thought I was getting you home before your mother realized you'd snuck out, but I was actually aiding and abetting *fugitives?*"

"More like stealing Lakeview property." Waverly shrugs. "The Administrator will probably consider it corporate espionage."

"This isn't funny!" her mother snaps.

"I know. It's a social, legal, political *nightmare.*"

I stare at her, stunned. "Nearly five thousand people *died* yesterday."

Waverly's mouth snaps closed. Her focus narrows on me, as if she's just now considering that her trauma might not be the most tragic aspect of this.

Lorna clears her throat and turns back to Trigger and me. "So you're saying there *were* five thousand of you, but you're the only one we still have to . . . deal with?"

"I don't think that's exactly what we were saying." Nor am I sure I want to know what it means to be dealt with by Lorna Whitmore.

"Okay, well, it's late." She stands, and when she pulls her translucent tablet from the pocket of her robe, her sleeve falls

35

back to reveal a beautiful scrolling pattern tattooed on her forearm in blue ink. In the center of the design, made out of those very swirls, is a six-digit number, divided into three sets of two figures. After a second of staring, I realize it's a date.

Lorna taps through a series of menus on her tablet as she speaks. "In the morning, we'll look at things through fresh eyes." She pockets the tablet and motions for Trigger and me to follow her as she heads for the door. "I'm having rooms prepared for you, and I'm sure we can find something for you to sleep in—"

"Wait." I stand. "We have questions of our own." Even surrounded by the evidence, it's difficult to comprehend the scale of the lie Trigger and I have been living, and before we escape, I *need* to understand. "Lakeview isn't a city at all, is it? It's a . . . a garden, in which to grow . . . servants?"

The concept lurks at the back of my mind, out of focus like something seen from far away, because I took the history class that gave me access to this vocabulary word very long ago. "Clones work not on their own behalf, but on yours? Not to glorify the city, but to . . . what? Why do you need gardeners?" I glance at Trigger. "And soldiers? And street cleaners and bakers and drivers? Are you not capable of cooking and cleaning for yourselves? Why does Lakeview exist? Why do *we* exist?"

"Existentialism from a clone." Waverly huffs with bitter amusement.

"I . . ." Hennessy frowns, as if he's having trouble coming up with an answer. "I guess we don't *need* clones. We buy

36

them to make life easier. And Lakeview . . . you're right. It's not a city. It's a corporation. A business. Clones are a . . ." His gaze flickers with guilt. "They're a product."

"Like fruits and vegetables?" Those are the products I understand. The products I am trained to produce.

"Yes. And like shoes, and cars, and houses. Like anything else that can be bought and sold." Waverly grabs my arm and pushes Margo's jeweled cuff back to expose the bar code on my wrist. "What did you think this was for?"

I pull my arm free and frown at the bar code, confused. "For identification and access. You just hold your wrist under the scanner in the cafeteria and your tray comes out of the chute. The scanner by the dormitory door unlocks your room. The scanner in the dorm room wall dispenses clean shoes and clothing."

Waverly shakes her head. "Bar codes are on things you *buy.*" She turns up the hem of her shirt and shows me a square of stiff material sewn into it. "Does this look familiar?"

She rips the tag free and hands it to me. On one side is printed instructions for laundering the shirt. On the other side . . . there's a bar code. It's virtually identical to the one on my wrist.

"I . . ." I glance at Trigger, but his focus is caught on the bar code. "I don't . . ."

"There's a catalog," Hennessy says. "Lakeview puts one out every year. It has pictures and specs on every genome that will be available for purchase and what skills the clones

37

are trained for. You can place an order up to nine months in advance. Sometimes there are waiting lists."

"Oh my God," Waverly moans. "Am I in the catalog?"

"Of course not," Lorna says. "If you were, we would have known about this months ago."

Hennessy's gaze flicks back to me and he looks . . . conflicted. "It sounds like Dahlia's genome won't mature until next year."

Not that there are any of us left to "mature."

"It was all a lie." My voice sounds hollow. I'm looking right at Waverly, but what I see is every friend I've ever had. Everything I've ever known. "Graduating and working with my friends, for the glory of Lakeview. It was *all* a lie." No matter how many times I say it, the grief feels brand-new.

"Lakeview is a business." Lorna says. "And as with any business, the object is to turn a profit. I know that must come as a shock to you, but—"

"That's all we are to you?" I ask, and Lorna blinks, evidently surprised by my softly worded question. "Is that all *she* is to you?" I nod at her daughter.

Waverly flinches. "I'm not a clone," she insists. "And I sure as *hell* am not a servant."

"If you don't believe me, take a blood test," I say. "You deserve the truth as much as I do."

Waverly rears back. "I can't . . ." She turns to her mother. "We can't send samples to a lab, Mom. Someone would sell the results—"

"I'll take care of it," Lorna assures her, but I don't understand what she's going to take care of. What I *do* understand is that everything—even information—is for sale here.

"It's nearly two in the morning." Lorna gestures at the door, and it slides open. "We all need some sleep. Tomorrow, I promise we'll have answers."

But tomorrow, Trigger and I will be long gone—well on our way to exposing the truth about Lakeview to its "citizens."

FOUR

WAVERLY

The moment the door closes behind my mother, I head for the liquor cabinet.

"Waverly." Hennessy's footsteps clack behind me on the reclaimed wood floor, and I turn on him.

"If you say a word to my mother—"

He plucks the glass from my hand and gives me that gallant little smile that makes my insides melt. And turns millions of viewers into obsessed fangirls and fanboys. "I was going to say 'Allow me.'"

"Thanks." I settle onto the couch again and run my hands through my hair. "I was half-afraid you were going to demand the ring back and bolt on me." I don't know what to believe about Dahlia yet, but if any of this were to get out, it would be just as damaging to Hennessy as it would be to me.

He pours two inches of my father's imported whiskey into

my glass. "If you don't know me better than that by now, then we have bigger problems than that other girl wearing your face." He swallows half the whiskey in one gulp, then sits next to me and gives me the glass.

"I'm sorry. I'm just . . ." I drink the rest of the whiskey and squeeze my eyes shut against the burn in my throat. "This is a nightmare, and you're taking it so well. *Too* well."

"It hasn't really sunk in yet," he admits. "Nor has it been verified."

"I think her face pretty much verifies it, Hen."

"That you look alike? Yes. But that doesn't mean you're actually clones. I don't see how either of you could be. You both talk like normal people—well, relatively normal, in her case. Neither of you walks around staring at the ground. And I've never seen you wash a dish or sew a scrap of clothing in your life." He's grinning now. Teasing me. But he has a point.

"She's definitely not like any clone I've ever met. Trigger isn't either." Though the only soldiers I've really interacted with are my personal guard, and while they typically work in silence, they don't stare at the ground and try to blend into the walls like other clones.

"That's what I'm saying. I think this is more complicated than simply, 'Waverly's a clone.' And even if that's true, I'm certainly not ready to believe *Dahlia's* the prototype."

"Me neither." I tuck my bare feet beneath his thigh on the couch, to steal his warmth. I feel cold all over. "So you really thought she was me?"

41

He shrugs. "She sounded a little . . . odd, but certainly not clonelike. And you're Waverly Whitmore, of *those* Whitmores." His teasing smile draws one from me, in spite of the circumstances. "The fact that you might have a clone or be a clone never occurred to me or to anyone else. It still sounds ridiculous. Like some crazy Labor Party conspiracy theory."

"Thank goodness. I can't even process the thought of Dahlia at a social event. What did she *say?*"

"Nothing that gave herself away, obviously. Though the more I understand of this, the more of a miracle that seems. She showed up in a trainee uniform." He laughs. "I thought it was a costume! I lent her Margo's backup dress. My sister was *furious.* But I think that'll be the worst of the fallout."

I set my empty glass on a coaster. "I still don't understand how there could have been five thousand copies of me running around Lakeview for sixteen years without anyone noticing."

Hennessy shrugs as he slides one hand up my calf, beneath the loose cuff of my pajama pants. "Seren and Sofia aren't allowed on the training grounds, and I doubt their mother's actually seen every one of the hundreds of genomes she puts into production. The Administrator strikes me as more of a delegator than a micromanager. So I guess it's *possible.*"

"If this had gone on for another year . . ."

"Hey." He takes my hand. "That didn't happen. There's only one of them left, if the others ever even existed, and she's a little weird, obviously. But I don't think she's going to go running to the networks."

That possibility hadn't occurred to me until the words fell out of his mouth. "What are we going to do with her? She can't stay here! Someone will see her. She can't stay anywhere!" Hennessy and I have two of the most recognizable faces on the planet. Our show is a hit *worldwide*—except in Lakeview, obviously, because no one actually lives there, except the Lockes and several hundred thousand clone servants-in-training, with no connection to the outside world.

"Hey. It's going to be fine, Waverly." He squeezes my fingers, smiling at the gorgeous vintage twelve-carat circle-cut diamond weighing down my left hand. "Your mom will sort this out, and *we* will live happily ever after."

"Yes, you will," my mother says as the door opens again. She practically floats into the library, her robe flaring out behind her, and as usual, she sucks up all the oxygen in the room. She doesn't do it on purpose. She's just the kind of woman who commands attention. And holds it, in her silk-gloved, iron-fisted grip. "Hennessy, I assume you'll be staying the night?"

"If you don't mind." He stands, and immediately I miss his warmth on my feet. His hand in mine. I wish we were already married with a house of our own. I wish we weren't sleeping in separate rooms.

I wish tonight had never happened.

"I've had a guest room made up for you in the south wing," my mother says. "I know you're of age now, but please let your parents know where you are so they won't worry."

"Of course." He pulls his tablet from his pocket, and

43

before he can message his mother, I pull him into a hug. "Good night, Waverly." His kiss feels a bit formal, as if our audience is the whole world, rather than just my mother. But I let him go without demanding a better one because I have questions for my mom that I don't want to ask in front of him.

He clearly intends to stay with me, despite the potential for scandal. But I don't want him to hear anything that might give him—or his parents—any reason to change his mind.

Even in the middle of the night, under an obvious load of stress, my mother looks perfect. Without makeup. But now when I look at her, I don't envy that. I don't study her face, hoping I'll look as good as she does when I'm her age.

Tonight when I look at my mother, all I feel is anger. Betrayal.

"How could you do this?"

She holds my gaze, unmoved by my judgment. "I had no choice, Waverly. You, of all people, should understand that. I would have done *anything* to have a child. And look what a smart, beautiful daughter I got out of it." She tries to brush the backs of her fingers down my cheek, but I lean out of range.

"Look what else you got!" I point at the ceiling, where Dahlia and Trigger are presumably sleeping on the second floor. "And considering that yesterday there were nearly five thousand more of me, I'd say you got more than your money's worth!"

"Are you finished?" My mother folds her arms, waiting for my rant to exhaust itself. She never raises her voice. She doesn't have to. Investors and executives alike have withered beneath the silent warning in her outwardly patient, polite gaze.

Normally, I would push right past it. Surely I inherited the ability to be just as intimidating as she is. But I don't even know how true that is anymore. "Am I even really your daughter?"

Her expression softens. "Of course! You are one hundred percent the product of my own and your father's genes! I carried you myself and I have the stretch marks to prove it." A frown flickers across her face. "Well, I did until I had them surgically corrected. We just couldn't conceive you the standard way. Everything else about you is on the beautiful and exceptional end of *normal*."

"Except for the fact that there's an exact replica of me upstairs. I still don't understand how this is possible. She's not a clone, Mom. She can't be, and neither can I. Clones aren't capable of normal social interaction."

"Actually, that's not true. Wexler 42, the genetic engineer she mentioned, is a clone. His speech is perfectly normal, and he acts like you and I, though he's a bit sheltered from living in a self-contained clone factory. And he's not the only one. Clones are produced for different tasks and with different specifications and abilities. Some, like Wexler, are highly functional and *very* smart, because they have to be. Trigger 17 seems to be evidence that at least some soldiers fall into that category as well."

"But how is that possible? I thought the process of reproducing a genome degraded it. That no copy could be as functional as the original."

My mother gives me a wary frown. "Where did you hear that?"

I can only shrug. "That's just what people think." Clones aren't like us by virtue of the very fact that they're clones. They're not capable of anything other than the menial tasks they perform. "If that's not true, why aren't our servants like Dahlia?" Why aren't they like *me*? "Or, I guess, why isn't she like them? Why would a gardener need to function socially on the same level as a geneticist?"

"I don't know. Dahlia's clearly different. Maybe her whole genome was. Maybe that has something to do with how and why it was designed. Speaking of which . . . I guess I owe you an explanation."

"Yes. Please explain to me how I came to be mass produced like a cheap suitcase, rather than conceived as an *individual* by my *individual* parents."

She sighs, and a strand of dark hair—just like mine—falls over her shoulder. "Waverly, lots of couples have trouble conceiving."

"Yes. And they go see a fertility specialist. Not a genetic engineer—and a *clone*, at that."

"We went to fertility specialists. We saw the best doctors in the world," my mother says. "But they all told us the same thing: that your father is infertile. Completely without hope." She pauses to let the gravity of that fact sink in.

Noble families *must* have an heir. A *genetic* heir. It's as true for Hennessy and me as it was for my parents, Lorna Emsworth and Dane Whitmore, when they married.

The Emsworths pioneered instant encrypted data transfer and the Whitmores developed the first e-glass technology. My parents were famous before they got married, but afterward?

The world was *obsessed* with them—their fledgling marriage, their glamorous clothes and travel and lives. And with watching her stomach for any sign of a baby bump. I've seen the old footage. *Hundreds* of millions of views. Tens of millions of followers. And hardly a second of privacy.

I know the feeling. I decided to embrace it rather than fight it. To give people an official glimpse into my life—one that *I* control—and the world has welcomed my choice more enthusiastically than I ever anticipated.

"Your father and I are both only children," my mother continues. "Without an heir, we'd have been the end of both the Whitmore and the Emsworth lines. We would have had to hand DigiCore over to the investors or name a nongenetic successor. I couldn't let that happen."

"So you what? Went to see the Administrator?"

My mother actually smiles. "Amelia Locke wasn't the Administrator then. Her father, Oliver, was still running Lakeview. But back then, as now, the Administrator brought an annual delegation to Mountainside—and to all the other major cities—to help his most important customers assess their needs and place orders. The envoy is mostly

47

high-ranking management, but they also bring a geneticist, to answer technical questions."

"And those are all clones?" Before tonight, I'd never heard of a management or a scientist clone.

"Yes, but they're not for sale. Lakeview produces them in very small batches and only uses them to manage the training grounds and to design and produce the rest of the clones. That way the Administrator maintains total control over the proprietary process and over the clones who run it. They're considered intellectual property."

"Like DigiCore's patents?" The company has registered hundreds in my lifetime alone.

"Yes. Like living, breathing patents. And the Lockes are so paranoid that their process will be stolen that they only employ their own clones. The Lakeview compound is Amelia's own little universe, where she plays God."

"If the Administrator is so controlling, how did you manage to hire a clone geneticist to . . . make me happen?"

"That year, Oliver Locke led the envoy to Mountainside, and Amelia accompanied him, preparing to take over the family business. The geneticist they brought was called Wexler 23. He was young and overwhelmed by all the differences between Lakeview and the rest of the world. And he developed a . . . well, a fascination with me." She shrugs. "As he was explaining his job, I realized he could do for your father and me what the fertility specialists could not. So I got Wexler alone for a few minutes and asked him to design an embryo using my DNA and your father's.

"I thought he'd refuse, or report me to the Administrator, because if he'd been caught, they would have executed him and every one of his identicals."

"Wait, *you* asked Wexler to design an embryo?" I sit straighter, frowning at her. "Alone? What about Dad?"

"I didn't tell your father. What I asked Wexler to do was illegal, and I couldn't drag him into that."

"So he still doesn't know?" My head feels like it's about to explode. There's a clone in one of our guest rooms, and my father has no idea she exists. Or how *I* came to exist.

"No. But obviously I'll have to tell him tonight." My mother looks more irritated than nervous at that realization.

"But how did . . . ? How did you get pregnant? How could he not know?"

"Wexler sent me the embryo—he sent me *you*. I went back to the fertility specialist I trusted the most, and I paid her double her typical fee to sign a nondisclosure agreement and perform the implantation. When I was sure it had taken—that I was pregnant—I told your father we'd beaten the odds. Science doesn't always know best." Her smile is almost nostalgic. "He was overjoyed, and happy men are quick to believe anything that lets them remain happy."

She lied to my father. She broke the law. But if she hadn't, I wouldn't exist.

I can't decide whether to stomp out in a storm of profanity or hug her.

"Okay. But what about the rest of it? I mean, we don't

49

know that Dahlia's the prototype. I can't be the clone if I'm a year older than she is, right?"

My mother sighs. "Honey, I suspect there were routine delays—inspections, approvals, and previously set schedules—that slowed down the production of five thousand . . . um . . . trade laborers, even though the embryos were all produced at once. That's why you were born before Dahlia and her identicals."

"But Wexler could have lied, couldn't he? She could be *my* clone?" I can't make sense of this any other way. I don't feel like a clone.

"He could have lied, but I don't think he did," my mother says. "The other identicals were euthanized because of the anomalies they found in Dahlia's DNA. If she were another clone, rather than the prototype, there wouldn't have been any anomalies to find."

"Maybe what they found in her really *were* flaws," I insist, clinging to what feels like my last hope. "We need to verify this for ourselves. I want to see a geneticist. Or a doctor. Someone we can trust."

My mother takes my hand, and the somber, sympathetic look in her eyes terrifies me all the way into the pit of my stomach. "Waverly, you're already seeing a doctor we trust. And finally, what he's been telling us makes sense."

My last thin thread of hope dies. "*This* is what's wrong with me? This is why Dr. Foster said Hennessy and I shouldn't wait to get married?"

My mother nods. "Dr. Foster and I have always assumed that your hormone deficiency was something similar to your father's infertility. Something we could fight with money and technology, like I did to get you. So it made sense that the younger you started trying, the better. But Waverly, the hormone therapy isn't working, and now I understand why."

My eyes begin to water, but I blink away the tears, determined not to mourn a loss I might not even be suffering. "You're going to have to explain that."

"It has to do with one of the changes Wexler made to Dahlia's genome—one of the 'anomalies'—so he could clone it. This probably never occurred to her, because embryos in Lakeview are artificially incubated, but clones are genetically engineered to be infertile, so that we can't just . . . let them multiply. So that we become the Administrator's repeat customers. Since Dahlia's not a clone, she's fertile, though none of her identicals are. Including you."

Goose bumps form on my arms. "You're saying I'll *never* have children of my own? No matter what?"

My mother takes my hand, and the unusually touchy gesture does not bode well. "Waverly, I'm saying you're never even going to get your period. You're not built for it."

This time, I can't stop the tears. Deep down, I've always believed the doctors could fix me. That the hormone injections would eventually work. "How am I going to tell Hennessy?"

My mother reaches for me, and I let her pull me into

a hug. "He already knows fertility is an issue for you. If he knows that clones are infertile, then he'll probably make the same connection I made. If he doesn't know that, you don't need to tell him. Just don't lie about it, because he'll find out when you two place an order for your own household staff."

"Mom!" I sit up, looking at her in fresh panic as a whole new set of horrors crashes over me. "I can't staff my house with clones. I'm *one* of them."

"*No.*" Ferocity shines in her eyes. "You are *not*. Lakeview's geneticists assemble genomes from a central cache of random genetic material. From samples preserved generations ago. The Administrator holds the patent on that process. She owns the genes. Her clones are her intellectual property.

"*Your* genes do not come from a central cache. You are my daughter. Your father's daughter. You are the perfect combination of his bloodline and mine, and no matter how you came to exist, I carried you. I gave birth to you. I fired every nanny my mother ever sent my way and changed your diapers myself, because I wanted you so badly that I *broke laws* to get you. You are the sum of every unique thought and experience you've ever had. Of every single time I've yelled at you for being careless and your father has spoiled you with some ridiculously expensive treat, to balance out my firm hand. *You* are a Whitmore. For better or for worse."

My panic begins to ebb. She's right. No matter how my genes were assembled, they came from my parents. No matter how my mother got pregnant, I am her natural child.

"Then so is Dahlia 16." I glance up at the ceiling toward

the north wing, as if I can see her through all the walls separating us. "She's the one you were supposed to get." She's special in a way no one raised in Lakeview has ever been. In a way few people born in the *real* world have ever been. "Dahlia's every bit as much a Whitmore as I am."

My mother frowns. "Yes, I guess she is. Technically."

"What are we going to do with her?" My hand begins to tremble, and I can't make it stop. Even knowing that Dahlia has as much right as I have to everything I own and everything I am, I am *terrified* by the thought that the public might discover that I'm a cheap genetic copy. A designer knockoff, flaunted in ignorance by my parents for eighteen years.

"For now?" my mother says. "We're going to hide her. Here in the house."

Alarm spikes in my pulse. My gaze drops to the stylized numbers permanently inked on her forearm—the date of my parents' wedding. "My ink ceremony is tomorrow! There will be cameras everywhere!"

Her thumb brushes absently over the date on her skin. "No one will see Dahlia. I'll make sure of that." A slow smile turns up my mother's perfect mouth, and I recognize the birth of an epiphany in the sudden shine in her eyes.

"What?" Suspicion echoes in my voice. "What are you thinking?"

"Dahlia has what you're missing, Waverly. I have an idea, and if it works out, we're going to need her. *You're* going to need her."

"Why? What's your idea?"

53

"I'll explain after I've had time to do a little research." My mother stands and pulls me up by one hand. "Right now, I have to go fill your father in on a secret I'd hoped never to have to tell him." Her smile falters at the thought. Then she cradles my face in her hands and wipes my tears away with her thumbs. "And you need to get some sleep. Unless you want puffy skin and dark circles for the shoot tomorrow."

She's right. Tomorrow's a very big day.

"This is why you wouldn't let me go to Lakeview, isn't it?" I ask as she guides me firmly toward the door with one arm around my waist.

"No, honey, I had no idea there were five thousand replicas of you running around the training ward. I wouldn't let you go because I was afraid you'd somehow run into Wexler. That he would see you and recognize you." She smiles. "In case you haven't noticed, you and I look alike."

"You thought he'd see me and confess to a crime that could get him executed?"

She shrugged. "I couldn't take the chance. And it's a good thing I didn't. What if you'd been at Seren's party when Dahlia and Trigger showed up?"

I shudder at the thought. Then another eclipses it. "What's the other difference between me and Dahlia? The other 'anomaly'?"

She tugs me closer to the door and it slides open. "Let's talk about that tomorrow."

"No, Mom." I pull free of her grip and capture her gaze,

terrified of the fear I see swimming in it. "Tell me. It can't be any worse than total infertility, right?"

My mother's smile fades. "Waverly, things can *always* get worse. All you need to know right now is that I told lies and broke laws to bring you into the world, and there is *nothing* I wouldn't do to keep you here."

FIVE

DAHLIA

The door slides open, and I stare into a bedroom unlike anything I've ever seen. The space is huge, yet there's only one bed, and it's big enough for several people to sleep in at once.

Will Trigger 17 be sleeping here with me?

I feel strangely nervous at the thought, yet I wonder what he wears to sleep in. Not that either of us has anything to change into.

"There are pajamas in the dresser," Lorna says. "Hang your gown in the closet, and I'll send it to the laundry tomorrow." She frowns with a glance at my dress. "Where did you get that?"

"It's Margo's," I tell her. "Hennessy lent it to me when he thought I was Waverly."

"Well then, I'll have it returned." Lorna gestures to a door on the far wall of the bedroom. "The restroom is through there. Make yourself at home. Trigger, you'll be down the hall—"

"He's not staying here?"

Lorna actually looks amused. "I can't allow you and your boyfriend to sleep in the same room. He'll be just a couple of doors away."

"But—"

"It's okay." Trigger squeezes my hand, then lets it go. "Just get some sleep, and I'll see you in the morning." But his beautiful, dark eyes seem to be telling me more than he's actually saying out loud. He steps into the hall with Waverly's mother, and the door closes behind them.

I am alone. I can count the number of times I've been truly alone on two hands, and most of those have happened in the past couple of months. And I've never slept in a room by myself.

I study my surroundings as I step out of Margo's high-heeled shoes, and my feet sink into a plush rug with splashes of blue in every possible shade.

This whole room is blue, from the sleek, featureless walls to the intricately patterned rug. The bed is a platform in the middle of the floor, made up with a puffy, oversized cobalt comforter and six matching pillows. I have to walk around the strange square bed to get to the dresser against the rear wall, where I find several sets of underwear cut into sparse shapes I hardly recognize, as well as a blue tank top and a matching pair of stretchy pants.

It takes me a minute to work my way out of Margo's dress—the latches in the back are difficult to reach—then I try on the soft blue pajamas. They're a perfect fit. Which means they probably belong to Waverly.

The bathroom door slides open when I approach; then it closes behind me and beeps. Before I can figure out what the beep means, my attention is captured by the bathroom itself. It's huge.

In the middle of the floor stands a long, asymmetrical tub made of polished black stone. The counter is shiny and black, and to my left is a large frameless glass shower stall with a black polished stone floor and a large round showerhead.

To my right, across from the sink, an open door reveals a closet as big as the bathroom Poppy, Sorrel, Violet, and I shared. Both long clothing racks are empty, except for a row of hangers and a single fluffy blue bathrobe.

I hang up Margo's dress and set the jeweled cuff on the counter, then contemplate the tub. I've been taking showers since my class aged up into the intermediate dorm, and suddenly I want nothing more than to fill this huge tub with hot water and sink into it.

But there are no knobs on the tub or the shower, so I wash my face at the bathroom sink—the water comes on when I hold my hands under it—then brush my teeth with the toothpaste and brand-new toothbrush laid out on the counter.

Despite my exhaustion, I'm not actually sleepy. Still, I fold back the covers and climb into the big blue bed, and the moment my head hits the absurdly soft pillow, the lights in the room go off, except for a soft glow around the floorboards, outlining the room with dim light.

I roll onto my side and close my eyes, but sleep does not come. This space feels too big. This bed feels too soft. This room is too quiet. There are no roommates rolling over in their bunks or getting up to use the restroom. And now that I've thought about them, I can't get Poppy, Sorrel, and Violet out of my mind.

Did they suffer when they died? Did they know the whole thing was my fault?

I sit up, and the lights come back on. When I slide onto the floor, the comforter rustles behind me, and I turn to see the wrinkles ironing themselves out, leaving the bedclothes turned down, yet perfectly neat.

I can't sleep here alone.

Determined, I head for the door, but it remains closed even when I'm inches away. "Um . . . open the door," I say to the room, though I have no idea whether or not it's voice-controlled.

"You are not authorized to operate this door," a voice says, and I jump back, looking for the source in the empty room.

"Does that mean I'm locked in?"

There's no reply.

"Hey!" I shout. "Open the door!" When that doesn't work, I bang on it with both fists. "Open the door!"

Why would Lorna lock me in? Is she turning Trigger and

me over to the Administrator? Are we about to be recalled? This room is nicer than my Lakeview prison cell was, but this is still imprisonment.

"Open the—"

"Dahlia," Trigger's voice calls from behind me, and I spin around to find him watching me from an e-glass screen I hadn't even noticed on the wall facing the bed.

His face takes up most of the wall. When he steps back from the camera, the space that comes into focus around him is a bedroom similar to mine, only decorated in shades of gray rather than blue—another fancy prison.

"Where are you?"

"Across the hall and one door down." Which means he probably heard me yelling.

"Are you locked in too?"

"Yes, but I'm working on that." Trigger's focus slides to my left, as if he's looking at something beside me, but the intricate dance of pokes and swipes his hands are performing tells me that I'm only one of the things being displayed on the screen in his room.

He's actually deep inside the Whitmore security system. Again.

"We've been denied access to all the doors except the closet and bathroom doors in our own suites, and I'm going to have to hack my way back into the security system to fix that. Since the mother brought us upstairs, we've also been locked out of communication with the outside world and any other room in the house, except each other's. Which means we won't be ordering late-night snacks or having secret conversations with Waverly or Hennessy."

"So she knows you can work the e-glass?"

"That, or she assumes we'll figure it out. Or she's just being cautious."

"Then why would she let us communicate with each other?"

"My guess is she knows that if we can't, we'll bang on the doors and wake up the whole house. This direct line of communication seems to be an attempt to pacify us, for the moment."

"Can you get us out of here?"

"I'm going to try." His gaze is focused to my right now, studying a security system I can hardly even fathom. "But it'll take some time. You might as well get some sleep while you can."

Sleep hardly seems possible. But Trigger's right, so I leave the e-glass on and curl up in the big blue bed. The lights go off again when I lie down, and I watch Trigger hack his way through the Whitmores' security system, pretending he's actually here in the room with me, until I can no longer hold my eyes open.

SIX

WAVERLY

My mother lets me into her home office at six a.m., still wearing her pink robe over a matching set of satin pajamas. But her hair is pulled back from her face in a neat bun and she looks wide awake. I'm not sure she even went to bed last night.

"Why do we have to do this so early in the morning?" I ask, yawning.

"Because the film crew will be here in an hour to set up. I assume you'd rather have this settled before you and Hennessy commit to your union in permanent ink, on camera." My mother swipes one hand in the air, waking up the e-glass on the far wall. "You should really be thanking me."

"I know. I'm sorry." The early hour isn't really the problem. I'm actually terrified to talk to the Administrator. To hear her confirm that regardless of my elite private high school, custom wardrobe, and online following of tens of millions, I was never meant to be anything more than a common laborer.

I can count on one hand the number of times I've seen the Administrator in person. She rarely leaves the Lakeview compound, and Sofia and Seren hardly see her for nine months out of the year because they're boarders at my school.

I've heard her called Mom by her kids and Amelia by my parents, but I've never been able to think of her as anything other than the enigmatic, reclusive, domineering Administrator. And that's even more true now that she holds my fate in her hands.

"Have you spoken to her yet?" I ask as my mother clears the wall screen of the documents, charts, and applications she left running last night.

"No. I scheduled this through her office—they were up late for the same reasons we were. But I *have* confirmed that Dahlia and her identicals are not in this year's Lakeview catalog. No one outside of our house and the clone compound knows about this."

A soft chime echoes through the room and a large chat window appears on my mother's e-glass, blinking with a silhouette of a generic female head. The text beneath the silhouette says that the call is coming via a secure signal from Lakeview.

My pulse spikes. My foot begins to tap on the floor.

My mother calmly settles onto the couch next to me, her

spine straight, her ankles crossed. She lays one hand on my knee, and I make my leg stop bouncing.

"Accept the call," my mother says. A second later, the Administrator's face appears in place of the silhouette. The room behind her is made of straight lines and glass surfaces, giving her office the cold, sterile feel of a laboratory, despite the fact that, according to Sofia, she doesn't actually run any of the scientific divisions of her corporation.

"Amelia." My mother's greeting is crisp but polite.

The Administrator nods. "Lorna." Her gaze narrows on me, and my skin crawls while she studies my face, as if she's never truly seen me before. "I wasn't aware that you knew about our little problem until you contacted my office. I assumed *I'd* get to break this news to *you*."

"When did you find out?" my mother asks.

"Yesterday. I received a report when Dahlia 16 was arrested, and I recognized her the moment I saw her picture."

"But not before? Almost seventeen years, and you never knew you were raising five thousand copies of my daughter? *Your* daughter's best friend?"

The Administrator leans forward, pale arms crossed over the glass top of her desk. "Lorna, this facility trains hundreds of thousands of clones at a time. I personally approve every strand of DNA based upon chromosomal traits and a genotype report, but I don't walk the training grounds, inspecting faces, for the same reason you don't go down to your e-glass factory and watch tablets roll off the assembly line. I haven't seen any of your daughter's clones since I inspected them at year five. Which was before Sofia even met Waverly."

"Seriously?" I demand as outrage gets the better of me. "You don't know what your own product looks like?"

My mom shoots me a warning glance, but the Administrator's full attention feels like an hour locked in the walk-in freezer. "My time is spent managing the compound and overseeing orders." She turns back to my mother, and I feel limp with relief. "Once the clones are in production, I rarely see them until I start putting together the annual catalog, unless something goes wrong. Obviously, yesterday something went wrong." Her pointed left eyebrow rises. "Though it would appear that that 'something' actually went wrong more than eighteen years ago. Care to tell me how you wound up raising one of my clones, Lorna?"

I shift on the leather sofa, uncomfortable with the descriptor, but I'm not going to interrupt again. This discussion may be about me, but it doesn't have to *involve* me.

"How can you be sure she's a clone? You haven't analyzed Waverly's DNA."

The Administrator dismisses my mother's bluff with a roll of her eyes. "Dahlia 16's genetic test said she isn't a clone. But her identicals were. I know what Wexler did for you, Lorna. I know he put *your* baby into production to fulfill *my* order. And I know he sent you the wrong embryo."

"Then you must also know that you authorized mass replication of DNA you didn't own. That's a felony."

I glance at my mother in surprise. Threatening the Administrator seems like a very risky move. But my mom isn't done yet.

"If we bring charges, the court will shut down Lakeview for the duration of the investigation, at a minimum. *Years* of lost productivity and profit, Amelia. Along with the bad press a trial would bring."

The Administrator aims a pointed glance at me. "Do you really want the world to know the Whitmore family made unauthorized use of Lakeview's facilities and clone labor as well as unauthorized use of proprietary technology? That you *stole* biological tissue belonging to Lakeview? That your daughter is nothing but a cheap replica of a hydroponic gardener?" She pauses dramatically, and her cold gaze hardens. "Clones can't hold citizenship, Lorna."

My face burns, and I blink away the tears.

Though I can feel anger radiating from her in silent waves, my mother looks unmoved by the Administrator's threats. "I suggest we come to an agreement that will leave us both unscathed by this whole mess."

The Administrator seems only mildly interested, but I'm not buying it. She'd *never* let anyone shut down Lakeview. "What do you propose?"

"You destroy all records and evidence that a certain class of trade laborers ever existed. And that any Whitmore DNA was ever in your possession. In return, we will destroy the evidence in *our* possession."

"What evidence would that be? Other than the sole Whitmore heir?" The Administrator's focus finds me again, and this time it feels like a threat. I hold her gaze, to make sure she knows she's not dealing with an obedient, submissive trade laborer.

I may look like Dahlia and her identicals, but I am a Whitmore through and through.

"Dahlia 16," my mother says, as if it should have been obvious. "Amelia, we have your missing gardener."

The Administrator blinks, and for just a second, a crack in her poised facade hints at the chaos and anxiety that must be wreaking havoc behind the scenes at Lakeview.

"You . . . ? We're also missing a cadet. Do you have him?"

"Trigger 17. We do. How else would we know about any of this?"

The Administrator clears her throat. "I assumed Waverly saw or overheard something at Seren's party last night. My security team followed the Chapmans' car all the way to the gate to question them, but the car didn't stop." She turns an accusing gaze on me.

"I didn't go to the party. Your gardener stumbled into it and faked her way through, pretending to be me. Then she left in Hennessy's chauffeured car, like one of the guests."

The Administrator's jaw tightens—the only sign of how frustrated she must actually be. "Send them back."

"No," my mother says, and I glance at her in surprise again. "I *will* fulfill my part of the agreement, as soon as I'm able. But for now, we need Dahlia."

"Why?"

"Because her genome wasn't altered to fulfill your order, her body produces hormones that Waverly's does not. A series of biological donations might let us develop a custom hormone therapy for my daughter."

I glance at my mother in surprise.

The Administrator's brows rise. "Interesting. That might help with fertility, if that's your goal, but hormones won't fix—"

"But once we have what we need . . . ," my mother interrupts, her entire frame suddenly tense. "You have my word that we will destroy all evidence of her existence."

"Mom!" The blood drains from my face, leaving me cold.

She shoots me a brief, hard look, and my mouth snaps shut. But I can't focus on another word said as she and the Administrator negotiate, coming to terms on an agreement that will affect the rest of my life.

Maybe it's callous of me to feel nothing about the deaths of all those other girls who looked just like me, but I never met any of them. By the time I knew they'd existed, they were already gone. But Dahlia 16 is real, and she's here, and I've seen her. I've spoken to her. She's not a clone. She's not a servant.

She may not be a Whitmore—I may not even like her—but she's a *person*. I can't believe my mother would just . . .

She's lying to the Administrator. She has to be.

"Agreed." The Administrator gives my mother a reluctant nod, and I force myself to focus on the discussion going on without me. "Send the cadet back, and you may have limited, temporary custody of Dahlia 16, for biomedical purposes. On the condition that her existence *never* comes to light."

My mother returns her nod. "I'll send the cadet back to Lakeview with an armed escort this afternoon."

The Administrator leans closer to the screen in her white leather chair. "I understand that your daughter leads somewhat of a public life. If Dahlia 16 is ever seen, on camera or off—"

"She won't be," my mother snaps. "We stand to lose just as much as you do if that were to happen."

"You stand to lose *much* more than I do, Lorna. If your little science project threatens Lakeview in any way, I will have you and your husband arrested. Then I will reclaim custody of my stolen biological tissue." The Administrator's gaze slides toward me again and she gives me a slow, cold smile.

The screen fogs over as she ends the call.

My mother exhales. Her entire body seems to deflate.

"What does that mean?" My hands are clenched so tightly my fingers have gone white. "What stolen biological tissue?"

"You need to go get ready." She stands and smooths already perfect hair back toward her bun with one trembling hand. "We'll discuss this after the Chapmans and the camera crew have gone."

"No! What biological tissue?" My mother turns away from me, and I grab her arm. "Mom! You're not really going to *kill* Dahlia, are you?"

She rips her arm from my grip and her gaze burns into me. "I don't have any choice, and neither do you. If the world finds out you're a clone, you'll lose your citizenship. Do you understand what that means?"

I blink at her, trying to bring the looming question mark into focus.

"Clones can't own property. They can't go to school. They can't marry. They can't inherit multibillion-dollar tech conglomerates. If *anyone* ever finds out about Dahlia, your life will be over. Literally, Waverly."

Chills race up my arms and down my spine. "What does that mean?"

My mother exhales slowly. "*You* are the stolen biological tissue, honey. Wexler used the DNA I sent him, but he implanted it into an egg stripped of its original genetic material. That's how Lakeview creates embryos. And that egg—that original biological tissue—came from a cache that belongs to Amelia Locke. Which means she might have a legal right to custody of you."

My head spins with the implications. "But I'm eighteen. *No one* has custody of me."

My mother shakes her head slowly. "The Administrator's custody claims wouldn't be parental. She literally owns the base material that created you, just like she does with all the clones at Lakeview. She could ask the court to return possession of that material to her as if it were a stolen chair or tablet."

The reality of what she's saying crashes into me like a car

at full speed. "If she owns me, she could have me euthanized, like she did with all the others."

My mother presses her lips into a grim line. "And if we don't destroy her gardener, that's exactly what she'll do. It's Dahlia or you, sweetheart. And I choose you."

SEVEN

DAHLIA

"Dahlia." Someone shakes my shoulder, and I open my eyes to find Trigger 17 staring down at me. The room is bright, and it takes me a moment to place the blue walls behind him. Then I sit up, and yesterday comes back to me in a sudden rush of grief and adrenaline.

My identicals are dead. Lakeview was a lie. Lorna Whitmore locked me in this room.

"We have to go back to Lakeview. We have to tell them." I throw back the blankets and slide onto the floor, where my bare feet sink into thick carpet. And that's when I truly register Trigger's presence. "You got the door open!" I throw my arms around him.

"Good morning to you too." He smiles and kisses me. "This is how I'd like to start every day, only without the need to flee for our lives."

I kiss him again, lingering in the contact longer than I

probably should. He's the only thing I have left, and being unable to get to him had felt like losing him too.

Then his greeting sinks in. "Morning?" I whisper, even though we're alone. He's not supposed to be in here, and I'm afraid that speaking loud enough for the room to hear us will get us caught.

He nods at the exterior wall, and I turn to see that a thin line of sunlight now outlines the drapes covering the windows. "It took longer than I expected."

"How late is it?" It doesn't feel like morning without the beeping of the dorm-wide wake-up alarm and three identicals jockeying for space at the sink in our bathroom. "Do you think people are up yet?"

"I know they are." He sweeps one hand in the direction of the e-glass, and it fogs over, then lights up. "Live feed. Exterior cameras. Show me the driveway."

The screen blurs again, then clears to show a grid of four camera feeds, each offering a different view of the front of the house, including the circular drive. Where six black vehicles are now parked in a line.

"They pulled up half an hour ago," Trigger says. "Something's going on."

"Are they from Lakeview?" I squint at the screen, my heart hammering against my chest, but I don't see a city seal on any of the cars. "Did Lorna turn us in?"

"I don't think so. There weren't any soldiers. Just women with tablets and satchels, and men carrying equipment."

"Workers? Are they clones?"

"Definitely not."

"Great. We're not going to be able to sneak out with the house full of people." But we can't just sit here and wait for Lorna to call the Administrator.

"I don't know. . . ." Trigger scrolls through more camera feeds, then spreads his fingers to enlarge one showing a group of people milling around a spread of food in a large dining room. Equipment I don't recognize sits in the corners of the room, and bright lights have been aimed at a chair at the end of the table, where two women are laying out tiny brushes and an assortment of small containers. "They're all gathered in one place, downstairs. We could use whatever they're doing as a distraction."

"Where are Waverly and her parents? And Hennessy? Do they know you've hacked the security system?"

"The parents are in their suite, and I think if they knew, I wouldn't have access to these cameras." He scrolls through more feeds, then enlarges two of them. The first shows Waverly's mother and a man who could only be her father chatting as he knots a tie around his neck. She appears to be drawing lines around her own eyes, in front of a mirror. "According to what I've gleaned from playing around in their system, the father's name is Dane Whitmore."

"That still feels so strange to think of. That everyone here has parents, except the clones. It seems so inefficient— making people one at a time."

"Everything they do is wasteful and inefficient."

"It certainly looks that way." Yet it's hard for me to think of Lakeview's efficiency with much nostalgia or respect, knowing that we were taught to maximize effort and streamline processes not for our own benefit, but in order to better serve people like Waverly and her parents.

Trigger gestures to the other feed, where my clone is staring straight at the screen as if it were a mirror, turning to admire her own clothing. "Waverly's in her room, and Hennessy left before dawn. But I get the impression that he's coming back."

"So if we go now, we can sneak past all the new people. And if they see us, they'll just assume I'm Waverly and you're my security." I shrug. "It worked last night, and it should work again today, if we can avoid the Whitmores."

Trigger lifts my arm to show me my own bar code. "Last night, this wasn't visible."

"Easy enough." I cross into the bathroom to grab the cuff from the counter where I left it, but . . . "It's gone. So is Margo's dress. Lorna must have sent someone for them." It gives me chills to think that someone walked right by me while I was asleep, and I had no idea.

"Are there any other clothes in here? Something with long sleeves?" Trigger heads for the dresser and starts pulling drawers open.

"No, but look." I point at the feed from Waverly's room, where at least a dozen articles of clothing have been tossed across her bed, rejected in favor of the outfit she's wearing. As

I watch, she heads into her bathroom, and the door slides shut behind her. "Trigger!" I turn to him, an idea pulsing through me. "Can you lock her in there? Just long enough for us to grab a long-sleeved shirt?"

He's already gesturing at the screen, minimizing the camera feeds in favor of menus I don't recognize. "I'll have to revoke her access to the entire system to keep her from calling for help. But yes." He gives the screen one last, victorious poke. "Done."

"That was fast."

Trigger pulls me close. "I'm *really* good at what I do," he whispers against my neck, right below my ear, and with my hands pressed against his chest, I can feel every line of muscle standing out beneath his thin shirt. He lets me go with obvious reluctance, but the ghost of his body heat lingers against my palms. "Show me a floor plan of this house," he says to the e-glass.

A blue three-dimensional map of the house appears onscreen, cluttered with symbols I don't understand.

"Plot a route from here to the nearest exit, with Waverly Whitmore's bedroom as a waypoint."

On the map, a line made of red dashes trails out of the room we're evidently standing in and winds its way down the hall and around the corner to another room, which must be Waverly's. A second line of green dashes leads away from her room, down a curving flight of stairs, then out the front door.

"Alternate route," Trigger says. "Avoid the main entry."

A new green path appears, this time leading to an exit at the back of the house. Trigger and I study the route, and I commit the turns to memory.

"Are you ready?" He takes my hand, and I squeeze his.

"As I'm ever going to be."

This time when we approach the door, it opens. Trigger lets go of my hand as we step into the hallway, and I mentally tick off every turn we make and each room we pass. My pulse races with every step; I'm privately certain that we'll be caught and re-arrested.

There's nothing to distinguish Waverly's door from any of the others, and when it doesn't open the moment we step close to it, I wonder if we've been caught. If Lorna has already reprogrammed her security system to keep us out. But then Trigger waves one hand at the door, and it opens.

Of course. They don't auto-open from the outside, to keep every door in the house from sliding open any time someone walks down the hall.

I spare a second to make sure Waverly isn't standing in the middle of her bedroom; then I tug Trigger inside. The door closes behind us, and I exhale. We are one step closer to escape.

"Hey!" Waverly shouts from the bathroom, and I jump, startled. "Is someone out there? There's some kind of glitch and I'm stuck in here!"

Trigger gives me a wink and a smile, and I swallow a twinge of guilt at having locked up my own clone. She may be my identical, but she's not my sister. She's made that clear.

Her room is beautifully furnished and I would love to study all the pictures on the walls, but there's no time, so I head straight for the huge bed. I paw through the clothes discarded on the comforter and grab the first long-sleeved blouse I find. It's blue, with thick black leather wrist cuffs and a thin black ribbon lacing up the center.

Trigger turns around to give me privacy, and I pull off the borrowed tank top, then tug the silky blue blouse over my head.

The e-glass in Waverly's room is set to function as a mirror, and I gasp when I look at myself in it. The ribbon threaded down the center of the blouse leaves a half-inch strip of my flesh exposed, from neck to navel, and I can't make the material close. The ribbons are sewn in place.

Trigger appears next to me in the mirror, holding a pair of black leggings. "Here. You'll give yourself away in pajama bottoms." Instead of taking the pants, I cross my arms over my chest, trying to close the gap in the shirt, but he only gives me a heated smile. "I know it's just a costume, but you look amazing."

"Really?" I whisper.

His smile grows as I let go of my blouse to accept the leggings.

"Hey!" Waverly shouts again from the bathroom. "Who's out there?"

Trigger turns around again, and I step out of the pajama pants, then shimmy into leggings that are just as snug as the PJs were. Which is when I realize my feet are bare.

In the mirror, I spy a pile of discarded shoes at the end of Waverly's bed. One pair is the same blue as the blouse, with spiky, shiny black heels. I slip my feet into them. I'm ready to go, and running in these heels will be impossible, but Waverly doesn't seem like the kind of girl to walk around barefoot—or in the wrong shoes.

Waverly is still shouting as we leave the room, and I sigh again with relief when the door slides closed behind us and I realize we can't hear her from the hallway.

My first few steps are shaky in her shoes, and I'm tempted to grab Trigger's hand, but Waverly would never hold hands with her security team. So I stand up straight and press on, dreading the staircase as it comes into view at the end of the hall.

Then voices echo toward us from the first-floor foyer. Footsteps clack up the stairs. My heart slams against my sternum. I don't recognize the woman coming toward me, dark ponytail swinging behind her head, large tablet clutched in one hand.

"Waverly! There you are!" She loops her arm through mine without even a glance at Trigger, who falls back into the proper security position, his expression carefully blank. "Let's get your hair and makeup done. This is going to be the best episode yet!"

EIGHT

DAHLIA

I have no idea what to do as the woman with the ponytail half-guides, half-pulls me toward the stairs. "The crew is setting up for a sound check. We *really* want to get everything right for the ink ceremony," she says, "since we can't do a reshoot."

"Um . . ." *Tell her you have to go to the bathroom. Tell her you feel sick. Tell her something—anything—to keep her from dragging you into . . . whatever an ink ceremony is.*

But what if she wants to escort me back to "my" room and hears Waverly shouting from the bathroom? What if she wants to call a doctor? Or Waverly's mother?

Trigger trails silently behind us as the woman with the ponytail leads me down the first-floor hall past the room with all the books, into the dining room we saw on the e-glass. Two women stand to greet me the moment we step into the room.

"Waverly! Great blouse!" a blonde says as she pulls out the chair at the end of the table for me. "This is Chesca, who's come on board to do your makeup for this special episode."

I sit in the chair, and Chesca adjusts a tabletop lighting fixture to aim it more directly at my face, which makes me squint. At the edge of my vision, Trigger stands with his back against the wall, watching both me and the room's two exits.

"It's so great to meet you," Chesca says, and I stifle a relieved exhalation. She's never met Waverly. Which means she won't notice any minor differences in our faces. But the *other* woman . . .

"I'm pleased to meet you as well," I say as Chesca begins opening a series of small tubes and bottles.

The blond woman moves behind me and begins to comb out my hair. "Your hair's grown," she comments. "And the ends feel a little dry. Are you still conditioning every day?"

I nod in answer to a question I don't even understand.

While the blonde works on my hair with a series of spritzes and hot metal wands, Chesca pins a paper bib to my blouse and begins to paint my face and neck with tiny brushes and smudging tools. It doesn't take me long to realize that this is how the girls at Seren's party looked like they did. They wore makeup.

Both women work quickly, chatting with each other, and I'm grateful that they don't expect "Waverly" to join the conversation. When I'm not following directions to look up or suck in my cheeks, I watch the door, terrified that at any moment Waverly or her parents will walk in and expose my charade.

Half an hour later, Chesca and the blonde hold up several mirrors, angled to show me both my face and the back of my head at once.

I'm stunned by my own reflection. I look like myself, but smoother. Even. Flawless.

"Wow," I whisper, and both women beam at me in the mirror, pleased with my reaction. Chesca removes the bib and I stand, wobbling a little in Waverly's heels. I cast a meaningful glance at Trigger, hoping he's ready to escape, now that—

"She looks great!" The woman in the ponytail loops her arm through mine again and leads me toward the door. "But then, she always looks great. Hennessy and his family are in the library with your parents. Your mother stood in for you during sound check. So we're all ready to roll!"

Before I can process any of that, we're walking down the hall, headed toward some event that has the woman next to me practically humming with excitement.

"You okay?" she whispers so that the six men gathered around the library entrance won't hear her. "You should be excited! You've been waiting for this your whole life!"

"I'm thrilled," I whisper, forcing a smile, but her frown only deepens.

"Nervous about the pain? Do you want me to get you a drink? There's some champagne in there for the celebration, but I can go find something else—"

Pain? "No, thank you. I'm fine." Except for the fact that I'm about to pretend to be Waverly in front of the people who know her best. At least three of whom now know that the real me actually exists.

This will *never* work.

I glance back at Trigger, who's taken up his position behind us. As if Waverly would need security in her own house. But the woman with the ponytail is so focused on her task that she hasn't noticed anything out of the ordinary. She gives a hand signal to one of the men in the hallway.

He gestures to the rest of the crew, and they part to make way for me, but the woman with the ponytail hangs back, watching me expectantly. Without even noticing that she's blocking Trigger's path.

One of the men aims a piece of shoulder-mounted equipment at me while the other holds a microphone mounted to a long pole over my head. "Let's get rolling," the first man calls. "And keep it as unobtrusive as possible. This is a tender moment, people!"

I continue toward the library, as I'm obviously expected to do, and they all watch me as if I'm about to perform some kind of trick. The microphone follows me overhead, and suddenly I understand. I'm being recorded. Whatever this ink ceremony is, Waverly is having it documented, like the historical films we saw in class and the instructional videos that taught us how to use new gardening equipment.

If I run now, my attempted escape will be caught on

camera. Though that would probably be true anyway, considering that every corner of this house seems to be under surveillance as part of the security system.

"Hey, Audra, do you want us to get a setup shot of her coming down the stairs?" the man in charge of the crew asks.

The woman with the ponytail—Audra—shakes her head. "We can shoot that afterward. For now, let's capture the ink bonding as honestly as we can. I want four different angles so we don't miss anything. And this time, make sure the equipment doesn't intrude on the reality of the moment."

The crew seems to close in around me, herding me toward the library. Cutting me off from Trigger.

I hesitate in the doorway. Inside, Hennessy kneels on a pillow on the floor, his left forearm resting on a cloth spread over the coffee table in the center of the grouping of furniture. Kneeling next to him, a woman is making adjustments to a piece of equipment that looks like a hefty cylinder. Like a long, heavy steel sleeve.

Waverly's father stands at the end of the coffee table, talking to a man and woman with mostly gray hair, and all three of them hold narrow stemmed glasses half-full of the champagne Audra mentioned. The gray-haired man has Hennessy's nose, and the woman has his eyes. They can only be his parents.

Margo sits on the couch at her brother's back, scrolling and tapping on her tablet, as if she can't see the camera crew or the parents obviously gathered to celebrate.

"—and the Caruthers sisters have designed a union ink pattern unlike anything we've seen before," Lorna says to the camera aimed at her. A woman on her left holds a metal sleeve identical to the one the woman next to Hennessy is adjusting. "Or so I hear. I haven't actually seen it yet, but I know that designs have evolved quite a bit since Dane and I got ours!" Waverly's mother holds up her left arm, showing off the date written in scrolling numbers on her skin.

Union ink. Understanding washes over me.

Waverly and Hennessy are here to have matching dates applied to their arms, to commemorate their upcoming wedding—a legal union of two people for the purposes of affection and procreation. An archaic tradition, according to my teachers in Lakeview, yet one that is obviously still alive and well in the rest of the world.

Hennessy's parents' cuffs have been rolled up to show off matching dates. Dane Whitmore's right sweater sleeve has been pushed halfway up his arm, exposing a date that matches Lorna's.

My feet freeze to the floor, my heart pounding in my ears. I can't step into this room.

Hennessy's gaze meets mine, and relief washes over his face. "Waverly." He starts to stand, but the woman with the steel sleeve grabs his wrist to stop him.

"Sorry," she says. "I'm still calibrating."

Waverly's mother sees me, and my pulse races. Surely she'll know with one glance at me that I'm not her daughter.

She'll make up some excuse to get me out of there and find Waverly.

Being caught now seems like the lesser of two evils.

But Lorna only gives me a tense smile, then ushers the woman carrying the sleeve toward the coffee table. "We're ready for you over here," she says as she sets the cylinder on the table.

Dane Whitmore and the Chapmans turn. Silence descends from the crew, and when I look up, I realize that this moment is already being recorded not just by the camera that followed me in here, but by crew members stationed all over the room, wearing small, thin cameras mounted to their shoulders in rigs supporting a bunch of equipment I've never seen before. Microphones. Display screens. Long, segmented lenses.

It feels like a million eyes are on me right now. How can none of them realize I'm not Waverly?

I never mistook any of my identicals for one another. We might have looked alike, but we weren't the same people. We had different gestures and habits. Different speech patterns. Different expressions. And that's doubly true for Waverly and me, having grown up in different worlds.

Yet the people closest to her are only seeing what they expect to see. Which can only mean they're not really paying attention.

I let Lorna lead me to the coffee table, mentally scrambling for a way out of this. But maybe the best way out is straight through: if Waverly's parents are fooled, surely the rest of the world will be too. Maybe I should just ride this out. Try not to say or do anything she wouldn't say or do. That *has* to be easier now that I've actually met her and heard her speak.

"Kneel on the pillow and put your left arm on the table," the woman holding the cylinder says to me.

Slowly, I kneel and hold my arm out.

Hennessy smiles at me, and he looks almost as terrified as I feel, even though he's really supposed to be here. Margo leans forward on the couch behind him, peering over his shoulder.

"Wow, I can't believe you guys are really going through with it," she says. "No turning back after this."

"That's the whole point, Margo," he says, but he's still looking at me, a tender smile on his lips. "We're not scared, are we?" And to his credit, his steady voice doesn't even hint at the fear in his eyes. I wonder if the cameras can see that?

I wonder if Waverly's seen it.

"No," I whisper back. Two of the camera men move for a better view of me. I remember what Audra told me on our way here. "I've been waiting my whole life for this."

"Aww," Mrs. Chapman says, and two cameras shift to focus on her, taking some of the pressure off me. They concentrate on the parents' sweet smiles as Lorna hooks her arm around her husband's, her expression glazing over with a haze of nostalgia.

Dane Whitmore smiles at me, but his posture is stiff. He's holding himself apart from Lorna, despite her grip on his arm, but no one else seems to have noticed the tension between them. Because everyone else is looking at me.

The woman next to me unbuttons the cuff of my left sleeve and rolls it back. "Okay, slide your hand through here," she says, holding out the metal cylinder while the woman attending to Hennessy does the same thing.

I hesitate, staring at the smooth steel sleeve. But I can't back out without exposing myself as an imposter. So I'll get the ink, and then Waverly can get it too. Later. In private. No one will ever know she wasn't actually present for what's obviously supposed to be a monumental moment in her life.

I feel almost as bad about her missing it as I do about being trapped here in her place.

Left with no other choice, I slide my arm into the cold cylinder, and it tightens immediately, drawing a gasp from me.

The woman laughs. "I know you're nervous, but in just a minute, you'll be able to show the world what all the fuss has been about." She smiles for the camera. "This is the single most intricate design we've ever done. Truly one of a kind. And it means the world to my sister and me to know that it will be forever worn by Waverly and Hennessy."

"The honor is all ours." Hennessy lays his right arm across the table, his palm open, fingers grasping for mine. I put my free hand in his, and he squeezes it, amid another round of "Awws" from the parents.

Margo rolls her eyes and leans back on the couch, but her gaze is glued to the sleek machines encircling her brother's arm and mine.

"Any last words?" the woman next to Hennessy asks, and everyone else laughs.

Hennessy looks right into my eyes. "To the start of forever," he whispers, and though I'm not sure if the cameras can hear him, the families certainly can.

"Forever," I echo, because I don't know what else to say.

"Okay. Now hold very still." The woman next to me leans over the device wrapped around my arm. "Relax your hand."

I try to comply as Hennessy's grip on my free hand tightens until my fingers ache.

"Three . . ." The woman leaning over me positions her finger over a small screen on top of the device, where the word *deploy* is flashing in red letters.

"Two . . . ," her sister says from across the coffee table.

"One!" The woman standing over me taps the screen on my device just as the other woman taps on Hennessy's.

Pain shoots through my forearm, and I suck in a sharp breath.

"Son of a—!" Hennessy bites off whatever he was going to say and squeezes his eyes closed.

My fist clenches involuntarily as fire contained by the metal sleeve races across my arm in a thousand pinpricks.

A second later, the pain recedes, leaving only a sharp,

residual ache, and the screen on the device flashes green. Something cold and instantly soothing is sprayed over my arm inside the cylinder.

I glance at the doorway, hoping for a glimpse of Trigger. Instead, between the shoulders of two of the crew members, I see a thin slice of a face I'd know anywhere. Waverly's tear-filled left eye blinks at me. Then she disappears down the hall while everyone else is still staring at me and Hennessy, eagerly awaiting the revelation of an ink design that should be on *her* arm.

The woman next to me slides the metal sleeve free.

All four parents gasp. Margo drops her tablet on the sofa as she stands to peer over her brother's shoulder. One of the cameramen steps closer, coming in for a better shot.

I look down at my left arm, and everything else seems to fade into the background. In the center of my forearm, several inches from my wrist, is a beautifully colorful, amazingly intricate series of swirls, arches, and tiny loops forming a pattern I can't quite make sense of.

Until Hennessy slides his arm toward mine across the coffee table.

Somehow, though our markings appear identical, when our arms are placed next to each other, inverted, the hundreds—thousands?—of individual ink markings join to form a date.

Waverly and Hennessy's wedding date.

And after a second, they begin to pulse with color in time

with my heartbeat, each stunning shade fading into the next with an odd rippling effect I should be able to feel. But I cannot.

"Oh . . ." Lorna sinks to her knees next to us. "It's *beautiful*, darling."

"Stunning," my father agrees.

"I've never seen anything quite like it," Mrs. Chapman says, her drink momentarily forgotten.

I can't look away from my own arm, and as I watch, the throbbing of color begins to speed up, along with my pulse.

"There's more." Hennessy stands, and as he pulls his arm away from mine, the colors stop pulsing. He rounds the table, then reaches down to help me up and holds his arm next to mine.

The cameramen move closer.

Somehow, even though our arms are now oriented the same direction, the patterns still form the same date they made before.

"Whether we're side by side or face to face, we are one. That was the idea, anyway," he says to the room around us, with an almost shy smile.

"That's beautiful, son." His father raises his glass in salute.

"And it's entirely unique." The artist next to me picks up the metal sleeve that inked my arm, cradling it like something precious. "Eight months of work. And though I'm sure pulsing ink will become a trend, there has never been, nor will there ever be, union ink like yours." She and her sister each press a button on the steel sleeves, and a tiny chip pops out of each device. "Just like there will never be another couple like Waverly and Hennessy."

"Ready?" the other sister asks as she lifts the chip.

Ready for what?

The sisters each place a chip between their front teeth, then pull down with a sudden snapping motion. Breaking the chips in half.

The room erupts in applause.

I don't understand what's just happened, but a sick feeling churns deep in my stomach. That felt . . . irreversible.

"Champagne!" Lorna announces, and the cameramen move aside so she can get to a table set up on one side of the room, where two more open bottles sit in buckets of ice, next to a row of empty glass flutes.

"Now, your skin has been numbed, but that'll wear off in a few hours, and there's bound to be a little swelling," one of the Caruthers sisters tells me while the parents refill their glasses. She dons a pair of sterile gloves from a sealed package, then squirts a dollop of blue foam on my forearm. "This is an antibacterial moisturizer," she explains while she spreads it into a thin layer over the ink. Then she applies a clear, flexible protective wrap over my entire forearm and gives me instructions about how and when to wash the new ink.

I'm not processing a single word she's saying.

When Hennessy's arm is similarly treated, he smiles and

takes my hand, then frowns when my grip doesn't relax in his. He looks into my eyes, and recognition dawns in his expression, swift and horrible. He leans in, as if he'll kiss me, and instead whispers what must look like something very sweet in my ear. "Dahlia 16?"

I nod, holding back tears with sheer will.

He whispers angry words I've never heard before; then his hand tightens around mine again and he turns to both sets of parents. "Will you excuse us for a moment? My future bride and I would like to admire our ink in private."

"Of course." His mother hardly glances up as she accepts another glass of champagne from Waverly's mother.

"Hurry back!" Lorna calls after us as the cameras part to let us pass.

Trigger is not in the hallway, and I only have a second to hope he followed Waverly to her room before Audra gives a signal to one of the cameramen, who follows us into the foyer.

"Sorry. Not for public consumption," Hennessy tells him with a sly smile as he slides one arm around my waist.

Audra pouts, but she and the cameraman settle for filming us as we head up the stairs.

"I should have known. You're not wearing your ring. *Her* ring," Hennessy whispers as we disappear down the second floor hallway. "How did none of us notice that? What the hell happened?"

"Audra thought I was Waverly. I didn't know what to do."

"Anything," he snaps. "For future reference, the answer is *anything* that will get you out of the room. Off camera."

"And go where?" I demand softly. "I'm not authorized to open the doors!"

"*Damn* it," Hennessy whispers. He holds his arm out, staring at the ink as we walk. "Waverly's going to *lose it* when she sees this."

"She already saw. From the hall. I don't think anyone other than Trigger noticed her, because they were all staring at us."

"There *has* to be some way to fix this." We stop in front of Waverly's room and he waves his hand, but the door doesn't open. He makes the gesture again, and again nothing happens. "She revoked my access. *Waverly!*" he half whispers, knocking on the door. "Let us in before someone sees us!"

The door slides open, and he tugs me into her room.

My clone stands in the center of the thick white rug, alone, wearing a beautiful, lacy red blouse, her hands clenched into fists at her sides. "How *could* you?" she growls at me, fury and grief warring behind her accusing gaze.

Hennessy swipes one hand at the door, and it closes behind us, though we're hardly a foot inside the room. I'm afraid to go any farther. Waverly looks like she'd like to claw my eyeballs out and display them impaled on little toothpicks.

"Audra thought I was you, and I didn't know how to get

out of that." I hold out my sore arm. "I didn't mean to take your ink. I don't even really know what this means."

"It means that until we can get the Caruthers sisters to replicate work it took them eight months to do in the first place"—she growls at me through clenched teeth—"*you* are Waverly Whitmore."

NINE

WAVERLY

"This can't be happening," I mumble as I pace across the plush rug between my bed and my bathroom door, waiting for my mother to arrive after my frantic message to her. "This *can't* be happening."

Dahlia 16 stands near the door, her hands clasped tightly in front of her. "Where's Trigger?"

"It wasn't Dahlia's fault," Hennessy says. "Audra pulled her into the library, thinking she was you."

"Why are you defending her?" I shout before it occurs to me that anyone walking by my room would know something is terribly wrong. "This is *totally* her fault. She and her soldier boyfriend locked me in my bathroom, stole my clothes, and impersonated me on camera, on *my* own show!"

Hennessy turns on her. "You . . . ?"

"We were only trying to get out of the house." Dahlia gives

him a wide-eyed, innocent look, but I am *not* fooled. "Lorna locked us up all night, and we need to . . ." She bites off the rest of her excuse. "We don't belong here." Her gaze finds me. "We were trying to get out of the city, and the only way to do that safely was for me to pretend to be you. But then Audra saw me, and . . ." She shrugs, leaving me to fill in the rest with what I already know.

"How did you know I was in the bathroom? And how the hell did you revoke my access to my own house?" I demand. But Dahlia 16 only shrugs. Not as if she doesn't know the answers, but as if she's not going to give them to me. This is no naive, innocent hydroponic gardener. No typical Lakeview servant. "Do you have *any* idea what you've done?"

She can't possibly, because she doesn't know what the Administrator threatened to do to *both* of us if the world ever saw her.

"It was an accident," Hennessy says.

"How could you let this happen?" I turn on him, more hurt than angry. "Could you really not tell you were pledging to spend the rest of your life with the wrong girl?"

"Waverly, calm down." He reaches for me, and when I back away, he looks crushed. "We're in this together, no matter what. Remember?"

"No, now you're in this with *her*. It's not like I can go on camera without that ink." My gaze settles on Dahlia again. "I hope you liked pretending to be me, because you just scored a starring role in *my* life. Every on-screen moment and every public appearance, until we can get the Caruthers sisters to replicate that pattern."

Dahlia's chin trembles while she stares at the design, which is already starting to puff up a little as her skin swells. I pull my tablet from my pocket, trying not to get my hopes up. "Maybe they haven't destroyed the chips yet, and we can—"

"They destroyed them on camera," Hennessy says. "You told them to, remember? To emphasize the permanence of the moment. The uniqueness of the design."

My finger stills on the surface of my tablet. "So this is *my* fault?"

"No." He pulls me into a hug, and this time I let him hold me. "I'm just saying we need to work together. All three of us. What's done is done, and we need to look forward. We need to figure out how to fix this."

"You're right." I sniffle and step out of his embrace, wiping away my tears, suddenly aware of the fact that my imposter's makeup is perfectly done, but my face is still bare. And probably puffy from crying. "Okay." I push past my anger and frustration and force myself to focus on finding a solution. "The real problem is that she has the ink"—I glance at Dahlia's arm, at the gorgeous, exorbitantly expensive, unique pattern that was supposed to be mine—"and I need it."

"And you can't get it because . . . ?" Dahlia still looks confused.

"When they destroyed the chips, they lost their ability to

program this pattern into the ink sleeves," Hennessy explains. "And we asked them not to keep a backup."

"That's the whole point of our design," I add through clenched teeth. "It was supposed to be as distinctive and unique as Hennessy and I are. As our relationship is. I didn't want people to be able to hack into the Caruthers' database and steal it after the show airs." I reach for her arm, then snatch my hand back without touching her, because I can't stand for this horrible moment to feel any more tangible than it already does. "It took *eight months* to draw. To get every line perfect. And it was all for nothing."

"What's a show?" Dahlia asks. "Audra said they were recording an episode—"

"What's wrong?" my mother says as the door slides open to admit her into the room.

"Show her!" I demand as my mom swipes the door closed.

Dahlia holds up her arm, and my mother's confused gaze travels from the ink to her face, then to mine. She still doesn't get it, and after a second, I understand why.

The gardener is wearing my makeup. And my clothes. She no longer looks like the demure, tech-deficient identical my mother's only keeping around as my personal hormone bank.

"*Dahlia?*" Shock echoes in her whisper.

"She went *on camera*." I give my mother a pointed look; she's the only one other than me who will understand how very bad this is.

"How did this happen?" my mother demands in the deceptively soft tone she reserves for employees who've *really* pissed her off. "How *the hell* did you get out of your room?"

"Your household system seems a bit glitchy today," Trigger 17 says as my door opens to admit him. Which should *not* have happened.

"*They* did this." I fold my arms over my chest as he moves near Dahlia in a blatantly protective stance. "I don't know how, but they locked me in my bathroom and stole my clothes. Then she stole my tattoo. My show. She stole my *life*."

Dahlia looks terrified, cradling her arm as if her puffy new ink is sore, though she shouldn't be able to feel it yet. "This wasn't supposed to happen." She turns to my mother. "I don't want her life or her . . . show. We just wanted to leave."

"Well, that's no longer a possibility." My mother pulls her tablet from her pocket and I watch as she reinstates my access to the house system and revokes Trigger's. "Has Waverly explained to you about the ink binding? About what this means?"

Dahlia nods. "I don't want to be her. I *can't* be her. I don't know—"

"Hennessy." My mom turns to my fiancé. "Your family is waiting downstairs to celebrate with you. Will you please go make apologies for Waverly? Tell everyone she's not feeling well, but as soon as she is, we'll all get together and celebrate the ink binding properly."

"Of course." Hennessy pulls me close and drops a kiss on

my forehead, his standard classy but affectionate public display of affection. The ratings people tell me that plays well on camera, but he's been doing it since before I signed on for the show. It's just part of who he is. One of my favorite parts.

"And may I trust that you'll keep all this between us?"

Hennessy squeezes my hand in moral support. "Mrs. Whitmore, I know we haven't said our vows yet, but I love Waverly, and we're in this together, all the way."

My anger at him melts like ice in the sun.

"Thank you, Hennessy," my mother says as he heads into the hallway. When the door closes behind him, she turns on Trigger and Dahlia. "Are you not aware that the Administrator wants to have Dahlia executed?"

"We're very well aware," Trigger says. "That's why—"

"Most people who are in danger of execution would know to keep a low profile, but you decided to go on camera instead! I can't protect you if you're *trying* to get yourself killed."

"You were trying to protect me?" Dahlia sounds skeptical, and with good reason. But I can't scrounge up much sympathy for her since she locked me in my bathroom and stole my life.

"Why else would I confine you to your room on a filming day?" my mother demands, and it's a little creepy how easily the lies seem to roll off her tongue.

Trigger does not look fooled. "Why didn't you just tell us what was going on?"

"Because it was after one in the morning and we were

all exhausted." My mother waves all three of us toward the cluster of white leather furniture in my sitting area, and the dismissive gesture makes it clear that she owes him no further explanation. She's scrolling through a document as she sits in the chair nearest the window, and though I can't read any of it, I recognize Trigger's picture, even in reverse. "Special Forces," my mother reads. "The Administrator was kind enough to send me Trigger's file this morning."

He doesn't look surprised.

Dahlia's frown looks more scared than angry. "You spoke to the Administrator?"

"At length." My mother scrolls through the file, then looks at me. "This explains how they got access to our system." She sets her tablet in her lap and leans back in her chair to study Dahlia and her boyfriend. "But what's done is done, and controlling the damage will mean changing our plans."

"What plans?" Dahlia's voice wavers, and Trigger takes her hand. The gesture looks so much like what Hennessy would do for me that for a moment, I'm transfixed, my gaze caught on their intertwined fingers.

"I'm sending Trigger back to Lakeview this afternoon, under armed escort."

"Just him?" Dahlia frowns.

"No." His hand visibly tightens around hers. "We stay together."

"Even if that means sending her to her death?" my mother asks, though I know she has no intention of sending Dahlia anywhere. This is why she's so much better in board meetings than my father is. He's good at manipulating ideas and technology. She's good at manipulating people.

Trigger hesitates, and I frown at the soldier. Why would he drag Dahlia back if—

He wouldn't. And suddenly I understand. "You think you can escape again," I say. "Together."

Trigger doesn't reply, but my mother gives me an approving smile, pleased that I've come to the same conclusion she has. Then she turns back to the soldier and the gardener, standing tall in front of us, facing their fate as one. "That is one of your options—I can send you both back to Lakeview, where Dahlia will face execution. But the Administrator knows what you're capable of now and she'll never give you another chance to escape. Or you can accept the offer I'm about to make."

My mother shoots me a look, silently ordering me to go along with whatever she says. "Dahlia, before the ink bonding, my daughter and I had planned to ask you to stay with us for a while. One of the 'anomalies' they found in your genetic code is the production of some hormones that her body can't make. A biological donation from you could literally change her life. And since you've managed to get yourself marked with her wedding date . . . well, we need your help now more than ever."

"By pretending to be her for this . . . show?" Though it's clear she doesn't really know what that means.

"And for a few other live appearances."

A *few*? I do several a week, when school's out. There's *no way* she's ready for that.

Dahlia exhales slowly. Then she looks right at me. "I wish I could help you. But Trigger and I . . . we need to go. Now." The waver in her voice says she's not used to making demands, but her gaze shows no hesitation. "It's not safe for us here."

"It's safer for you here than anywhere else," I tell her. "Here, people think you're me."

She and Trigger look skeptical.

"The Administrator knows we need your help with the medical issue," my mother says. "She's already agreed to let you stay, if we send Trigger back."

He tenses, ready to stand his ground. "No—"

"Do you love her?" my mother demands.

Trigger frowns, as if he's not sure he understands the question. Which makes sense, considering that clones aren't even supposed to have a sex drive, much less the capacity for romantic feelings. But then he looks at Dahlia, and I can see it in his eyes.

"I think you do," my mother says. "You two risked a lot for each other, and I don't think you're the kind of guy who would drag her into danger just to keep you company, when she could be safe and happy here without you."

"That's not what I'm . . ." The conflict raging behind his features is almost painful to watch. "Dahlia, they're right." He takes both of her hands. "I'm not going to put you back in the Administrator's grip."

"You wouldn't be," she insists, clearly still convinced that they could escape again. "And anyway, that's not up to you." Dahlia fixes a surprisingly strong gaze on my mother. "Send us both back, or let us go. Either way, we're leaving."

Panic burns like fire in my veins. Locking Dahlia up is no longer an option, not that I was ever really on board with that. She'll have to be an active and *willing* participant to take my place on camera. And if she leaves or refuses to play along, I'm *so* screwed.

"Before you decide to do something stupid . . ." My mother picks up her tablet and taps rapidly through a series of screens, then opens an attachment in an email I can't see well enough to read. A video feed opens on her tablet. My mom stands and makes a swiping gesture from her tablet toward my e-glass screen.

The feed appears on my wall, nine feet tall. Larger than life.

For the half second it takes to come into focus on the bigger screen, Dahlia, Trigger, and I stare, puzzled. Then the image sharpens, and Dahlia gasps.

"If you won't do it to help Waverly—or to help yourself— then do it for them," my mother says.

On-screen, in an empty concrete room, sit *dozens* of girls wearing my face.

TEN

DAHLIA

I stare at the wall, my hands steepled over my nose and mouth, stunned beyond speech. This can't be real. They can't be . . .

"Is this real?"

"Very real. It's a live feed," Lorna says. "From one of the Administrator's 'acclimation facilities' in Valleybrook."

"How are they still alive? Are there more? Or is it just these few?" I'm looking at three dozen of my sisters, at most, and while that feels miraculous, assuming Lorna isn't lying, it leaves thousands unaccounted for.

"All 4,999 of your identicals are alive and well in the facility," she says. "They were scheduled to begin 'acclimation' for their lives outside of Lakeview until you escaped the compound, at which point the Administrator put the entire process on hold."

I don't realize I've wandered closer to the wall until I'm

less than a foot away, trying to figure out which of my identicals I'm staring at.

Isolated in that featureless concrete room, identically dressed with nothing to do but sit and stare at the floor, they've become what the rest of the world believes us to be. Indistinguishable. Interchangeable. Unworthy of notice or consideration on an individual basis.

Still . . . "They're alive." My amazement and relief are quickly eclipsed by confusion. Distrust. I turn to Lorna. "How is this possible?"

"The Administrator lied." Trigger steps up to my side, studying the screen. "That shouldn't be much of a surprise, considering that she's lied to us about everything else. But this is . . ."

"Unbelievable," I finish for him.

He nods. "Yet at the same time, it makes sense. There's nothing wrong with your identicals. She had to tell us they'd been recalled, to keep us all believing that breaking any rule could get us killed. But that's no reason to throw away the profit from nearly five thousand sales." He turns to Lorna. "That's it, right? She's still going to sell them?"

"Probably at a discount, because they missed out on that final year of training," Lorna says. "But that's better than the loss she'd take from actually having them euthanized."

Waverly groans, and her mother shoots her a censuring glance. They don't want us to see how badly it upsets her to know there are still five thousand copies of her—of me—alive and well out there.

"Why are you showing us this?" I turn back to the screen. I'm mesmerized by it. "How would me helping Waverly benefit the rest of my identicals?"

"If you cooperate—if you donate your hormones and learn to be Waverly on camera—you have my word that I will buy all 4,999 of your identicals."

Waverly stares at her mother, aghast, but Lorna doesn't seem to notice.

I refocus on her, trying to understand. "You couldn't possibly need that many trade laborers."

"I wouldn't be buying them as servants. I would be buying their freedom." She shrugs. "After all, they're my flesh and blood too." But her tone lacks the conviction of her words.

"Mom, what are you—? Where would we—?" Waverly can't seem to finish a thought, yet I know exactly what she's asking.

"I don't know yet," Lorna admits, and that feels like the most honest thing I've heard her say. "We can't bring them to Mountainside, of course. No one can ever know about them. But maybe we could build someplace for them in the wild. Their own little secret clone town." She sets her tablet in her lap, but leaves the live feed open on the wall, so I can see what she's offering. What I could be giving the sisters I thought I'd lost. "If you agree, we could start the project next week. The construction crews would never have to know what they're building. And once you've done what you can for Waverly, you can join them."

I can hardly even process what she's offering. Life. Freedom. Community. We could have the future the Administrator told us we'd be getting, without the lies of Lakeview.

Without Trigger.

And without exposing the true nature of Lakeview to its residents. Shining light on the compound would mean exposing Waverly as a clone, and her mother's sudden generosity would evaporate—at best.

I'll have to choose. Life and liberty for my identicals and me, while Lakeview remains a training center for slaves, or returning to Lakeview in handcuffs, with Trigger, for a *slim* chance of exposing the Administrator's lies to my fellow clones. And a strong chance of execution for us both.

"May we have some time to discuss?" I'm far from sure we can trust Lorna.

"Of course." She gestures for us to follow her toward the door. "But I'll need to know by dinner. There will be a lot of preparations to make and plans to set in motion, either way."

"What's the alternative?" Trigger asks, without moving to follow her. "If Dahlia says no, what will happen to her identicals?"

Lorna's smooth forehead wrinkles as she considers. "I need some time to think about that as well, if you don't mind."

I do mind. How can I weigh my options if I don't fully understand the repercussions? But I'm not in a position to make demands. I've *never* been in that position.

"I'll take you both back to Dahlia's room and have some

food brought up." Lorna gestures toward the door, and as Trigger and I comply, she glances at her daughter. "I'll have lunch sent up for us as well, but put on a long-sleeved blouse, please. You can't afford to walk around with your arm uncovered, even here."

I can't tell how much of this Waverly is processing. But as Lorna peeks into the hall to make sure no one's around to see us, my clone closes the live video window with an angry swipe of one hand.

The moment we're alone in the blue bedroom, Trigger disables the outgoing audio feeds, so no one can hear us or record anything we say. "I activated an alarm to let us know if anyone turns the audio back on," he tells me.

"Clever. What about the video?"

He shakes his head. "I don't want to mess with anything other than the audio for now, because the more I interfere with the system, the greater the chances of someone noticing what I've done and reversing it."

Within minutes, the door opens to reveal a clone in a gray servant's uniform, carrying a tray that holds two covered dishes and two glasses of ice water. The name tag pinned to her shirt reads Julienne 20, and I recognize her face from a class of manual laborers that graduated two years ago. But I can't tell whether she recognizes me or Trigger because she never looks up from the floor. Nor does she speak a single word. She just sets the tray on the dresser, moving as if she were in a mental fog.

"Julienne 20?" I say.

She turns toward me, but doesn't look up. She still hasn't seen my face. "How may I serve you?"

Her question gives me chills. It has the feel of the prescribed greetings in Lakeview, which were the only things we were permitted to say to members of another bureau. This is all Julienne 20 is allowed to say to us, unless her duties require additional communication. Yet the Whitmores, the Chapmans, and the camera crews may say whatever they like to one another. And to the clones who work here.

The disparity sits like a lump in my throat—I can't swallow it.

"I don't need anything. Thank you," I say, still puzzling through the discrepancy.

Julienne leaves, and Trigger uncovers the dishes, then sets the heavy tray on the end of the big blue bed, because there's no table in this room. We both climb onto the tall mattress and sit cross-legged with the lunch tray between us. Each plate holds a large serving of chicken and pasta in red sauce, which doesn't seem to cool off no matter how long I stare at my food instead of eating it.

I should be starving, but watching Julienne serve lunch has killed my appetite. I grew up alongside manual laborers on the training ground, and they were as aware and sociable as the rest of us—nothing like the withdrawn woman who just left the blue room, seemingly unaware of anything going on around her.

"So . . . ," Trigger begins as he contemplates his food.

I spear a piece of rotini and a chunk of tomato on my fork. "Do you think we can trust Lorna?"

"No." He dips a piece of his garlic bread in a smear of red sauce, then eats it. "Her 'clone town' in the wild is as much of a lie as Lakeview ever was."

"So whether I cooperate or not, there's nothing stopping the Administrator from selling my identicals."

"*Lorna* is what's stopping that from happening." Trigger spears three pieces of pasta and a cube of sautéed chicken on his fork. "She won't let them go to sale and expose her daughter. But there's nothing stopping her from buying and killing them all if you don't play along."

"You think she would just *murder* them?"

Trigger's fork goes still. "I think that if she buys them, she will own them, and she can and will do whatever she believes is necessary to protect Waverly."

"Which means I'm going to have to play along." I push pasta around in the sauce on my plate, but can't bring myself to take a bite. "And while I'm pretending to be Waverly, you and I can work on a plan. Some way to keep my identicals safe permanently."

"Dahlia . . ."

"No. You're staying. That's my demand, in exchange for my cooperation."

Trigger frowns as he chews his food. "Don't get your hopes up." But it feels like there's something more he wants to say.

"What's wrong?"

He meets my gaze over the lunch tray. "I agree that this is the best way forward. Possibly the *only* way, for now. But pretending you're Waverly means pretending you're going to marry Hennessy." He sounds disappointed. Hurt. "It means spending time with him and pretending that's where you want to be. As badly as I want to be here with you, I'm not looking forward to seeing that."

"Trigger, pretending is *all* it will be."

"You can't know that for sure," he insists. "I'm the only guy you've ever spent any time with. The only guy you've ever kissed. So I guess I'm worried that it isn't actually me you like. That maybe what you really like is having the option to . . . fraternize. And that's understandable—"

"No." I push the tray out of the way and scoot closer to him on the foot of the bed. "That's not true. I spent time with Hennessy at Seren's party, and I felt nothing for him. He didn't smuggle wild peanuts into the city so I could taste them fresh from the ground. He didn't sneak into the equipment shed to kiss me. He didn't risk his life to help me escape from Lakeview. That was you." I run my fingers along his chin, and though we've spent the past two days together and have been free from Lakeview's rules for at least eighteen hours, that contact still feels daring. Still makes my pulse race. As does the admission I lean forward to whisper into his ear, so that he can't see the self-conscious flush in my cheeks. "I only want to kiss *you*."

Trigger slides his hand around my neck and his fingers into my hair. He pulls me closer and his mouth presses against mine, sucking gently on my lower lip until my mouth opens. His head tilts, giving us a better angle, and this time when his tongue sweeps into my mouth I greet it with my own.

He groans and pulls away for a second. "The only good thing about this place is that we seem to be allowed to do this." Then his mouth is on mine again, and suddenly I'm fascinated with his lower lip. With tasting it. Feeling it between my teeth, for one teasing second before—

The door opens with a whisper, and we jerk apart. My face flames, and I suck in a startled breath. Trigger looks confused for a second before we both turn to see Waverly's father standing in the doorway.

"Hello. I'm Dane Whitmore." His gaze travels to Trigger, then back to me, and for a second, I'm afraid that maybe we're not allowed to kiss here either. That maybe I've ruined any chance of keeping Trigger with me. "I'm sorry." Wrinkles appear on his forehead and he looks flustered. "I guess I should have knocked. I just . . . I had to see you for myself."

I'm not sure I've ever heard an adult apologize.

"You've already seen me." I hold up my left hand, and the

unbuttoned cuff of my borrowed blouse slides down to expose the fresh tattoo, slightly swollen beneath the clear film protecting it.

"So I heard." He glances at the ink. "But this morning, I didn't realize . . ."

Trigger slides off the bed onto his feet while Mr. Whitmore eyes me with a more open curiosity than either Waverly or her mother did when we met. His interest seems unencumbered by either dread or fear. He seems, quite simply, intrigued.

"I can't believe it," he says. "Even though I'm looking right at you."

"I don't really understand that." I stand and venture a little closer, staring at him as frankly as he's staring at me, because he doesn't seem to mind. "You're the first father I've ever met, but you see clones every day, right? Here in your home? Working in Mountainside? Patrolling the city wall?"

"Yes." His gaze seems caught on my face. "But that's different. The clones working among us fade into the background by design."

He strikes me as honest and uncalculating in a way that neither his wife nor his daughter seems to be, but the casual disregard in his words ignites an ache deep inside me.

"Yet somehow, in spite of her origin, Waverly stands out in any room. And based on the fact that you made it out of Lakeview in one piece, I'm guessing the same is true of you."

Mr. Whitmore clearly means that as a compliment, yet

the idea of standing out still sends a shiver up my spine, after a lifetime of belief that getting noticed is dangerous. That being different means being flawed, and that flawed genomes must be recalled.

"Are you . . . ?" He pushes the sleeves of his sweater up and crosses his arms over his chest. "Is there anything I can do for you? Anything I can get you?"

I must look puzzled by his question, because he glances around the room briefly before his gaze is drawn back to my face. "I'm sure Waverly has clothes that will fit you, and I'm pretty sure some of them have never been worn. But if there's anything else you need, please let me know."

I glance at Trigger and find him staring at Waverly's father's forearms. At what we can see of them, folded over the front of his sweater. "May I see your ink?" Trigger points, and I realize he couldn't have actually seen the bonding ceremony from his position in the hall.

Mr. Whitmore unfolds his arms and looks at them as if he were hardly aware of the ink on them until it was pointed out. "Oh. Of course."

He extends his left forearm, and we step closer to study a beautiful scrolling pattern, about two inches in diameter. In the center of the design, made out of those very swirls, is a six-digit number, divided into three sets of two figures. "It's the day Lorna and I got married. She has one just like it."

"It's beautiful," I breathe, resisting the urge to reach out and touch the design. I saw it in the library, of course, and I've seen its mate on Lorna's arm, but up close, though the design doesn't swirl with color, it's quite stunning.

"We often get temporary ink to commemorate a special occasion. A birthday or graduation," he explains. "But for a wedding, the birth of a child, or the loss of a loved one, we use permanent ink." He holds out his other arm and shows us another elegantly drawn date, this one more than eighteen years ago.

"Waverly's . . . birth?" I guess, though the word still feels odd on my tongue.

He nods. "One of the best days of my life. And this one is my mother's death, last year." He pushes his sleeve up farther to show me another date.

"Because it takes a couple of weeks to heal, union ink is usually done well before the ceremony so there won't be any swelling in the pictures," Mr. Whitmore explains as he rolls down his sleeves. "These days, the inking itself has become one of the pre-wedding events, and Waverly and Hennessy were very excited about the special matching designs they had commissioned."

"We have matching designs." Trigger holds up his right forearm and lifts mine, showing Waverly's father our bar codes. Our ink marks us as property, to be bought and sold.

Mr. Whitmore shifts on his feet, as if the reality of our origin hadn't really sunk in until that moment. "Yes, well, this is somewhat different."

I wonder if it's occurred to him yet that I've now received *two* ink designs originally intended for his daughter. And that if not for a case of mistaken identity when we were little more than a handful of cells, she might have wound up cleaning his floors, rather than bearing his name.

ELEVEN

WAVERLY

I closed the video feed when everyone left my room, and I had no intention of reopening it. Yet here I am again, staring at the screen, where I've been studying Dahlia's identicals— *my* identicals—for twenty minutes. Because of the size of the screen, I'm seeing them at their true height. My height. The feed is clear enough that I can see the striations in their brown eyes. The seams in their gray uniforms.

If the video weren't being shot from overhead, it'd be easy to forget that I'm not just looking through a doorway into the next room.

I can't quite wrap my mind around how bizarre this really is. Hearing that I once had five thousand identicals was unsettling and alarming, but seeing them? Even just a few of them? It's like looking into a carnival mirror full of reflections that refuse to play their part. To mimic my movements. Though the truth is that they're hardly moving at all.

They might be sedated.

Yesterday, the thought of a room full of sedated servants-in-training probably wouldn't have bothered me. But now? Knowing that I was supposed to be one of them?

Someone knocks on my bedroom door, and I swipe the video window closed again as my mother comes in. Behind her, a servant named Julienne 20 is carrying a lunch tray. I watch the clone as she crosses my bedroom to set the tray on the table by the window, and for the first time in the two years we've had her, I wonder what her life is like. What her life was like before she was a servant.

She's only four years older than Dahlia. Did they know each other on the clone compound?

Would I have known Julienne 20 if I'd grown up there, instead of here?

"I spoke to the Caruthers sisters, and there's a little bit of good news," my mother says as Julienne removes the plates from the tray, then the domes from the plates. She stacks the domes on the tray and carries the whole thing into the hall.

"Waverly," my mother says as the door closes behind Julienne 20. I blink and force myself to focus on what she's saying. "They adhered to our original wishes, which means there's no backup of the ink pattern."

I groan as her announcement sinks in. "How is that good news?"

She settles into one of the white chairs and motions for

me to take the one across from her. "The good news is that since we have access to the pattern itself, on Dahlia's arm, they believe they can re-create it in a fraction of the time the original took. We just need to send them some close-up pictures."

"How long is a fraction of the time?"

"Two months."

I groan again. "I can*not* spend the next two months hiding out in my room while she pretends to be me."

"Right now, the Caruthers sisters think we've changed our minds and want a copy of the pattern for posterity. To be preserved in family records." My mother cuts into her chicken breast with her knife and fork, the perfect picture of etiquette. "If I rush them any more, they'll start to doubt that explanation."

"So I'm just supposed to let Dahlia play me on camera?" That seems like my only option, but . . . "There's no way she can pull that off. She doesn't understand the concept of global connectivity. Or fame. Or monetary value. She hardly understands the concept of *currency*. The first thing she says will make me sound like an idiot."

My mother blots her mouth with her napkin. "So teach her. I think we can buy you a little time for that if you go to the florist yourself tomorrow. You can wear long sleeves and put a bandage over your arm in case the cuff rides up. Hennessy will do the same." She shrugs. "You don't want anyone to see the pattern before the show airs anyway, right?"

"But the show airs next Tuesday," I say. "After that, people will expect me to show it off."

"That gives you just over a week to teach Dahlia to play the part on camera. And in public. Where she'll be vulnerable to recording by anyone holding a tablet. To footage we can't control or edit."

"And after that? What about the engagement party?" I lay my napkin in my lap and pick up my fork, but I'm too upset to eat. "The bridal shower? The rehearsal dinner? The ceremony? I can cancel most of my other appearances, but I am *not* going to miss my own wedding."

She arches one brow at me. "Then I hope you picked a wedding dress with long sleeves, because that's the only way you'll be able to appear on camera at the ceremony."

Hearing the words out loud makes me feel like someone's just punched me in the chest. "Will Hennessy even be married to me, if she's the one who says 'I do'?" Tears fill my eyes, and my mother's expression softens.

"He'll be married to you because you'll be the one signing the marriage certificate. And if it truly comes down to this, Waverly, we can have a private ceremony here, off camera. You can already be married before the televised event. It's all for show anyway. It's the certificate and the official filing that matter."

No. It's the memories that matter. And I don't want to remember standing behind the scenes, watching someone else wear my dress and "marry" my husband.

"Has she even agreed to this?"

"Not yet, but she will." My mother takes another bite of her pasta, and if not for her too-tight grip on her fork, I might not even know this was bothering her. "I'm sure she and Trigger 17 are discussing it right now, and when we're done here, I'll play back the footage from her room and we'll know where we stand."

"What about the Administrator? What if she figures out it's Dahlia on camera?"

My mother sets her fork down and gives me a grave look from across the small table. "It is *crucial* that you don't let that happen. From now on, the most important member of your audience is Amelia Locke."

That thought makes me feel vaguely sick.

My gaze strays to the e-glass. It's transparent now, but every time I look at the screen, I see dozens of girls wearing my face, milling aimlessly around a featureless concrete room. "You're not really going to buy them all, are you?"

My mother exhales slowly. "Waverly, I've already put in an offer. For the entire batch." She hesitates. "But obviously there won't be any clone city. I'm not buying them for Dahlia. I'm buying them for you. To keep them from ever being seen. And there's only one way to do that."

"Don't say it," I whisper.

My mother takes another bite of pasta, and while I try not to think about what she's not saying, I listen to the soft sound of her chewing.

It was one thing when I thought Sofia's mother had killed thousands of girls who looked just like me. When it was over before I even knew about it. But knowing it'll actually be *my* mother . . . Knowing I might be able to stop it . . .

Can I really let my mother kill five thousand people to protect me?

TWELVE

DAHLIA

The whisper of the door sliding open startles me awake. Which is when I realize I fell asleep with my head on Trigger's shoulder. And that I may have been drooling on his shirt.

We both sit up as Lorna marches into the blue bedroom. "The audio feed from your room seems to be malfunctioning," she announces, and though she's clearly speaking to me, she's looking at Trigger. "It must be another 'glitch.'"

He stands and takes up a semiformal bearing, his hands clasped at his back, but he offers no explanation or commentary. So I don't either.

Lorna's irritated gaze narrows on me. "I assume, since you were both napping, that you've already discussed your options and come to a decision?"

"Yes. I'll do it." I slide off the bed onto my feet. "But I have a couple of requests." My pulse rushes in my ears. I've never made demands from an authority figure, and though Lorna is neither my instructor nor my mother, that's very much what it feels like I'm doing.

She crosses her arms over her blouse. "Such as?"

"Trigger stays here. With me."

"No. I gave the Administrator my word."

"Then take your word back. If you want me on camera, Trigger stays."

"Here, in this house," she concedes through gritted teeth. "Not in this room."

I fight not to look too pleased by my victory. "As a guest. Not as a prisoner."

Lorna's left brow arches. "I can't let either of you just wander the house. But you may take meals together, in either this room or his."

"I want to accompany her on appearances," Trigger adds. "As security."

"No." She offers no reason or explanation.

"I'll be more relaxed and better able to concentrate on my performance with him there," I insist. "And that benefits everyone."

She scowls. "We'll take that on a case-by-case basis. What else?"

"I'd like access to the video from the facility in Valleybrook. Not just the one you showed us. I want to see all my identicals. So I know they're still alive."

Lorna's bearing relaxes, and I wonder what she thought I was going to ask for. "I'm not sure that's possible at the moment. The Administrator isn't one to indulge requests without being given a satisfactory reason. But I can give you that one feed now." She pulls her tablet from her pocket, taps through a few menus, then opens the video and slides it onto the e-glass in "my" room with a flick of her wrist.

Hesitantly, I lift my hand and poke in the direction of the video open on the screen. The border around it lights up. I poke one of the lower corners of the window and drag my finger down and out to enlarge the screen, as Trigger showed me earlier.

The video now takes up half the wall. I can see my identicals clearly.

"Are there any other requests?"

I shake my head, but I'm not even looking at Lorna now. I'm watching my sisters, wishing they could know that I'm here. That I'm doing everything I can to keep them safe.

"So we have an agreement?"

"Yes."

"Good." Lorna extends one hand toward the door. "Waverly's ready to teach you everything you need to know to pass for her on camera and in public."

We follow her into the hall, where she opens the door to the gray room and seems to expect Trigger to go inside. "Wait, can't he come with me?"

"It's okay." Trigger steps close and leaves a lingering kiss on the corner of my mouth. "You don't need me for this part." Then he steps into the gray room and lets the door close between us.

Lorna's frown says she was expecting him to put up more of an argument. As was I. Which means he's probably planning to use the alone time to get better acquainted with the security system.

As I follow Lorna toward the family wing, a new question occurs to me. "What's the other anomaly?"

"Excuse me?" Lorna doesn't even slow down.

"You said one of the anomalies they found in me is hormone production. What's the other one?"

She waves off my question. "We won't have to worry about that for more than a decade, so we'll cross that bridge when we get to it."

A decade?

Waverly's bedroom is empty when her mother lets me in, but the bathroom door is closed, and I hear water running. Lorna stays in the hall, and when the door closes at my back, I turn and wave one hand at it experimentally.

It doesn't open. So I turn and study the room, which I hardly got a look at this morning.

Waverly's bed is even bigger than the one in the blue room, and it's made up with a puffy pink-and-white comforter and an entire army of coordinating pillows with elaborate stitching and buttons.

In one corner of the room is a sitting area with furniture

upholstered in white leather, peppered with yet more small, fancy pillows in colors that match the bed.

One wall is nearly covered with an artful arrangement of frames, each showing a picture of Waverly frozen at a different moment in her life. Toddler Waverly, blowing out a tiny candle lit on top of a huge cake, has Violet's mischievous grin. Child Waverly frozen in mid–soccer kick looks like Poppy when she's concentrating really hard. And Laughing Waverly, with her head thrown back, one arm in the air, looks like Sorrel when she finally—

I step closer for a better look, and Laughing Waverly begins to move, tossing her hips from side to side while she waves her arms in the air. The frame isn't just displaying a picture; it's playing a video. Laughing Waverly is actually Dancing Waverly.

As the clip plays, two other girls dance into the frame, both laughing. I recognize Margo and Sofia, though they look younger in this video. All three girls are wearing shinier, shorter versions of the dresses worn at Seren's party, and—

"That was four years ago," Waverly says. I spin to find her standing behind me. "It was the last day of school before the break, and we went out that night to celebrate."

"The break?"

"The end of the spring term, before summer . . ." She frowns. "You guys didn't get breaks, did you?"

"We got one day off every week," I tell her. "For organized recreation."

"Well, we get a lot more time off here." She nods at the frame, where the video clip has started over. "That was the first night of filming my show."

"What is this show, exactly?" I've committed to being on camera, but I don't really understand what that means.

Waverly drops onto one of the chairs in the sitting area. "Yeah, I guess that's where we should probably start. So the biggest difference between Lakeview and the rest of the world, other than the whole clone factory angle, is that Lakeview is totally socially isolated, while the rest of the world is connected through a digital network. Most of us are on it pretty much constantly. Every time we look up something we don't know, or send a message to someone, or buy something, or order food, or read a book, or listen to a song, or watch a show. This network is our access point for just about everything. And everyone."

"Connected . . . how?"

"The network is a series of digital signals connecting every single digital device in the world. Every tablet. Every camera. Every audio feed. In houses. Stores. Offices. Think of it like a giant spiderweb. Every signal is like one of the threads in the web. And every place they intersect is a connection. All together, it forms one massive network, through which you can communicate with anyone or anything—if you have the necessary equipment, passwords, and authority. One of the things people do on the network is watch videos, on their tablets or their wall screens."

"Oh. Like watching our identicals in Valleybrook," I say, pleased to have made the connection, but Waverly flinches at my reference to them as "our" identicals.

"Not really," she says. "That's just a security camera feed, which is different from livecasts and shows. Livecasts are posted spontaneously, in real time, when someone has something to say or something exciting is happening around them. People just connect to the network and start broadcasting from their tablets. But shows are filmed on professional equipment, edited, then released to the public. Some of them are fiction—made-up stories, like watching a novel play out on the screen."

I'm familiar with the concept of a novel, from history class, but I've never read one because fiction—like kissing, parties, and everything else the outside world seems to enjoy—has long been banned in Lakeview as a pointless and inefficient expenditure.

"But others are more like documentaries," Waverly continues. "A video record of something real. My show, for instance, is like a window into my life. Basically, a camera crew from Network 4 follows me around a few days out of the month, recording everything I do from every possible angle. Then a team of editors compiles the footage and trims it into a series of twenty-minute episodes." She shrugs. "Any longer, and people get bored. Any shorter, and they think we're hiding something."

"So the recordings from this morning are going to go on this network, for strangers to see?"

Waverly nods. "After they're edited."

This world gets stranger with every second I spend in it. "I understand people wanting to watch the ink ceremony." Clearly that's something special to those who already understand the custom. "But why would anyone want to watch you eat, and . . . do other everyday things?" Suddenly I realize I have no idea what Waverly does on a daily basis if she's not taking classes or learning a skill.

Another shrug. "Because I'm famous. Because I'm young, and beautiful, and I can afford a life most of them can only dream of." She frowns. "I know my life is the only thing you've really seen since you got here, but this isn't the norm. Hennessy, Margo, Sofia, and I . . . we're the exception. That's why regular people are interested in our lives." Her frown deepens. "As weird as it sounds, now that I'm saying it out loud, people like to think they know me."

"But they don't?"

"They know the good things. The parts of my life that are funny, or glamorous, or self-deprecating in a funny or glamorous way. Everything I show them is real. It's just . . . edited. To take out the parts that make me look too normal."

"Why?"

"Because their own lives are normal. When they watch me, they want to see extraordinary. Which is why we usually film parties and charity events. Work I do for my official platforms. You know, feeding the homeless and reading to orphans. Stuff like that."

"Homeless and orphans?"

"People who don't have anywhere to live. And kids who don't have parents."

No one I grew up with had parents. But homelessness? "Why don't people have homes?"

"Some people don't have enough credits to pay rent."

"Why not?"

Waverly looks exasperated by my questions. "Because they don't have jobs. But they're not, like, on the street or anything. Not in Mountainside. We have a lot of homeless shelters. Hennessy and I go there all the time to donate clothes and serve food on camera. The network mostly shows when things go wrong in a cute way—like if I drop a whole tray of peas and they roll everywhere—but I think people would watch anything we do. Everyone loves Hennessy. He has almost as many followers as I do."

I must look confused again, because Waverly waves an arm at the e-glass, then pokes one of the large icons. It grows to take up most of the screen. "This is my public message feed. Where people can go to see videos and messages I post."

Row upon row of text fills the screen, divided into colored boxes, each of which is labeled with the photo of whoever sent the message. In the left and right margins, boxes flash with images or silenced videos entreating me to buy a dress or watch a livecast, and the display is so disorienting I can't process much of it. So I concentrate on the messages filling the main portion of the page.

"They're pings," I say, relieved to recognize a similarity between her world and mine. "Though in Lakeview, only adults get pings. Mostly messages from Management."

"That sounds like a private inbox," she says. "This is my public feed, and these"—Waverly swipes up with her hand, and the messages scroll up, and up, and up, too fast for me to read—"are from my followers." She scrolls up again, and the messages roll on and on, with no end in sight.

I stare at the screen, bewildered. "How can you ever answer all these?"

She laughs again. "Oh, I don't even read most of them. I just filter them, so that I only see the ones from friends, or from other famous people, and I answer those." She pokes at a symbol at the top of the screen, and most of the messages fade until they look like shadows; then they disappear. The still-bold messages slide together to close the gaps, and though there are far fewer of them now, they still fill the huge screen. "Regular people like to see famous people interact with one another. They feel like they've become a part of some special relationship." She shrugs and smiles. "It's my job to make sure they keep feeling like that, so they keep watching my show."

At five thousand girls, my class at the training ward was among the largest commissioned. But Waverly has millions of fans. Millions. I can hardly even conceive of that many . . . followers. What I *do* understand is that even if her followers don't truly know her, they probably know her well enough to spot an imposter after more than a few minutes on camera.

I got lucky at Seren's party, and again at the ink ceremony. But that luck can't possibly last.

I stand closer to the screen, scanning the messages. Trying not to feel completely overwhelmed. "I don't think I can do this. Can't you be yourself on camera and just . . . wear long sleeves?"

"That's what I'll be doing for all of my appearances this week, as well as the recap interviews for the ink ceremony episode. But after the network airs the footage they shot this morning, people will expect to see the design. Union ink is something to be shown off, like an engagement ring. If I hide it, everyone will know something's wrong."

I run the fingers of my right hand softly over the clear film covering my left forearm. "Waverly, we may look alike, but I can't pass for you. I don't understand your life. Or this place."

"That's why you're here." Her voice has gone hard. "To learn how to be me." I start to argue again, but she cuts me off. "I don't want this any more than you do, but believe it or not, you're getting the better end of the deal here. You've taken *everything* that's supposed to be mine. My health. My show. My name and my fiancé, for all practical purposes. And now you get to be in *my* wedding, while I have to hide out in the house for the next two months.

"You've pushed me out of my own life, Dahlia. The least

you can do is see it through. And maybe stop acting like being rich and famous is such a hardship."

I don't think I truly understand either of those concepts, but I *do* understand that Waverly's asking me to make the best of the situation.

"Fine." I suck in a deep breath and sit straighter, trying to dig up some enthusiasm. "Show me how to be rich and famous."

THIRTEEN

WAVERLY

"Good morning," I say, sounding more cheerful than I feel. Julienne 20 sets a plate in front of me at the breakfast table, then disappears. "Lobster eggs Benedict. Yum."

"Morning," my dad says, but neither he nor my mom looks up from their tablets.

"Okay, I'm just going to take a guess," I say as Julienne 20 returns with a steaming mug of coffee, doctored with sugar and cream until it's the color of butter pecan ice cream. Just the way I like it. "This silent treatment is about Dahlia 16?"

My dad sets down his tablet. "Honey, this has nothing to do with you."

My laughter sounds harsher than I intended.

"Okay, this has everything to do with you," he concedes. "But it's not *because* of you. I just need a little while to process what's happening. This whole thing was thrown at me out of nowhere."

"It was thrown at *all* of us out of nowhere," my mother snaps.

My father's chair squeals against the floor as he scoots away from the table. "Yes, but at least *one* of us must have known it was a possibility when she enlisted the aid of a clone geneticist to design our daughter! How did you think he'd fit your little project into his schedule without letting the work do double duty?"

"Dane, I swear I had no idea—"

"*Little project?*" The words feel like ice on my tongue. "That's what I am to you?"

"No!" My father takes my hand. "Waverly, you are all your mother and I ever wanted. You are everything we could have hoped for, and I don't care how you came to be here. I just wish I'd known the truth from the beginning." He turns back to my mother without letting go of my hand. "We'll deal with this like we deal with everything. Together. But I'm going to need some time to process."

"Of course." She gives him a tense smile.

He turns to me and clears his throat, as if maybe that's enough to press the reset button on this entire day. "What's on the schedule for the people's princess this morning?"

"We're shooting at Bloom World in a couple of hours."

My dad gives me an amused look. "Didn't you order flowers for the wedding last month?"

"Yes, but they're all custom, and footage of me staring at holographic blossoms with the shop owner in our dining room would be monumentally boring. So today we go in with the crew to look at the selection of real flowers in person, then pick out the arrangements we actually custom-ordered last month." I shrug. "It's good press for the florist, and it makes for a much more interesting episode."

"I see. Well, have fun fake flower shopping," he says with a smile.

"It's not fake." We're *actually* buying flowers shown on camera, from the *actual* florist. "It's just . . . scripted."

"Whatever you say, honey." He slides his tablet into a large pocket inside his suit jacket, then offers his hand to my mother. "Lorna, I don't want to fight."

"Neither do I." She accepts his hand and stands to hug him.

He turns to me, his arms still around my mother's waist. "What's done is done. Dahlia is your sister, Waverly. The one thing in the world we thought we'd never be able to give you. And I want her treated well while she's here."

He heads out of the breakfast room toward the garage, where our driver is waiting to take him to work, his words echoing in my head long after his footsteps have faded from my ears. A *sister*.

"She's your real daughter." The thought slips out before I even realize I've said it.

"No!" My mother pulls her chair closer to me and sits. "*You* are our real daughter. And I know your father means well, but he and I see this issue very differently. Dahlia is not your sister. She's a stranger. But she's a stranger we need."

"She's everything I was supposed to be."

"*You* are everything you were supposed to be."

I nod, because my mother seems to need me to acknowledge what she's saying. Whether it's true or not.

"You didn't tell Dad about the identicals, did you?" He would never have called Dahlia my sister if he knew about my mother's plans. "He'll figure it out eventually."

She exhales slowly, as if she's buying time to think of a response. "When this is all over and you're safe because of the decisions I made, he'll agree that I did the right thing. But he isn't capable of making choices like that himself. And he shouldn't have to be." My mother's eye contact deepens, taking on a heavy significance to make sure I *truly* understand. "Your father is a dreamer. A creator. A wonderful man. But he's the kind of man who can't know about decisions like this until they've already been made. By someone else."

And strangely, I *do* understand. We're keeping this from my father not just to protect him from any legal liability, but to protect him from his own conscience.

I wish we were doing the same for me.

My mother stands. "I need to make sure Trigger 17 hasn't taken over the security system again; then I have some work to do before I escort him to Dahlia's room for lunch. Have fun at the florist, hon. And don't forget the talking points."

"I know, I know. Support local businesses. Donate to Project Orphan. Watch Network 4."

As soon as my mother leaves, Julienne 20 comes to clear my parents' plates from the table. She works in silence with her eyes on the task and never once looks at me, even when brushing crumbs from the table into her palm puts her hand less than an inch from my arm.

She's been our cook since I was sixteen, when our previous cook, Blanche 27, was retired. But I know nothing about her. I've never even spoken to her, other than to order something to eat or drink.

I take another bite of my breakfast, kept warm by the heated plate, and when Julienne comes back from the kitchen to refill my coffee, my curiosity gets the better of me.

If not for a random twist of fate, I could be where she is right now. Working for someone else. Wearing a uniform. Staring at my shoes as if they were the most fascinating things I've ever seen.

Why do clones always look like they don't really know where they are or where they belong? And why *don't* Dahlia and Trigger look like that?

"Julienne?"

She stands up straight, still holding the coffeepot. Staring at the floor. "How may I serve you?"

"I—I just wanted to ask you something."

Confusion flickers across her face for a moment; then her features relax into her usual distant expression, as if in her mind, she's somewhere else. She looks blank. Like how I feel first thing in the morning, before I've had food or caffeine. Only less cranky.

"What do you like to eat?" I ask her.

"Food."

Okay. "Yes, but what kind of food?"

Her forehead wrinkles, her brows drawing low. She looks like she knows the answer to my question, but can't quite remember the right word.

Clearly I'm going about this all wrong.

"Never mind. Here. Have a seat." I nudge my father's chair out for her with one bare foot, but she only stares at it with a deepening frown. "Put down the coffeepot."

Julienne sits. But she keeps holding the pot.

"Tell me something about yourself. What do you like to cook the most?" I ask, but she still looks confused. "Wait, *do* you like to cook?" Maybe she wasn't given any choice about that. Maybe she would have been happier as a seamstress, or a driver, or a gardener, like Dahlia.

"I like to cook," Julienne says.

I'm encouraged to hear her say something other than "How may I serve you?" but her answer sounds more like an echo of the question than a true reply.

Maybe I'm expecting too much of her. But if she's smart enough to cook gourmet meals, how can she be having so much trouble with simple questions?

"What's your favorite part of cooking? Eating the left-overs?" That would be my favorite part.

Her brows dip until I'm afraid they're going to slide right into her eyes. "A man comes every day to take uneaten food to the homeless shelter."

Oh. "So then, what do you eat?"

"My meals come in a . . . box." She frowns, as if that's not exactly the right word, but it's the best she can come up with.

Clone food comes in a *box*? Prepackaged? I had no idea.

New subject. "So what was it like growing up in Lakeview? Did you have many identicals?"

Julienne nods slowly, still staring at the floor. Her frown relaxes. "There were five thousand of us."

I lean forward, trying to catch her gaze, but it remains glued to her feet. "And they were friends? Like . . . sisters?"

She nods again. She's still holding the coffeepot.

"Do you miss them?"

Julienne's eyes narrow until she seems to be frowning at her shoes, and for the first time since I've known her—at least that I've noticed—she looks frustrated. Then her expression clears again, like a pane of e-glass fogging over. "May I take your plate?"

I glance at my breakfast. I've lost my appetite, but Julienne probably got up at five in the morning to cook, while I was sleeping in my big bed, alone in my huge room. And if not for that random twist of fate . . .

"No, thanks. I'm going to finish it. It's delicious."

"Which ones am I supposed to like again?" Hennessy asks as our car rolls to a stop in front of the flower shop. The camera crew is already waiting to get a shot of us walking through the doors, and they've attracted the usual crowd of onlookers.

"Crimson and white tulips for the church pews," I say as fans rush at the car. Some of them knock on the windows. Others cup their hands on the glass, trying to see in, but it's set to be opaque from the outside. "White tulips for the bridesmaids' bouquets, to contrast with their crimson dresses. Red calla lilies for the groomsmen's boutonnieres. And red calla lilies *and* white tulips for my bouquet."

He groans and lightly rubs his left arm through his sleeve, because his freshly inked skin itches. "I don't even know what a calla lily looks like."

"That's okay." I give him a quick kiss as the driver gets out of the car and walks around to let us out, opening a path through the crowd. "You can like everything she shows us. The shopkeeper will love it." As will the cameras. And the fans. They love everything he does.

The driver opens the door, and Hennessy gets out first, smiling at the crowd. He holds one hand out for me, and I take it as I step onto the sidewalk and pause to let the breeze blow my hair back from my face. The cameraman by the door is already rolling; the network loves footage like that. Shots where nature itself seems to be celebrating our union.

"Waverly!" someone shouts as our private security clears a path to the door. I turn to the crowd and wave with a big smile, letting my sleeve ride up a little to expose the bandage we've strategically applied on my arm. Then I smooth down my skirt.

"I love you!" a voice shouts from the crowd.

"Who designed your dress?"

"What are your wedding colors?"

"Can you say happy birthday to my cousin?"

Hennessy and I just smile and nod on our way up the sidewalk while the camera tracks us. He pulls the door open for me, and we pause as we enter the shop, to take in the sight. And the scents.

My look of astonishment is real. The florist has pulled out all the stops for us. There are flowers on every available surface—hundreds of arrangements, tulips in every color of the rainbow.

The display isn't just because we've already ordered thousands of credits' worth of standing arrangements and pew flowers, when most people have to make do with holograms for everything except the bouquets they actually carry.

It's because her business will triple after being featured on my show.

That's the talking point. Waverly and Hennessy shop local. The Whitmores and Chapmans support Mountainside businesses. That's what the world needs to see, to balance out headlines criticizing DigiCore for using automated and clone labor instead of hiring local citizens.

I gaze slowly over the shop, giving the camera a chance to capture my amazement. "Wow, Mrs. Roberts, you've outdone yourself! These are all gorgeous!"

"Stunning," Hennessy agrees.

"Thank you!" The shopkeeper loops her arm through

mine and smiles for the camera. "We're so honored that you've come to us for your wedding flower needs. I thought we'd start with roses, and work our way up to your favorite: tulips."

"That sounds perfect," I tell her.

"I love them all!" Hennessy proclaims, and she laughs, delighted. He plucks a champagne-colored tulip from the nearest display, pinches off the stem, and tucks the flower behind my ear. Then he caresses the side of my face and moves in for a kiss.

An audible sigh rings out from the people staring in through the front window, and Audra, our producer, looks ready to melt into a puddle on the floor.

I know how they feel. Hennessy is beautiful, and kind, and perfect. And he's all mine.

Even if he deserves a future I may never be able to give him.

"I think you've chosen very wisely," Mrs. Roberts says as she finishes our mock order on her tablet. As if we haven't already placed one and paid for it in full. "This is going to be *the* most beautiful wedding. . . ."

"My bride deserves nothing less," Hennessy declares.

"Still, you put so much work into all these sample arrangements!" I turn in a circle, inviting the cameras to pan the shop. "I think we're going to have to take them all."

"You . . . what?" The owner frowns, as if she's misheard me. "They're all so beautiful, and I know just who'd appreciate them most. The patients at Mountainside Pediatric Hospital. Ring us up, please, Mrs. Roberts. Do you think your delivery van can handle them?"

"Of course, but . . . all of them?"

"Yes." As she starts another order on her tablet and begins scanning the tags from the bouquets, I make a mental note to make sure that the camera crew follows the delivery van to the hospital, for some footage of the flowers being delivered to sick children.

I would have sent them even if there were no camera crew, but since there *is* a camera crew . . .

On our way out of the shop, I kneel next to an adorable little girl waiting in the crowd on the sidewalk with her mother, eager for a glimpse of us in person. I pluck the tulip from my hair and tuck it behind her ear. "A beautiful bloom for a beautiful girl."

"Thank you." Her mother smooths the child's hair over her shoulder. "It means the world to her to get to meet you."

"It means the world to me too," I tell her. Then security ushers us toward our car, where the driver is already holding the door open.

"You were great," I tell Hennessy as he slides onto the seat next to me. I take his hand and drop a kiss at the back of his jaw, just below his ear. That's my favorite spot, because it makes him shiver.

"You are *always* great." He squeezes my hand, then pulls

his tablet from his pocket. "I assume you want to check the optics?"

"We probably should."

He holds his tablet where I can see it as he scrolls through the feeds, scanning subject lines.

"Damn it," I breathe as one message catches my eye. I take his tablet and click on the story. "This one says Bloom World uses clone gardeners in its hothouse." I turn to him, brows arched. "Is that true? I didn't see any clones."

Hennessy shrugs. "Well, it's not like she would have paraded them in front of us."

"It doesn't do us any good to support local businesses if those local businesses aren't employing local citizens!"

"You want to cancel the order? I'm sure there's at least one florist left in the city who hires citizens."

I sigh. "It's a little late now. But we have to vet better next time."

"Doesn't that make us a little hypocritical?" Hennessy says. "Considering that both of our houses are staffed by clones?"

"Those are our parents' houses," I point out. Then I take a deep breath and plunge in. "I can't have clones in *our* house, Hennessy. I just . . . can't. Not knowing what I know."

He takes my hand again. "Whatever you want is fine with me. But you know my dad already bought our household staff as a wedding gift. They're in transition now." He hesitates, and I understand what he's going to say before he even opens his mouth again. "What's going to happen to them? Best-case scenario? Sold to someone else?"

Refusing to take the clones won't be helping them. "Okay. I'm going to have to think about that."

"So what's the plan for Dahlia and Trigger?" Hennessy says as our car pulls through the gate in front of my house. "What are you guys going to do with them after you get your ink?"

"It looks like they'll be secret houseguests for a while. My dad says I should treat Dahlia like a sister, but my mom thinks she might be useful on the medical front." I don't want to go into any more detail, because this doesn't feel like the best time to tell him that I'll never be able to give him kids on my own. But I'm not going to lie to Hennessy. I'm not *that* much like my mother. "Because in theory we have identical physiology."

Hennessy meets my gaze, as if he's waiting for more. Then he takes my hand. "Waverly. I know you're infertile."

I hold my breath. "You do?"

He nods. "The Lakeview catalog says clones are designed that way. I didn't think twice about that until Dahlia showed up. Then the problems you've been having suddenly made sense."

Did *everyone* figure that out before I did?

I clench my teeth, determined not to cry anymore. Tears never solve anything. "My mom thinks we can fix it. She thinks Dahlia's hormones will help me—"

"Waverly." Hennessy lays one hand along my jaw, then

149

leans in to kiss me. "It doesn't matter to me." He shrugs. "We were going to adopt anyway. There are plenty of babies out there whose parents can't afford to keep them, and we'll have plenty of room."

"But your parents will—"

"Screw my parents. Screw yours, if they can't be happy for us in whatever decision we make."

"Thank you." I kiss him again. I kind of want to crawl into his lap, even with the car still moving. "My mom thinks we can fix this, but it's good to know that even if we can't, you're still with me."

"There's no place I'd rather be." Hennessy clears his throat and his gaze seems to be searching mine for something. "Waverly, I don't care about the fertility issue, but I *am* worried about that other thing."

A chill washes over me at his suddenly somber tone. "What other thing?"

"Your expiration date."

FOURTEEN

DAHLIA

"Pause," I say, and the image of Waverly freezes on the e-glass.

My clone smiles out at me from the steeply sloped streets of Mountainside, holding the small ceremonial shovel she's just used to "break ground" on a new facility intended to provide food and shelter for the homeless.

I've seen six episodes of Waverly's show since breakfast, but this is the first time I've seen her give the camera a real smile. She's having fun digging in a pile of loose dirt with Hennessy, even though the wind keeps whipping hair into her face and her ridiculously high heels are sinking into the ground.

"Mirror," I say, and a reflective box opens in another window next to the video feed. I smile into it, trying to imitate Waverly's expression. Her carefree posture. The easy way she balances in shoes that make me feel too tall and clumsy.

"Play."

The video resumes, and Waverly's laughter rings out across the room. She practically glows in the sunlight. She's so different on camera than she is in private. In public, she is gracious, and kind, and quick to smile. She laughs at herself when she does something clumsy. She doesn't trip over her own shoes, as I've already done twice today. She gets ice cream on her nose and glances at it, cross-eyed, until Hennessy kisses the smudge of chocolate away.

I wish I could meet that on-camera Waverly. And I *really* wish I could figure out how to *be* her.

The door slides open without warning, and I pause the video again as Trigger follows Lorna into the blue room.

She looks pleased to see that I've been studying Waverly's show, yet somehow she doesn't look particularly pleased with *me*. "Lunch will be here in half an hour. Also, I wanted to let you know that I've just heard back from Waverly's endocrinologist, who's agreed to help us under strict confidentiality. He thinks there's a good chance we can design a hormone therapy for her, using your donation. Or by using your donation as the model for an exact chemical replica of the hormones she needs. He'll be here tonight to do an initial exam and take a little blood for testing."

I glance at Trigger, but he seems as confused as I am.

"What kind of hormones do you need from me, exactly?" We didn't learn much about hormones in class because gardening doesn't require detailed knowledge of human physiology. "Why can't Waverly's body make them?"

Lorna crosses her arms over her chest, as if it's unreasonable of me to want to know what she plans to remove from my body. "Clones are designed with a hormonal deficiency that those of us conceived the normal, natural way don't have."

I frown at her. "Where we come from, genetic design *is* the normal way."

"Yes, but that's not the way the rest of the world works. And genetic design is, by definition, unnatural. Nature cannot make five thousand identical copies of anything."

"That's *why* genetic design exists," Trigger tells her. "To improve upon nature."

Her left brow arches in mild amusement. "They teach you that you're an improvement upon nature?"

"It's true," I insist as an unexpected bolt of pride straightens my spine. "Variances and mutations in nature lead to disease and dysfunction. To irregularities, which hamper efficiency." Yet even as I speak truths that have defined my entire existence, I am well aware that my identicals were all ripped from their lives and locked up in concrete rooms because I'd turned out not to fit that perfectly efficient mold on a genetic level.

What would the Administrator do with me if Lorna gave me back to her? Would she try to sell me too? Even though I'm not a clone? *Could* she do that? I don't operate in a compliant mental fog, like Julienne 20 does. But then, neither do any of the clones in Lakeview.

"What's wrong with Julienne 20?" I blurt out, and Lorna looks surprised by the subject change. "Why doesn't she ever look directly at anyone? The clones we saw on our way through town acted the same way. Like they were only half-awake." Yet somehow awake enough to work.

Lorna shrugs. "They all come that way. Until I met you, I assumed that's how all laborers were designed."

"Well, it's not. We're all normal in Lakeview," Trigger tells her.

My mind spins, searching for a rational explanation. "It can't be genetic, because Waverly is a clone raised like an individual, and she's not like that. It can't be environmental, because I'm an individual raised as a clone, and I'm not like that. Trigger's a clone raised as a clone, and *he's* not like that. So what's going on with the clones in this city?"

"It must be something to do with the transition process. All I know is that this is what they're like when they get here." Lorna leans with one hip against the desk near the door and crosses her arms. "But to answer your original question, clones are designed to produce too little of the hormones required for a body to fully mature, in a reproductive sense. That deficiency is mild, but when coupled with a suppressive substance served in their food, it keeps clones infertile and largely uninterested in physical relationships."

Her explanation triggers an epiphany for me, like someone's turned on the light in a dark room. *This* is why none of my identicals were attracted to anyone the way I feel drawn toward Trigger. Why the way I want to touch him at random moments felt so out of place.

But he looks unconvinced. "Cadets must lack this deficiency. We're allowed to . . . fraternize."

"Oh." Lorna glances from him to me, then back, as if she's just made some kind of mental connection. "It makes sense that soldiers would be the exception. Your job requires the kind of strength and bulk that can't be achieved without natural hormonal levels. And you . . ." Her gaze narrows on me. "You're not a clone, so you're perfectly functional. Or you will be, once those hormonal suppressants have cleared from your system."

That last bit, she seems to be saying to herself. And she offers no explanation.

"You and Waverly are opposite sides of the same coin. She's suffering from the genetic hormonal deficiency you were spared, but she hasn't been fed a lifetime of the suppressive substance in her food, which you and her other identicals were. The result seems to be that she developed normal interests, but abnormal physical capabilities."

I frown, trying to puzzle through several new concepts. "Meaning . . . ?"

"Meaning her body produces enough hormones for her to feel attraction—and love—for Hennessy, but not enough to enable them to have a child of their own."

To have a . . . ?

Of course she would want a child with her future husband. That's normal here. Yet the thought of one of my identicals incubating a baby inside her body is almost too bizarre to even imagine.

But Lorna is still talking.

"Once you've been here eating regular food long enough for the suppressants to leave your system, your hormone levels should rise into the healthy range, which will kick-start a late but hopefully normal pubescence. At which point an infusion of your hormones could do the same thing for Waverly, allowing her at least a limited period of fertility. So the short answer to your question is that Waverly needs the hormones your body will soon begin to produce in order to conceive and carry a child."

Wow.

I blink at her, trying to process everything I've just heard. So many questions are rattling around in my head that it's difficult to focus on any of them.

"How long does it take to incubate a baby the 'natural' way?" I'm not sure that was covered in any of my few history or biology lessons.

"Pregnancy is nine months, unless something goes wrong. I don't know how long the hormone therapy would take to develop, or how long she'd need to be on it in preparation, but of course, you and Trigger would both remain our guests the entire time."

Yet coming from her mouth, the word *guests* feels more like *prisoners*.

FIFTEEN

WAVERLY

As Hennessy's car rolls through the gate and onto the street, I head into the house. He wanted to come in with me. But my mother owes me answers, and I'm not sure I want him to hear them before I've had a chance to process them on my own.

My heels click on marble as I head for the back of the first floor, and though my steps sound steady, my hands are shaking as I wave open my mother's office door. "Mom? *How* could you not tell me I'm going to die at twenty-eight?"

Startled, she turns toward me from the center of the room, and for a moment, she only stares at me, her expression carefully guarded. "Waverly." She extends one arm toward her e-glass. "Say hello to Amelia Locke."

Oops.

I step into the room, cringing, and find the Administrator staring out at me from the wall screen, her severe features several times larger than they would be in person. Which makes her look even more intimidating. "Hi." I stand there like an idiot, not sure what to do with my still-trembling hands. "Sorry, Mom. I didn't know you were on a call." And suddenly I realize how disastrous my interruption would have been if she'd been speaking with anyone else when I burst in and basically outed myself as a clone.

The Administrator turns to my mother. "She didn't know?"

"Waverly, have a seat." My mother opens a cabinet and pulls out a chilled bottle of water from the beverage refrigerator inside. "I wanted to have a solution before I told you about the problem." She hands me the bottle and sits next to me.

"And by *problem*, you mean the fact that I'm just going to drop dead at twenty-eight?"

"Not exactly. Clones come with expiration dates." On-screen, the Administrator leans back in her chair. "Typically ten years from the date of maturity."

"An expiration date." I heave a bitter huff. "As if I'm suddenly going to be less effective when I turn twenty-eight. Like an out-of-date prescription. Or a stale box of crackers."

My mother shoots me a look, but the Administrator seems unfazed.

"Actually, in theory, it is kind of like that. Clones are genetically engineered so that a vital neurological protein degrades at a fairly rapid rate." The Administrator shrugs. "No one drops dead at the age of twenty-eight, but that *is* generally the time when peak performance as an employee is no longer possible. Shortly thereafter, the organs begin to fail, and the entire process gets kind of messy. Which is why Lakeview offers a 'retirement' service, which comes with a five percent discount on any new clones bought as a replacement for those being removed from service."

A terrifying numbness rolls over me as the Administrator's words echo through my head. *Retirement service.* So when we retired our previous staff members two years ago, they were euthanized? How could I not have realized? I mean, it's not like retirement could possibly mean sipping drinks on the beach for a clone. Or for me . . .

"I'm going to die at twenty-eight." I look up at my mother. "What's the point of hormone therapy? Why does it matter if I can have a baby if I won't live long enough to raise it?"

"I spoke to Dr. Foster about hormone therapy this morning, and while I had his attention, I also asked about gene therapy. It sounds like there may be a way to fix this."

"Dr. Foster's an endocrinologist. He knows nothing about genes." I twist the top off my water bottle, and a little spills over the neck to roll down my hand. "What we really need is the geneticist who designed me."

"That's what Amelia and I were just discussing," my mother says.

On-screen, the Administrator touches the top of her desk and when it fogs over, I realize the entire surface is e-glass, like my dad's. She taps through a menu and opens a document. Her eyes move back and forth as she scans it. "My soldiers tracked Wexler 42 several miles into the wild and they believe they're closing in on him."

"Wait." I set my water on the end table. "Wexler 42 is forty-two years old, right? Why didn't *he* die at twenty-eight?"

The Administrator leans back in her desk chair. "Management and specialist clones, including medical staff and geneticists, spend their entire lives on the Lakeview compound. They're engineered to live longer so I get more use out of them."

"Then why design the rest to die so young?" I ask. "Dahlia says everything in Lakeview is superefficient, but that sounds like a huge waste of resources to me."

The Administrator's left brow rises. "The expiration date means my customers come back every ten years instead of every forty or so. That's four times the profit in the same time period." Her arrogant smile is cold enough to give me chills. "I'd call that pretty efficient."

"Dahlia and Trigger don't know about the expiration date, do they?" I ask as I follow my mother up the stairs.

"No, and they don't need to, at least for the moment."

"Then we shouldn't talk about it in the house. If Trigger can turn off the audio feed in Dahlia's room, he can probably access the audio feeds from other rooms. He could be listening to anything, anytime."

She gives me a smug smile. "While he was having lunch in Dahlia's room, I had the screen in his disconnected. The gray room is now a digital dark zone—our own little version of Lakeview. Dahlia will be coming to him for lunch from now on, and he isn't allowed out of the gray room without my express permission."

I should feel bad about him being on lockdown. But I don't.

We pick Dahlia up from her room, then head into the basement, past the laundry facilities, storage, and a wine cellar, into the exam room my parents had built when it became clear I had medical issues that shouldn't be overheard by other patients and staff in a normal doctor's office.

"I can't get ahold of Trigger on the screen in my room," Dahlia says, standing awkwardly in the middle of the floor while I hop onto the heated exam table where I've received largely ineffective hormone injections once a month for the past three years. "I think there may be an actual glitch."

My mother smiles as she sits in one of the padded waiting room–style chairs. "I had his screen disconnected."

Dahlia doesn't ask for an explanation; she knows as well as I do why Trigger's been locked out of the system. And locked into his room.

A few minutes later, our butler escorts Dr. Foster into the exam room. I've been seeing him since I was fifteen. If there's any doctor who can be trusted, it's him. Especially considering what my parents pay him.

"Thank you for coming on such short notice," my mother says, rising from her chair.

"Anything for my favorite patient." Dr. Foster sets his medical supply case on the stainless-steel countertop, then turns to me with a smile. The friendly greeting freezes on his face when he sees Dahlia standing next to the exam table. "Oh my . . ." His gaze flickers between us. "When you said you had a biological donor, I thought you meant a distant relative. But . . . a twin? Or . . . ?" He grabs Dahlia's right arm and pushes her sleeve up to expose the bar code tattoo—a sight that makes my stomach pitch. "A *clone*."

Dahlia frowns, but leaves her arm in his grip while he studies the mark.

"Neither, actually," my mother says, and the doctor lets go of Dahlia's arm. "What good would a clone's deficient hormones do in hormonal therapy?"

Dr. Foster looks from Dahlia to me. "*Waverly's* the clone? How is that possible?"

"It's complicated," my mother says. "And I expect your discretion. All you need to know is that this is Dahlia, and she has the hormones Waverly needs."

Slowly, the doctor nods. "Okay. Well, this explains the source of Waverly's deficiency." He glances from Dahlia to me again, then takes a deep breath. "Let's get to work. I'll need blood samples from both of them, to compare." Dr. Foster waves Dahlia toward the exam table, and I make room for her next to me. He picks up an empty blood vial and an ink pen. "For discretion in the lab, we'll call Waverly Patient A and Dahlia Patient B."

"Doctor, until two days ago, Dahlia was consuming hormonal suppressants in her food. How long will that take to leave her system?"

Dr. Foster opens his mouth as if he's about to ask a question. Then he seems to think better of it. "I'm as interested in that answer as you are, Mrs. Whitmore. It could be days. Could be weeks. Which is why we'll need to take weekly samples and monitor the hormonal change."

We sit as patiently as possible while the doctor takes several vials of blood, and though Dahlia seems curious about everything, she doesn't ask any questions. She doesn't even speak.

"I'll give these a top priority at the lab, and I'll be in touch as soon as I've been able to isolate the necessary hormones."

"Thank you, Doctor." My mother opens the door and turns to Dahlia. "Steward 20 will escort you back to your room."

Dahlia says nothing as she follows the butler toward the basement stairs.

As Dr. Foster begins packing up his supplies, my mother closes the exam room door. "There's one more thing. With the discovery of Waverly's genetic origin, we've realized the hormonal deficiency isn't her only problem." She leans against the door, waiting patiently for him to come to the right conclusion on his own.

"The expiration date." The gaze he turns my way is heavy with sympathy. "I'm so sorry."

"Doctor, we wouldn't bother with hormone therapy if we didn't believe Waverly has a long life ahead of her. You were explaining to me this morning how gene therapy can be used to repair genetic protein and chromosomal abnormalities . . ."

Dr. Foster sinks onto the rolling stool. "I thought you were asking on behalf of the children's hospital charity." He exhales and his gaze flicks toward me again. "Lorna, I could sequence your daughter's genome in a couple of minutes with the proper equipment, but I wouldn't know what to do with that information once I had it. You need a geneticist. Someone experienced with gene therapy."

My heart sinks into my stomach. "Do you know a geneticist who can be trusted?"

He swivels on his stool to fully face me. "I know a couple who could do what you're asking. For the right price. But confidentiality that can be bought can also be sold down the road, if someone else makes a more generous offer."

"Send me a list. Not of those who can be bought, but of those most skilled in the field." My mother doesn't look concerned about loyalty being outbid.

"I'll do that. And I'll let you know when I have the results from those tests."

"Thank you, Doctor."

My mother and I walk Dr. Foster to the front door, and as we watch his car roll through the front gate, she takes me by both arms and looks straight into my eyes. "I *will* find a way to fix this, Waverly. I want you and Dahlia to focus on getting her ready to play you on camera and let me worry about everything else."

SIXTEEN

WAVERLY

"I'm not ready for this," Dahlia says as she steps into my bedroom.

I pause the video playing on my wall screen and roll off my bed, onto my feet. "It's been a week. You've seen every episode of my show three times. You've memorized my life story. You can walk in heels, eat with the proper fork, and recite all my friends' birthdays. You're as ready as you're ever going to get. Besides, Hennessy will be right next to you." I swallow the lump of envy lodged in my throat at the thought of my clone and my fiancé attending my engagement party without me. "You'll be fine. Now step all the way into the room so the door can close."

My mother gave her access to both her door and mine, so she can attend our daily "princess prep" sessions, as my father's started calling them, without needing an escort. But every time she leaves or enters either room, my mother gets

166

an alert. She still doesn't trust Dahlia, but after all the time I've spent with my clone, I'm pretty sure Trigger 17's the one we need to worry about.

Dahlia's become proficient at using the wall screen, but there's no way she could hack into the security system. I don't even know how to do that.

Trigger hasn't left his room in six days. I peeked at the feed from one of the cameras in his room a couple of times and found him doing push-ups. Lots and lots of push-ups. Dahlia says he's going stir-crazy, even with the unconnected tablet full of books, games, and music my dad gave him.

I don't care if he goes howl-at-the-moon crazy as long as he doesn't have the ability to eavesdrop or lock me in my own bathroom.

"Are you sure you can't go to the party yourself?" Dahlia asks. "You could just wear long sleeves again."

I roll my eyes. "We've been over this. That's like getting your nose done, then wearing a mask. The whole point of the ink is to show it off; it'll look like something's wrong if I don't. And inevitably, someone will ask to see my new ink, and I'll have no good reason to refuse."

"Getting your nose done?" Dahlia's forehead wrinkles.

"You know. Having it fixed, surgically."

She stares at my nose. "What's wrong with it?"

"Nothing," I say with a glance into the mirror. "I haven't had any work done, but a lot of girls—and some guys—get surgery to 'fix' things they don't like about themselves."

"If you'd done that, we wouldn't look alike." Dahlia seems blown away by that thought.

"Especially considering that what I wanted was implants."

"Implants?" she says, and I hold my cupped hands in front of my chest, miming bigger boobs. Her frown deepens. "Why would you want that?"

I give her a look. "Because I don't have any? The surgeon said I was just a late bloomer and told me to come back when I got my period. But that never happened, so I had to turn the tables. I convinced the world that this is the ideal." I gesture up and down my own body. "That rather than me trying to look like them, they should all want to look like me."

"Did it work?" Dahlia asks.

"I'm still famous, aren't I? Come on. Let's do your makeup." I grab my desk chair and lead her into the bathroom.

"I don't know how to use those little paintbrushes and pencils," she says as I set the chair next to my vanity stool, so we can sit side by side in front of the mirror.

"No need. For days when there's no professional makeup crew . . ." I open the trifold automated applicator and Dahlia leans in for a better look. "Illumination settings: camera ready," I say, and the light panels between the three mirrors brighten to the setting I've programed for filming days. "I tried out several looks this morning and settled on this one," I tell her, framing my perfectly made-up face with my hands. "The goal now is to make you look just like I do. Sit here."

"A machine did that?" She sinks onto my vanity stool. "How does it work?"

"When it was installed, the technician took a bunch of pictures of my face, then uploaded a three-dimensional model. You look just like me, so it should work for you too. Foundation, contouring, and blush are applied with a series of airbrushes—tiny paint guns—programed with each specific movement, based on that 3-D model. Eye shadow and brows are done the same way, with smaller airbrushes. The eyeliner applicator uses an actual bristled brush, depending on the desired effect. There are about a million different looks. More every day, actually. My stylist uploads anything she thinks I might like."

"Your stylist?" Dahlia seems to be tasting the word.

"The person who helps me pick out my clothes, makeup, and hairstyles. Normally, she'd have been here on Sunday, planning out what I'd wear on camera for the rest of the week. But I've been stuck here teaching you how to be me."

Dahlia frowns. "You shot the voice-over for the union ink episode and you went to dinner with Hennessy the other night. I saw about a thousand pictures of you drinking champagne."

"Yeah, but that was just one charity dinner." And a long-sleeved dinner at that—my last chance to be seen in public before the ink ceremony airs and I'm stuck inside for weeks. Watching Dahlia go out in my place. "I normally commit to a heavy schedule of appearances when school's out, and I've already had to miss a children's benefit, a celebrity tennis tournament, and the dedication of the new DigiCore annex building this week alone."

My friends think I'm avoiding them. My public message feeds are full of people speculating that I'm sick, or I'm having second thoughts about the wedding, or—irony of bitter ironies—that I'm suffering severe morning sickness.

"Anyway . . ." I turn back to the mirror. "I do my own lashes, because I don't want any machine that close to my eyeballs." I laugh at myself. "Weird, I know."

But Dahlia doesn't seem to think it's weird. Or maybe she has no idea what mascara is.

"And it doesn't hurt?"

"Nope. Um . . ." I study her face for a minute; then my gaze lands on her arm. "Let's cover up your bar code first."

"Makeup can do that?"

"You've clearly never seen Margo first thing in the morning. This stuff can cover anything." I take her right arm for a better look at the pattern of thin black bars tattooed across her wrist. "The surface is pretty flat and the area is small. A rough scan should work."

I hold her arm in front of the applicator. "Area scan for basic foundation—blemish cover."

A small sensor on a robotic arm slides out of the applicator, and I position Dahlia's wrist in front of it. "Cover drastic discoloration," I say, and the sensor runs a red beam of light over her arm in search of the "discoloration." When it finds the tattoo, it begins to scan.

"Scan complete," the applicator says. "Color match with the dominant skin tone?"

"Yes," I say. "Okay, hold your arm still."

An airbrush emerges from the applicator on another delicate robotic arm. It hovers over Dahlia's wrist, then sprays a fine coat of foundation over her tattoo in several strokes, carefully blending it with her skin on the edges of the coverage.

"Please approve," the voice says as the air brush retracts.

I study Dahlia's wrist, searching for any sign of her tattoo. But it's gone. "See?" I hold her arm up for her inspection. She looks stunned.

"You can't even tell I'm a clone," she whispers.

An odd ache echoes deep in my chest. "You're actually not a clone," I remind her. "Now you look like what you are. Yourself."

"Will it rub off?" She starts to run one finger over the foundation, but I catch her hand to stop her. "Not after we seal it." I turn back to the applicator and hold her arm in position again. "Approved. Seal the cover-up." Another airbrush emerges and sprays her wrist with a clear sealant, then disappears into the applicator.

"Give it a second," I instruct while Dahlia inspects her arm again. When the coat looks dry, I nod. "Okay, you can touch it."

She runs one finger over her wrist, but the foundation stays put. "I can't even feel it!"

I can't help but smile. She looks so pleased. So astonished. "Now it won't wash off, even in the shower, unless you use a special makeup-remover wipe." I hold up the packet for her to see. "These break down the seal. I'll have some sent to your room. You have to take your makeup off and wash your face every night with that soap I gave you, to maintain clear skin for the cameras. This is *crucial*, Dahlia."

She takes the wipe packet, then scans the directions.

"Okay, now for your face." I set the applicator for the look I've picked out, with a little extra attention to the eyes, since today's a special day. Then I talk Dahlia through washing her face with a special soap and applying moisturizer.

With her skin prepped, she sits as still as possible while the applicator sprays on primer, then foundation, then contours and applies blush. She holds her breath while the tiny eye shadow airbrush begins, and she looks more like a statue than a person while the eyeliner brush does its job, giving her a smooth, slightly smudged outline that fades around the middle of her lower lid.

"Wow," Dahlia says when she finally sits back so I can do her mascara. "I look like myself, only . . ."

"Better?" I suggest.

"Well, shinier, anyway," she agrees. But that's an understatement. She looks just like me. And we look stunning.

"Now . . . clothes."

Sofia and I help each other pick out new clothes all the time, but neither of us has ever looked anywhere near as excited by that prospect as Dahlia looks right now. "Come on." I throw open my closet door and pull her inside, where her eyes go wide as she looks around.

"Go crazy," I tell her. "With our hair and skin tone, we

172

look best in bold, strong colors, and you really can't go wrong with that . . . butt." Do I look that good from behind?

Somehow neither the mirror nor the Digiglass does justice to my body the way seeing someone else walk around in it does.

Dahlia picks out a flowing red blouse with broad lace cuffs—the color will look great with our dark hair—and a pair of snug white pants. She has good instincts. Not that there's anything in my closet that would look bad on either of us.

I take the clothes into my room and hold them in front of the e-glass. "Have I ever worn this on camera?"

Three dots scroll across the center of the screen while it scans the clothes and searches for them in every episode of my show, as well as in footage of me from hundreds of public appearances.

"No," it replies at last. "And may I suggest you add black knee-high boots and an onyx necklace to coordinate?" An image of me wearing the suggested ensemble appears on the screen.

"Yes. That'll work." I give the clothes to Dahlia and shoo her back into the bathroom to change. When she emerges, I hand her the boots, and while she steps into them, I fasten the onyx pendant around her neck. Her ears aren't pierced— we'll have to fix that, if she's going to become my full-scale mannequin/dress-up doll/live stand-in—but I have a pair of dangly silver clip-ons that will do the job.

"I haven't even worn this myself yet," I tell her as we stand in front of the mirror. "But I'm making a mental note to wear it as soon as it comes back from the laundry. It didn't look this good on me in the virtual dressing room."

"You would wear it even though I've already worn it?"

"I'm going to wear it specifically because you wore it, and I've seen how good it looks."

"Margo seemed to think she should light the dress I borrowed on fire rather than be seen in it after I'd worn it."

"That's different," I tell her. "That was a custom ball gown, designed specifically for her. If she wears it after you wore it, people might think we both bought the dress from the same place. Off the rack." I hesitate, trying to think of a way to explain one-of-a-kind fashion to someone who grew up as one of five thousand uniform-wearing identicals. "My friends and I don't go out in off-the-rack clothing. Designers show us their newest things, we buy what we like, then no one else gets to have that outfit ever again. Unless we auction it off for charity." Although, there are plenty of copycat discount designers.

Dahlia follows me into the bedroom, where I take a slim white box wrapped in a silver ribbon from one of my desk drawers and hand it to her. "This is for you."

She hesitates for a second. Then she pulls off the ribbon and opens the box. Her eyes widen as she stares at the contents. "You're giving me a tablet?" She pulls out the thin, hand-sized sheet of e-glass and squints at the lines of her palm through its surface. "For how long?"

"Forever. That's how a gift works."

Dahlia stares at me for a second. Then she throws her arms around me, still holding the tablet, and nearly bowls both of us over.

"Hey." I tap on her shoulder, and when she doesn't release me, I let myself hug her back. "It's just a tablet."

Dahlia lets me go. "We didn't give gifts in the training ward. Trigger is the only other person who's ever given me anything."

"Really?" It seems so sad to never have been given a gift before. I get gifts all the time. "What did he give you?"

"A carrot. And a peanut," Dahlia adds, as if those are the most normal things a soldier could ever give his secret clone girlfriend.

"Oh. Wow," I say, nodding. There is *so* much about Lakeview that I don't understand. And now I feel guilty, because the tablet isn't so much a gift as it is a prop. Part of the costume required to play Waverly Whitmore in public.

"Well, in lieu of vegetation"—*So. Weird.*—"I hope you'll accept the tablet. It's just like mine—same settings, apps, pictures, and videos. You can buy, read, and watch whatever you want, and purchases will go to both of our tablets. The only exception is social media. You're not signed into my message accounts because I don't need you to be me online."

I show her how to program her fingerprints so the tablet will respond to her touch instead of mine. "Why do we have different fingerprints if we have identical DNA?" I ask as she finishes with her last pinkie finger.

"Because fingerprints are influenced by environmental factors during fetal development, and you and I definitely did not experience the same environmental factors. I was gestated inside sterile lab equipment, in a controlled environment."

Does that mean her identicals all have the same fingerprints? If my mother gets her way, I'll never have a chance to find out.

"Okay," Dahlia says as a flash of light blinks from the center of her tablet. "I think it's done." She picks it up, and a soft green light blinks in one corner, acknowledging her fingerprints. The glass clouds over, then shows the image I have programmed into my own tablet as the background—a shot of Hennessy and me kissing in a field of flowers.

"He really seems to care about you," she says, staring at the picture with a wistful expression.

"He loves me," I tell her. "I know that's not a word you're used to using about non-sisterly relationships, but that's what's between me and Hennessy. I love him. And I should be there with him tonight."

Dahlia gives me a sympathetic look, and I stand, mentally shaking off gloom. I'm tired of feeling sorry for myself and I'm *really* not comfortable with her feeling sorry for me. "Okay. One last run-through of the details."

She slides her new tablet into a pocket hidden in the folds of her blouse.

"You can have *one* drink. But no red wine—it stains your teeth and lips. Stick to champagne, but wait for Hennessy to hand it to you. It's this gentlemanly thing he does, and people love it."

"You can't get your own drink?"

"Of course I *can*. But he likes to do it for me. It's polite, and supercute. Just like when I tie his tie. He can do it. But it's sweet when I do it for him."

"Okay." Dahlia shrugs.

"You can sample three snacks—they're called hors d'oeuvres—but only one of each, because that's all I would eat in public, and nothing—"

"With beef in it. I know." She rolls her eyes. "You don't eat beef."

"And you shouldn't either. It's not good for you."

Dahlia's brows rise. "I've never selected my own food."

"Of course you haven't." I'm such an idiot. "Well, you'll get to tonight. Have fun. Just don't go overboard, because I seriously don't eat much in public. There's too great a risk of getting arugula stuck in my teeth or spilling something on my clothes."

She nods, and where I saw only fear and dread in her gaze before, there is now a spark of interest. Excitement. "Anything else?"

"Yes. Speak to everyone, but small talk only. The statements you memorized about my platforms. Compliments for the other girls' clothing. But don't compliment any guys or look at any of them for too long, or the tabloid feeds will say I'm thinking of cheating on Hennessy. Or that I'm already cheating." Her look of incomprehension is starting to feel very familiar. "That I'm interested in another guy," I clarify.

"Just because you look at someone for too long?" Her frown deepens. "How long is too long?"

"Go with your gut. Hennessy will stay by your side and my parents will be nearby. And remember, you're *always* on camera. From the moment you get out of the car until the moment you get back into it. People will be recording you. Waiting for you to do or say something stupid, so they can sell it, or just post it themselves. *Don't* give them the opportunity."

Dahlia nods firmly, clasping her hands in front of herself like a nervous kid. Which is when I notice that her hands are bare.

A fresh ache grips my chest as I pull my engagement ring from my finger. I stare at it for a moment as I hold it up between us. "This is *very* important to me. It's the ring Hennessy gave me when he asked me to marry him. He designed it himself, which means that even if you had all the credits in the world, you couldn't buy me a replacement. So don't let *anything* happen to this."

Dahlia shakes her head when I try to give it to her. "If it's that valuable, you should just keep it."

" 'I' can't show up at my own engagement party without my engagement ring. Put it on the third finger of your left hand."

Dahlia reluctantly slides the ring onto her finger. Then

she stares at her hand as if she's never seen it before. "It's heavier than it looks."

I remember thinking the same thing when Hennessy put it on my hand. "That's because it's important. Be careful and don't gesture with your hands. It snags on things."

"Okay." Dahlia's forehead furrows with some new thought, and her fear is back. "What about dancing? There was lots of dancing at Seren's party."

"There won't be tonight. The hardest part will be a series of toasts to the couple of honor. It's a tradition. Just laugh when Hennessy laughs, raise your glass when everyone else does, and keep smiling." Thank goodness her teeth are perfect. "Ultimately, that's the advice you should fall back on, when in doubt. Waverly Whitmore is *always* smiling."

SEVENTEEN

DAHLIA

Trigger 17 is dressed and ready to go the moment Waverly opens his bedroom door. His soldier's uniform is a little different from what he wore in Lakeview, but it's similar enough to make me feel strangely wistful, in addition to the nervous excitement already buzzing just beneath my skin.

Waverly thinks having Hennessy at my side should be comforting, but I'm much happier about having Trigger at my back.

"Wow. You look . . ." Instead of trying to find words, he pulls me close for a kiss, but Waverly slides her hand between our faces at the last second.

"You'll smudge her lipstick." She seems pleased for the excuse to deny us our moment, and though Trigger looks irritated—and also *very* attractive in his new uniform—I understand her resentment. I'll be spending the evening in her clothes, at her party, with her fiancé, while she sits at home reading the public feeds. "Remember to ride up front with the driver and stay three steps behind Dahlia when you're walking," she tells Trigger. "The party's in a secure setting, so once you get inside, stay in the background. *Off* camera."

He gives her an amused look. "I think I can handle it."

Waverly flounces off toward the stairs, and when I start to follow her, Trigger takes my hand and pulls me close, delaying us by a few steps for at least a semblance of privacy.

"I'm so glad to be out of that room," he whispers, his lips brushing my ear, and I have to fight the urge to turn and kiss him. "I didn't think they were going to let me come, after they disconnected my screen."

"I convinced Waverly that I would be more comfortable with you there, thus better able to remember everything I've learned this week."

"Come *on*," Waverly calls from the top of the right-hand staircase.

Trigger lets me go, and we head down the steps side by side.

The sun is low on the horizon as we step outside, where Hennessy is leaning against his car. He glances from Waverly to me, then back as we descend from the front porch, and it's obvious that he can't tell which of us is which. Until his gaze trails over our clothing. Waverly's not dressed to go out.

Clearly relieved to have identified his fiancée, he greets her with an embrace and a kiss on the cheek. "I wish you were coming with me," he says softly, probably hoping I can't hear him.

"Me too." She sighs. "Don't let Dahlia have more than one drink," she whispers to Hennessy.

"I won't." He presses his forehead against hers and closes his eyes, as if they're communicating without speaking. Brain-to-brain. They look really sweet together, even though there aren't any cameras here to catch the moment.

Trigger opens the rear car door for me, then climbs into the front seat, next to the driver.

"I'll see you tonight." Hennessy squeezes Waverly's hand, and as I slide across the long rear seat, I hear him whisper something else to her. "I love you."

"Love you too." They kiss, long and deep—they don't have to worry about messing up her lipstick. Then Hennessy sits next to me and closes the door.

As the car pulls away, I twist in my seat to see that she's still standing on the front steps, staring after us.

"So, you ready for this?" Hennessy asks as we pull through the gate and turn onto the sharply sloped street. As its name implies, Mountainside is built into the side of a large mountain, and—as Waverly has already explained—the more credits or power one has, the higher up one lives.

The Whitmores live near the peak. As do the Chapmans. Yet the building we're headed for is even higher up.

"Waverly says I'm as ready as I'll ever be. I have a tablet now." I pull it from my pocket to show Hennessy, proud of my gift, and he laughs out loud.

Trigger turns to look. "May I see that?"

"Sorry, man," Hennessy says. "Waverly will kill me if I let you near any tech. Though I might be convinced to look the other way at least once tonight, if you show me how to lock my sister in her bathroom. . . ."

Trigger chuckles. "I'm sure we can work something out."

"You're not missing anything," I tell him. "The way Waverly explained it, I can download just about anything I want, but I can't upload anything or access the household system."

"Naturally," Trigger says. "They won't let you communicate with the world, unsupervised." Which means my new tablet won't be much use for helping expose Lakeview or for protecting my identicals.

"Why aren't we riding with Waverly's parents?" I ask as our car winds its way up the mountain.

"They're already there. We're the guests of honor, so we arrive a little late, to make a grand entrance." He winks at me. "Also so Audra can get some interviews with the people waiting for us."

I must look scared again, because he gives me a friendly shoulder nudge. "Don't worry. I'll be by your side all night."

Trigger stiffens in the front seat, and I want to remind him again that this is pretend. Acting, like in the scripted shows I've started watching on my wall screen when I'm trying to fall asleep alone in the blue room at night. But I don't know how to reassure him without making it worse.

"We're almost there." Hennessy leans forward to peer out

the window on my side of the car. "Protesters are always *near* the event, but not *too* near."

"Protesters?" I follow his gaze and find a crowd of people gathered on the sidewalk, pumping their fists in the air angrily. They're all wearing worn coats, their cheeks red from the cold. Some of them hold signs that show Waverly's name crossed through with red slashes. Others display slogans like "NO MORE CLONES!" and "CITIZENS DESERVE TO WORK!"

"The police hold them at least a block away. That doesn't keep them out of the news footage, but it *will* keep them off the show."

The protesters appear to be shouting, but . . . "Why can't we hear them?"

"Hang on." Hennessy taps on his own window, and when it fogs over, I realize that the windows are made of e-glass. A menu appears, and he deselects a box labeled *Mute*. Suddenly I hear the shouting, which is actually a synchronized chant echoing the slogans on the signs.

Hennessy moves his finger up a slider on the glass. The higher his finger moves, the louder the protest gets.

"The windows are interactive?" Trigger taps his window, but nothing happens.

"Just the ones back here. Sorry," Hennessy says. And he actually does sound sorry.

I twist to watch the protesters as our car passes them. "They're saying they don't like clones? Why?"

Hennessy looks conflicted for a moment. "It's not actually

184

clones they don't like. It's the system. It's more cost-effective in the long run for businesses to buy clones than to employ citizens."

"Really?" Trigger turns to give Hennessy a skeptical look. "Why?"

"Well, clones are expensive up front, but employees draw salaries and benefits, and they get time off, and there are legal limits on the number of hours that can be worked in a given period. None of that is true for clones."

"What kind of benefits do citizens get?" I ask.

"Childcare. Medical care. Dental. Days off work when they're sick. Days off for vacation." Hennessy frowns at my look of incomprehension. "That's time off to relax and be with your family. Take a trip. They also get maternity leave— time off when a woman has a baby."

"And clones don't get any of that." I've known that since the day we got to Mountainside, but it isn't what clones don't get that surprises me. It's what citizens *do* get. I know that Waverly and Hennessy and their friends live drastically different lives than their servants do, but until this moment, I didn't truly understand that the same is true of the other citizens.

Even those protesters out there who have no jobs and no credits have the freedom to choose what to wear. What to eat. They have the option of standing on the sidewalk and shouting about things they find unfair.

Clones just . . . don't. And because of the mental fog they operate in, they couldn't do those things even if they had the option.

"For a long time, clone labor was almost exclusively used for military and security, and for household staff for the wealthier families. But my dad says that a few decades ago, businesses started buying clones instead of hiring electricians, and bakers, and tailors, and . . . well, gardeners," Hennessy says with an awkward shrug in my direction. "The number of clones in service skyrocketed. Citizens started losing their jobs. That led to an unemployment crisis. And not just in Mountainside. It's pretty much all over."

"These protesters show up everywhere you and Waverly go?" I ask as we turn a corner and I can no longer see or hear them. "Why?"

"DigiCore's subsidiary companies used to be the largest employer of citizens in Mountainside. Then they made the transition to clone labor, and all those people lost their jobs."

My mind spins, trying to puzzle through the complexities. It's not the clones' fault that we—*they*—exist. But it's not the citizens' fault that they have no jobs, thus no way to earn the credits that pay for their food and housing.

The only ones winning under this system are the wealthy, like the Whitmores and the Chapmans. And the Administrator.

What would happen if all the clones in Mountainside could protest?

"Okay, here we go!" Hennessy sits straighter and stares out the windshield between the front seats.

A crowd has gathered in front of the building we're evidently headed toward, and most of the people have large cameras fitted with bright lights. Those who don't are already holding tablets up in our direction, obviously filming.

A sudden surge of nerves overtakes me.

"Breathe," Hennessy says. Then he leans forward and taps Trigger on the shoulder, just as the car pulls to a stop. "You're up."

Trigger gives me a reassuring smile. Then he opens his door and gets out.

While he walks around the car, Hennessy takes my chin and gently turns my face so that I'm looking at him. "Waverly says you're ready to pretend you're her, and I believe her. But there's another part to this. A part that's just as important, but that she would never tell you."

"What part?" My nerves are buzzing like bees beneath the surface of my skin.

"If you want people to believe what we're about to do, you have to sell them not just on you, but on *us*. You have to make people believe you're in love with me. Even if that means pretending I'm Trigger 17."

EIGHTEEN

DAHLIA

We get out of the car, and Hennessy takes my hand as he waves to the crowd. I wave too, just as I've seen Waverly do in several videos, but this time my wave shows off the union ink, free of both bandages and swelling, and swirling with color, because its mate is so close by. I give the crowd a broad smile and, taking Hennessy's advice, I pretend it's Trigger's hand in mine.

Though Waverly frequently stops to speak to people in crowds, Hennessy keeps us moving, and in seconds we're in the lobby of a tall building, where the e-glass spanning one large wall shows a series of silent video clips of my clone and her fiancé and declares that the Whitmore–Chapman engagement party is taking place in the Precipice Ballroom. Which evidently takes up the entire top floor.

Trigger follows Hennessy and me into the elevator, then

stands imposingly in the doorway, preventing anyone else from following us in. For which I'm grateful. My palms are damp and my ankles feel a bit wobbly in my high heels. "How many people will be at this party?" I ask as the elevator rises.

"Didn't you say the guest list was about four hundred strong?" Hennessy squeezes my hand and glances up at the corner of the elevator.

Oh. There must be a camera.

"That sounds about right," I mumble.

Trigger glances over his shoulder and gives me a reassuring smile, and suddenly I remember that he and I met in an elevator. I wish this were that elevator.

I wish we were back then and there, but knew what we know here and now.

The elevator stops and the door slides open. Trigger steps to the side to let us precede him into a large, elegant foyer. Across the open space are three sets of double doors. Audra, Waverly's producer, stands in front of the center set, holding a large tablet, and the moment she sees us, she begins whispering into her headset.

Hennessy places my hand on the crook of his arm and leans in as if to kiss me. "Some of the guests are friends from school, but most of them are our parents' business associates. I don't remember all their names, and neither would Waverly. So don't stress too much about that."

"Thank you," I whisper in return. Then I shoot Trigger

a smile, silently reassuring him that that moment wasn't as intimate as it may have looked.

Hennessy leads me across the foyer with Trigger 17 at our backs. Audra says something else into her headset. Then she gives us a big smile and throws the double doors open.

Music is playing from somewhere—the string quartet Waverly mentioned. The huge room is *full* of people. And they're all staring at us.

I inhale. Then I smile.

Applause breaks out as we step into the ballroom, and my smile feels frozen in place. My heels wobble, but my fears about tripping over my own feet seem misplaced because we're not really walking. The crowd closes around us a few steps into the room, and from that moment on, we're merely shuffling slowly across the floor, greeting couple after couple, group after group.

Some introduce themselves as friends of the Chapmans. Others as friends of Waverly's parents. I shake hands and compliment dresses. I laugh at jokes I don't understand and listen to stories about people I don't know. Whenever someone asks about Waverly's wedding dress, I smile and give the coy deflection we practiced in front of the mirror. Then I hold my tattooed arm next to Hennessy's tattooed arm and let people ooh and aah over the pulsing colors as a distraction and a change of subject.

Halfway through the large room, when I can't come up with an answer to a question from a woman my clone has apparently met several times, Hennessy interrupts my awkward reply to signal to a waiter carrying a tray of drinks. He lifts two tall champagne glasses—Waverly says they're called flutes—and hands me one.

I give him a grateful smile, and as I lift the champagne toward my mouth, I notice that there's something etched into the side of the glass in a beautiful scrolling print. It's Waverly's name, above the word *Bride* and the date of the wedding.

"Oh, how beautiful!" And as I glance around, I notice that everyone's glass either bears the same words as mine, or Hennessy's name and the word *Groom*.

The woman who was speaking to me frowns. "Didn't you know about the glasses, dear?"

"She picked them out." Waverly's mother appears at my side seemingly out of thin air. "She just hasn't seen them in person until now. And it was Waverly's idea to sell them as mementos after the wedding, with the funds going to her signature cause—the children's home."

"What a wonderful idea," the woman says. "And yes, they are beautiful. I'll take one of each!"

Lorna gives me a cold smile, then disappears into the crowd. But I suspect she won't wander very far, in case she has to save me from myself again.

After another half hour of mingling, Hennessy sees me eyeing a tray of hors d'oeuvres, and waves the waiter—a clone—closer. By some miracle, we're alone in the crowd for a moment while I study the selection.

The waiter lowers the tray. "This one is grilled watermelon, chèvre, and basil," he says, pointing to a delicate tower speared with a tiny stick that curls into a loop on one end. "These are maple-caramelized figs topped with bacon and chili pepper, and these are endive cups with beet, persimmon, and marinated feta."

They all look delicious. And elegant. And they're all *bite-sized*. I didn't know the food would be so tiny!

I take a caramelized fig—it looks the most filling—and thank the waiter. Hennessy watches me with a small smile as I put the entire morsel in my mouth. "Mmmm . . . ," I moan as I chew. It's sweet, and chewy, and crunchy, and a little spicy, all at the same time.

Hennessy's smile grows. "I wouldn't have guessed you for a bacon lover. Waverly won't touch it."

"We're only *genetically* identical," I remind him as softly as I can.

He laughs and snags a tiny pastry from a tray being carried past while I sip my champagne. "This was the only thing I requested for the menu," he tells me, holding up his bite-sized morsel.

"What is it?"

"It's a miniature beef Wellington." He takes a careful bite, then shows me the tiny portion of pinkish beef wrapped in what remains of his tart.

"It looks amazing. It *smells* amazing." My mouth waters as he chews. "But Waverly doesn't eat beef."

Hennessy takes a sip from his own flute and watches me for a second. "Play along," he whispers. Then he raises his voice to a normal level. "Oh, come on, Waverly. Just try a bite. I tried the snapper crudo for you." His lips are turned up into a teasing smile for Waverly, but his expectant gaze is for me as he brings the rest of his hors d'oeuvre toward my mouth.

Ah. Waverly wouldn't voluntarily eat beef, but she might take a bite that her fiancé feeds her. For the cameras.

I open my mouth. Hennessy places the morsel on my tongue. His fingers brush my lips as I close my mouth.

I moan again as I chew, and his smile . . . changes. His focus on me deepens, and I get the distinct impression that for the first time tonight, he's seeing *me*, rather than the girl pretending to be his fiancée.

"See?" His voice is above a whisper, yet still low-pitched, as if this is part of a private conversation. "Sometimes it pays to branch out."

"Thank you," I whisper while people all around us make sounds of approval, as if we're the cutest thing they've ever seen.

As I raise my glass for another sip, my gaze travels over Hennessy's shoulder and lands on Trigger. He's standing at attention along the wall, near a few other members of private security. He looks . . . hurt.

"Waverly!" A familiar voice calls, and when I turn, I see Margo and Sofia fighting their way through the crowd toward us, with Seren and a few others trailing behind them. These are Waverly and Hennessy's friends—the faces and names I've spent part of the past week memorizing. Most of them I actually met last week, at Seren's party, but I was too terrified and overwhelmed then to process much of anything other than the startling realization that they were all individuals.

That concept no longer seems as strange as it did. In fact, I can hardly even imagine there being a thousand other boys who look like Hennessy. And considering that Sofia and Margo's relationship with Waverly is as much competition as friendship, it's probably a very good thing that there's only one of each of them.

"We've been looking for you for an hour!" Margo squeals as she loops her arm through mine, sloshing champagne dangerously near the top of my glass. "Come on, there's some breathing room near the lookout."

Before I can decide whether I should know what the lookout is, she and Sofia are pulling me through the crowd, away from both Trigger and Hennessy.

I'm so focused on not tripping over my heels or spilling my champagne that I don't see the glass until we're feet from it, in the most open space in the entire ballroom.

"Oh . . ." I breathe as I stare at the view laid out before us. And suddenly I understand where the Precipice Ballroom gets its name. We're looking out over half the city, sprawling down the side of the mountain that gives it its name. The setting sun glimmers on rooftops and cars, and on miles of the metallic cruise strip tracing the roads in both directions.

I assume I'm looking through a huge window—literally

one entire wall of the long, tall ballroom—until I notice a video playing silently in the glass just below eye height, showing the installation of the huge wall.

While Margo and Sofia get drinks from a waiter, I read the text scrolling across the bottom of the video, lauding the installation of the two giant panes of e-glass—the largest in the world—as an architectural masterpiece.

Two panes? I spin to look across the room, and above several hundred heads I find another wall of glass, opposite this one. This building, I realize, sits at the very top of the mountain, in place of its peak, and through the huge e-glass windows, one can see *both* sides of the city winding its way from the foothills toward the summit.

"Waverly's father really outdid himself," Hennessy whispers, and I jump, startled to find him right beside me. "He personally designed these panels, working closely with several architects at my father's firm. It took them three years."

"Wow." This view deserves more, but I have no better words.

I wonder if Trigger has seen this yet.

I sip my champagne slowly and we chat with Waverly's friends—though my focus is split by the view out the glass as the sun sets—until Lorna appears again and ushers Hennessy and me toward a dais set up near the wall opposite the foyer entrance.

It's time for the toasts.

There are at least a dozen of them, and that's no exaggeration. Waverly's parents each speak. Then Hennessy's.

Then his sister. Then Waverly's maternal grandmother—her mother's mother, a concept that seems to encompass twice the strangeness of the idea of maternity itself. Then a series of people whose relationships to the bride and groom I can't even understand.

Some of the toasts are sweet, others funny. I smile and laugh, glad that I've seen lots of footage of Waverly at parties.

There are so many toasts that despite my very modest sips, Hennessy has to snag another glass of champagne for me about six speakers in.

By the time the toasts are over, I feel a little light-headed. Yet very pleasant.

"Speech!" someone shouts, and when I look for the shouter, I have to grab Hennessy's arm for balance. "Waverly! You always have something to say!"

The audience laughs, and in the second it takes me to realize that I'm being asked to speak to a room full of strangers, someone passes Hennessy the microphone, intending for him to give it to me.

I stare at him, wide-eyed with panic. Waverly said this wouldn't happen.

Instead of handing me the microphone, he keeps it. "Waverly gets to have her say all the time," he jokes to light laughter. "But tonight you guys are stuck with me." Hennessy turns to look at me. "Waverly Whitmore, I knew from the moment I met you that someday I'd ask you to marry me. I was a little less confident that you'd say yes."

"Aww . . ." comes a chorus from our audience. And though I know he's talking to my clone, not to me, something about the audience, and the champagne, and the knowledge that this should be a very special moment makes my heart feel suddenly swollen with emotion I can't quite define. As if I've been dropped in the middle of someone else's memory.

"But you said yes and made me the happiest man in the world. Now I'm going to spend the rest of my life making you the happiest woman in the world. I love you. I want you by my side every day. Even if that means having your camera crew, and your makeup team, and your one-hundred-fifty-bazillion followers at my side too."

The audience laughs, and my head begins to swim. I can see how much he loves her. What I can't see through the crowd is Trigger 17.

"I want the whole package. I want to give you the world. But I'm afraid you might already have it," Hennessy says, and more laughter bubbles up through the crowd. "So instead, I'll just give you myself. All of me. For the rest of our lives. This is how forever starts."

Then Hennessy leans in and kisses me, right on the mouth. On camera. On the stage, in front of hundreds of people.

And Trigger.

The audience roars with applause and boisterous approval, and for a moment, as my head spins and the applause closes in on me, I kiss him back.

Then Hennessy pulls away, and the reality of the moment

hits me like a knife shoved straight through my heart. Behind his head, I see that the huge glass wall on one side of the room has become a viewing screen, and our images are on display, live. At about ten times our actual size.

I look stunned.

That kiss wasn't meant for me. I know that. But it was *given* to me. Trigger saw. Waverly will see, if she hasn't already, thanks to this city full of cameras.

My image on the huge screen blinks.

Lorna takes the microphone from Hennessy and smiles at the crowd. "Clearly Waverly's a little dazed," she says. "Now, *that's* chemistry!"

The audience roars its approval again, and I manage a smile as I scan the crowd in search of Trigger. But there are too many people. I can't see him.

What I do see is a staff of gray-clad clones filing into the back of the room through a service entrance. They begin emptying trash cans and clearing trays of used glasses and napkins, staring at the floor when their job doesn't pull their gazes to the tasks at hand.

While everyone else eats, drinks, and laughs, the clones are working. And unlike citizen employees, they won't go home with an account full of credits in exchange for their labor. They won't change into casual clothes and greet their family members. The same is true of the clone cooks who made the hors d'oeuvres, the drivers who brought the guests to this party, and workers who will clean up after we've all gone.

Suddenly it all seems so simple.

This isn't right.

And it won't change unless someone does something. Someone people will listen to. Someone with an audience of tens of millions.

Or someone who looks just like her.

"Waverly, say something!" a voice calls from the crowd, and it sounds suspiciously like Sofia Locke.

"Waverly isn't feeling very well—" Lorna begins.

I turn and take the microphone from her before I can lose my nerve. Before she, or Dane Whitmore, or Hennessy can read my intention on my face.

"Thank you all for coming," I say, beginning the way Waverly starts most of her public addresses. "It means the world to me and to Hennessy that you've all come out to celebrate with us. I do have something to say, if you'll all bear with me." I stare out at the crowd without focusing on any one face. Hennessy takes my hand and squeezes it subtly, but I ignore his silent warning. "As you all know, the beautiful engraved glasses we're drinking from tonight will be sold after the wedding, with the proceeds to go to one of my favorite children's charities. But while I have you here tonight, I'd like to mention another cause. My new official platform."

Hennessy's hand squeezes tighter, and Lorna steps up to my side, her presence like a physical threat. But there's nothing she can say or do now without causing a scene.

I press forward, emboldened by my glass and a half of champagne and the indignation burning in my gut. "My new signature cause, which I'd love for you all to support with me, is"—I pause, letting anticipation build like I've seen Waverly do on her show—"clones' rights."

NINETEEN

WAVERLY

The screen on my wall plays a happy little melody, alerting me that the link my mother set up is ready.

Through silent feeds from three of the security cameras in the Precipice Ballroom, I watch Dahlia and Hennessy make their way slowly through the room, greeting guests, while on the other half of my wall, I monitor the public feeds for all mentions of the party. A bolt of jealousy surges through me as I watch him feed her an hors d'oeuvre.

The comments are all positive. People love her clothes. They think he looks hot and she looks gorgeous. I should be thrilled. Yet envy burns in my chest like indigestion.

The whisper of my door opening distracts me from the engagement toasts that are beginning on-screen, and I turn to see Julienne 20 coming in with a domed silver tray. She sets my meal on the table by the window. "Will there be anything else?" she asks, staring at the floor.

Why does she always stare at the floor? If Dahlia can convince a room full of people that she's me, why can't Julienne even give coherent answers to my questions?

A new idea flashes through my mind like lightning across the sky. "Yes, actually, there's one more thing. When do you eat dinner?"

She frowns at her gray canvas shoes. "Whenever time permits."

"Tonight, I'd like you to have dinner with me. Go get your meal, please, and bring it here."

Her frown deepens, but her gaze doesn't rise. "H-here?"

"Yes. Right now. Go get your food."

"Of course. Will that be all?"

"Yes. Thank you," I add.

A few minutes later Julienne comes back carrying a plastic fork and a small cardboard box with steam rising from the seam. Yet this time she hesitates just inside the door, as always, looking down at her feet.

I wave her forward as I settle into one of the chairs by the window, on either side of the small table. "Come eat with me."

Julienne looks confused as she sits across from me in silence. Her hands tremble as she sets her box of food on the table.

"Oh, you're not going to be eating that," I say, and her gaze snaps up to mine. "We're going to run a little experiment. For the next few days, you're going to eat your meals with me—

sharing my food—and we're going to see if that makes you feel any . . . different."

Julienne stares at me, brows drawn low. So I take her box dinner—noting the Lakeside insignia printed on two sides— and drop it into the trash can, untouched.

"Here." I push my plate toward the center of the table. "I only ever eat half of it anyway. The servings are huge." I motion toward her fork, but she doesn't reach for it. So I take my own silverware and cut my crumb-crusted sablefish fillet down the center and push half of it toward her. Then I carve a divide down the middle of my caramelized fennel and roasted cherry tomatoes. "Seriously." I tear the freshly baked crescent roll in half and set one hunk on her side. "That part's for you. It smells delicious. Dig in." Then I pick up my fork and take a bite of fish. "Mmmm . . . ," I moan. "Everything you make is *amazing*."

Julienne smiles, for the first time I can remember. It's a small smile. Shy. And she stares at the table the whole time. But I silently celebrate the victory.

"Eat," I say as I cut my next bite. "That's an order." But she doesn't take the first bite until I turn my attention to the e-glass. So I watch Dahlia on-screen and settle for studying Julienne out of the corner of my eye, which seems to make her more comfortable.

By the time I finish my fish, the toasts are over, and I notice tension on the dais. I can't tell exactly what's going on. Someone hands the microphone to Hennessy, clearly intending for him to hand it to Dahlia. Instead, he keeps it and begins to speak.

I *really* wish I could hear what he's saying, because though he's saying it to her, I know he means it—whatever it is—for me.

Then he kisses her, and I feel like my heart just cracked open and fell apart.

It's an act. It's a *necessary* part of the act. A dozen people just toasted to our marriage. Of *course* he kissed her. But he was really kissing me.

Yet he kissed her.

I stand and swipe the viewing window closed; then I drop my fork on my plate with a clatter. Julienne looks up, startled.

"Sorry. Finish your dinner. It's fine," I tell her. But it's not fine. If it's this hard to watch my fiancé kiss someone else, how am I ever going to watch him recite vows to her in *our* wedding?

Julienne chews her last cherry tomato as she stands and gathers the silverware and napkin onto the plate. She sweeps crumbs from the table onto the plate with her hand, then disappears into the hallway before I can remind her to bring her breakfast with mine tomorrow.

And honestly, right now I don't even care.

I pace across the room, and from the corner of my eye, the pink holographic tulip in a projector pot next to my bed withers and dies. In its place a stem emerges, growing rapidly until a bud at the top unfolds, reflecting my anger in the form of a single black iris with delicate, wavy edges.

Frustrated, I spin to face the screen again and reopen the video just in time to see Dahlia take the microphone from Lorna. She begins to speak, and the entire crowd goes still.

What is she saying?

Desperate, I turn back to the public feeds and scroll through until I find a video posted in the search column I've set up for the party. Though it's been forbidden, someone is shooting a livecast from the Precipice Ballroom. I tap on the video to play it, then enlarge the screen until the shaky view of the dais takes up a quarter of my wall. I've missed the first part of Dahlia's speech, but her closing statement makes it easy to fill in the blanks.

". . . citizenship for clones!"

What?

Noooooo . . .

TWENTY

DAHLIA

Waverly storms out the front door of her house as our car pulls to a stop in the driveway. "What the *hell* did you do?" she demands.

"You did the right thing," Trigger assures me from the front seat as he opens his door.

Hennessy hasn't said a word since he shuffled me through the crowd, out of the building, and into the car on Lorna's orders, leaving Waverly's parents to do "damage control." He looks angry. But he also looks worried.

Trigger opens my door.

"Dahlia!" Waverly snaps as I climb out of the car. "How— Why—" Finally she just stares at me, as if no more words will come.

Behind us, the front gate squeals open and another car pulls into the driveway. Waverly's parents get out. "Inside. All of you," her mother orders in a low, angry voice.

Dane Whitmore marches past us into the house without a word.

Trigger takes my hand on the way up the front steps. "They're mad now, but they'll understand soon," he whispers as we climb the curving staircase together.

"I doubt that."

Half an hour ago, I'd felt invincible, buoyed by champagne and emboldened by the microphone in my hand. By the hundreds of people waiting to hear what I had to say. But now . . .

After spending a week learning to be Waverly, I understand enough of her world to know that I've embarrassed and angered the Whitmores in a very public way. Which, in terms that Trigger would understand, is like stabbing them where they're most vulnerable.

I don't really care about the anger and embarrassment of a family that doesn't even notice the servants who make their meals, wash their clothes, or clean their house. But I do care about how they'll react to this.

Lorna still has all the power in the world over my identicals.

"Waverly's a clone. What you said is in her best interest," Trigger insists, too low for anyone else to hear as we head down the second-floor hallway. "She'll see that eventually."

But I don't think she will. I think she'll always believe that hiding the truth is what's in her best interest. Even if that doesn't benefit anyone else.

We follow Waverly and Hennessy past the blue room,

headed for the family wing, but Lorna stops in front of the gray room.

"Trigger isn't involved in this." She waves the door open and gestures for him to enter.

"I'll stay with Dahlia," he says.

"No."

"It's okay," I tell him. "I'll be fine." And I'm afraid that if he comes with me, Lorna will use him against me. That she'll threaten him like she's threatening the rest of my identicals, to get me to do whatever she wants.

Reluctantly, Trigger steps into the gray room, and the door slides shut between us. Suddenly I feel like I've just severed a lifeline. Like I'm stacking mistake on top of mistake, and soon the pile will bury me.

I follow Waverly and Hennessy into her room, but Lorna remains in the hall, tapping on her tablet.

"Do you have any idea what you've done?" Waverly demands the moment the door closes.

"I know you're angry, but—"

"You have *no* idea. I'm going to have to own this now. The only way I'm going to be able to convince the world that I'm not insane is to take what you said and run with it."

I exhale in relief. "Good. I think that's the best thing." While I hadn't given my speech much forethought, I *had* assumed that anything I said on camera, she'd have to stand by. Which was why I'd said it.

"This is *not* good," Waverly screeches.

Hennessy drops onto the white leather couch without even attempting to calm her down. He seems to be deep in his own thoughts.

"Mom!" Waverly stomps toward her door, but it opens before she reaches it and Lorna walks inside, sliding her tablet into her pocket. "Have you looked at the optics? Obviously we're going to have to own this. Call my publicist. I have to make a statement, and I need options for how best to approach this."

Lorna crosses her arms over the bodice of her dress. "Slow down, Waverly. The Administrator will never let you take on clone citizenship as a public platform."

"The *Administrator.*" Waverly sinks onto the couch like a deflating balloon. Then she groans.

I glance from mother to daughter, confused. "What does the Administrator have to do with it?"

"She's agreed not to tell the world that Waverly is a clone and we've agreed not to press charges against her for putting DNA she didn't own into production. We'll all get hurt, should either of those things be made public. But there's only so far we can push her before she's willing to break that truce, because the truth is that we stand to lose more than she does from all this. And she's a vengeful woman."

"What does that mean?" I understand the words, but the conclusion still feels fuzzy.

"It means you may have just gotten us both killed!" Waverly explodes off the couch, fear and fury warring behind her eyes. "If I'm a clone, she owns me, and she can have me euthanized anytime she wants. Just like the rest of your identicals."

I turn to Lorna, my heart thumping so hard my chest aches. "I thought you bought them. Don't they belong to you now?"

"She hasn't accepted my offer yet. They're still in her possession, both physically and legally."

"This is why you can't just go out in public and say whatever you want!" Waverly says. "Words have consequences!"

"So do actions," I say softly.

"What?" Waverly turns on me, and suddenly the righteous indignation shining in her eyes—as if *I'm* the problem—makes me so mad.

"I said actions have consequences too." I raise my voice until all three are looking at me, and this time, instead of shrinking away from the attention, I power through. "Buying human beings, producing human beings to be bought—those have *always* had life-or-death consequences for clones. The only thing my speech changed is that now those consequences could affect *you.*"

"She's right," Hennessy says, and we all turn to him in surprise. "And all that goes for me as well. I didn't really care about any of this until it started affecting Waverly. But that doesn't mean I *shouldn't* have cared."

"Okay. Yes." Waverly drops onto the cushion next to him, more moved by his admission than by anything I've said so far. "The world is a terrible place. Big surprise." She turns to me, brows dipped low over eyes reflecting my own kaleidoscope of emotions back at me. "But you can't fix it like this. You can't fix it at *all*. No one even knows you exist."

"But they know *you* exist. You're the people's princess—the most famous face in the world. People listen to you. You've spent the past week teaching me that. If anyone can change things, it's you."

"You don't get it!" Waverly stands again, and now she's pacing.

"When you couldn't make yourself look like other women, you convinced the world that other women should look like you. You changed the way people think, Waverly, and if you can do it once, you can do it again."

She gapes at me. "Dahlia, I don't think you understand the nature of my influence. I'm famous for cutting ribbons and donating clothes to the homeless. For visiting sick kids in hospitals. I can sell out designer purse lines and raise stock values on lip gloss, but I don't make laws. I don't work miracles."

"Well, you better learn how fast." I claim the chair by the window and watch her pace. "There were a lot of cameras in that room."

Something beeps, and Lorna pulls her tablet from her pocket. She reads with narrowed eyes and a clenched jaw, but she offers no input on the discussion.

"Okay. Let's think about this." Hennessy waves an arm to wake up the wall screen. "What's already out there can't be

211

taken back. So our options are to say that Waverly suffered a stress breakdown—"

"No," Waverly says. "My brand would never recover."

"—or develop the new platform Dahlia announced and find some way to leverage the Administrator."

"Not possible. The Administrator will fight 'citizenship for clones' with every credit she has in the bank. And every politician who's ever bought one will be on her side, because if the law decides that clones are citizens, they'll have been guilty of buying people."

"They're already guilty of that," I point out.

"Not legally," Waverly shoots back. But I can see the conflict eating away at her. "This is so messed up. I'm a clone. I *can't* go out there and tell people that clones shouldn't have any rights. I shouldn't want to do that. But this will ruin me. This could get me killed."

"It could *always* have gotten you killed," I say quietly. "Even if none of this had happened, next year my identicals and I would have gone to market, and you'd be facing the same problem. At least this way, you found out before the rest of the world did."

"Wait," Hennessy says. "We don't have to get the Administrator on board with Dahlia's statement. She doesn't have to support citizenship for clones. She just has to agree not to out Waverly."

Waverly frowns at him. "Why on earth would she agree . . . ?"

"Okay," Lorna says, and with that one word, she's taken

over the room. She lifts her tablet and swipes something from it onto the e-glass.

I gasp when I see Trigger staring up at me from the wall screen. He's still wearing his security uniform, but he's standing alone in a room containing only a single small cot and a door open to reveal a small restroom. He stares up at the camera and starts yelling angrily, but without audio, I can't tell what he's saying.

"What is this?" I demand, my gaze glued to the screen.

"Motivation." Lorna pockets her tablet. "Trigger is in the basement, in the holding cell. That room has no connection to the household system, other than the security camera we're seeing him through. I'm the only one authorized to open the door. Dahlia, if you don't do exactly as I say from here on out, I will send him back to the Administrator in chains."

"But she'll euthanize him for disobedience!" I cry, horrified.

"With my full blessing," Lorna confirms. Waverly stares at her feet in obvious discomfort. Hennessy puts his arm around her. "Do you understand what I'm saying?"

"Do what you want, or you'll kill Trigger." My voice echoes with defeat.

"Exactly. Now, what we're going to hope is that when the Administrator sees that video, she believes that finding out about her own origin has given Waverly a change of heart. Because if she realizes that was you on camera, there will be no way to stop her from ruining *all* of us." Lorna turns to

Waverly. "Audra, the network, and your publicist have been fielding calls and interview requests for the past hour. I've told them all to say that you will be making a statement on camera soon, and everyone will have to wait for that."

Waverly nods.

"And you'll be making that statement yourself. Wearing long sleeves." Lorna turns to Hennessy. "It's very important that you refer all questions to the network and that you give no statements yourself. The same goes for your family, if you can manage that."

"I can. But what do I tell my parents and sister? They've been messaging me since we left the party."

"Tell them that Waverly's been thinking long and hard about her official platform, and she's sworn you to secrecy. For now, at least."

He doesn't seem convinced that will work. Having met Margo, I suspect he's right.

Lorna heads for the hall with one more angry glance at me. "Now if you'll all excuse me, I have to go deal with the Administrator."

TWENTY-ONE

WAVERLY

When Julienne comes in with my breakfast tray, I close the document containing my prewritten, mother-approved interview answers and slide my tablet into my pocket, glad for the break. And for the distraction. In the week since the engagement party, damage control has become a full-time job. My public feed is overwhelmed with questions about my "clone citizenship" platform, whether or not Hennessy and I plan to staff our household with clones, and whether or not our parents will change the staffing arrangements in their houses and businesses.

I've spent so much time putting out social media fires—without actually answering any questions—that our "princess prep" sessions have dwindled to an hour or so a day. I've seen more of Julienne 20 this week than I have of Dahlia. And I'm fine with that.

Julienne hasn't betrayed me.

"Good morning," I say as the door closes behind her.

She doesn't answer, but this time she looks up when I speak. I blink at her in surprise, and then she smiles right at me. Eye contact and everything. It only lasts for a moment, but I swear, that tiny smile sparks a sense of triumph in me unlike anything I've felt before.

It's working.

I was right. Her prepackaged food isn't just laced with hormone suppressors. It's also full of some kind of sedative that lets her work but keeps her from truly engaging with the world. From really seeing anything beyond a job she can basically perform on autopilot.

"What's on the menu this morning?" I ask as she sets the tray on the table by the window.

"Pear and honey crostini with candied walnuts." Julienne pulls the domes from both plates. One contains my breakfast. The other holds hers—a paper bowl of instant oatmeal, labeled with the Lakeview city seal.

As I've done three times a day for the past five days, I drop her food into my trash can, then slide half of my meal onto her plate; she still makes more than I can eat in a single sitting anyway. "You've outdone yourself," I tell her. "It smells delicious!"

This morning, Julienne sits across the table from me without being asked. She even drapes her napkin over her lap and picks up her fork. But she waits until I cut my first bite before cutting hers.

"Is that blue cheese?" I ask as I cut another bite.

"And ricotta," she answers around a mouthful. I laugh, and she smiles as she chews. She's staring at the table again, but this is real progress.

Obviously Dahlia and Trigger themselves are proof that clones aren't born mentally muddled. But seeing a clone emerge from that mental fog—knowing what causes it and that it's *reversible* . . .

Twice, I've started to tell Dahlia what I'm doing. She deserves to know, especially now that my theory has panned out. But after what she did at the engagement party . . .

Julienne gives me another shy glance. For the past few days, I've been asking her small questions. Her favorite color. (It's purple.) Her favorite food. (It's chocolate ice cream.) But today, I think we're both ready for something bigger.

"May I ask you something?" I say while she sips from the glass of pomegranate juice I set in front of her, from my tray.

Julienne nods.

"What's your favorite thing about cooking?" I've asked her this before, but got no answer.

This time she seems to be thinking as she chews, her gaze aimed at the table between us. "I used to like trying something new. Making a substitution in the recipe."

That's more than she's ever said to me at once, and I have to hide my excitement. "Used to?"

"It's easier to just follow the recipe now," she says. "I haven't felt like experimenting in a long time."

"How long?"

She cuts another bite as she thinks. "Since the training ward. Cooking was fun then."

"What changed?"

Julienne's empty fork hovers over her plate. "I don't know. After graduation, I came here, and . . . nothing seemed to matter anymore." She glances at her plate with a thoughtful frown. "I wonder how this would taste with pistachios in place of walnuts?"

"Let's find out! Tomorrow for breakfast, why don't you bring something that you've altered. Or something you made up entirely."

Her eyes light up at the idea, and it bruises my heart to realize that after two long years of service to my family, I am just now truly meeting Julienne 20.

"Are you ready?" My mother taps the car window to mute the protesters as we drive past. There are more of them than ever this morning, but the signs have changed. Now the unemployed demonstrators are protesting clone citizenship, which, they seem convinced, would only add to competition in an already crowded job market.

I can't help feeling a little vindicated that they don't like Dahlia-as-me any more than they like the real me.

"I will never be ready for this," I admit as I turn away

from the window. I straighten the hem of my long-sleeved silk shirt.

"But you have your answers memorized?" my mother presses.

"Yes," I tell her. We've been setting the stage for this all week, releasing previously unaired footage of me feeding the poor, reading to sick kids, and hammering in nails on homeless shelters under construction.

The approach we've decided on is that Waverly Whitmore is a friend of those in need. *All* those in need. The new platform doesn't change that—it expands upon my existing humanitarian interests.

Which is why we're doing this interview at the new homeless shelter, which I opened by cutting a ceremonial ribbon last month. Nearly two weeks before the meteorite named Dahlia 16 slammed into my world and destroyed everything I'd ever known.

Our car pulls up to the shelter, a squat two-story building that houses dormitory-style sleeping quarters upstairs and common areas on the first floor. For once, there's no crowd to mob me when the driver opens the door to let me out, and I understand why when I hear the wave of cheers echo from the side of the building.

I can't resist a smile, in spite of my interview anxiety.

"I'll be watching from here," my mother says, holding up her tablet. Then the driver closes the door.

With one security guard at my back, I follow the sidewalk

around the building to the basketball court, where more cheers nearly drown out the sound of shoes slapping the pavement and the bounce of a ball.

I laugh when I see Hennessy with his sleeves pushed up and his arms outstretched, guarding the basket while a kid who can't be any older than twelve dribbles down the concrete court toward him, wiping sweat from his forehead with the back of one arm. He feints to the right, then moves left to take his shot. The ball soars over Hennessy's head and swishes into the basket.

The crowd cheers, and Hennessy laughs. Then he shakes the kid's hand. "Rematch!" he declares, to another round of cheers. "Next time!"

The kids love him. The cameras love him.

I love him.

I catch his gaze as he makes his way through the crowd, and his bodyguard tosses him a towel. Hennessy wipes sweat from his face, and as he gets to me, he leans in for a kiss.

An appreciative cheer rises from the kids in the crowd, and even from some of the parents.

We wave and call out greetings as we head into the building through a side door. "This one's live?" Hennessy whispers low enough that the echo of my heels on the tile floor should drown him out from more than a couple of feet away.

"Yes, but the questions were submitted in advance," I tell

him. "Most of them will be for me. You just have to look and sound supportive."

"That should be easy. I am supportive."

"And I love you for it." Hennessy didn't ask for any of this. But he hasn't even flinched.

Fifteen minutes later, we're seated in folding metal chairs, squinting into soft, flattering three-point interview lighting with the shelter's large, commercial kitchen—paid for by DigiCore—in the background. Hennessy no longer looks sweaty from his basketball game, and I'm wearing an apron over my silk shirt, because after the interview I'll be serving dinner to the twenty-eight homeless families lucky enough to be sheltered here while they're trying to get back on their feet.

A boom mike positioned overhead will pick up everything we say, so there's no need for individual microphones.

As part of the negotiation for this interview, we requested Deena Philips as the interviewer, because she's a friendly face who works for the very network that airs my show. Which means that she, the network, and I all have the same goal—to make us look good and avoid a ratings dip over Dahlia's moment of unscripted lunacy.

This is as safe as a live interview will ever get.

Deena starts off soft and easy, asking us about the wedding preparations and about my dress, giving Hennessy and me a chance to gush and smile at each other. Then she moves into the main event, and I mentally check off each question as she asks it.

"So, Waverly." Deena turns in her chair to face me directly. I wish I could check the stats on my tablet, to see how many people are watching. "I'm sure I'm not the only one out there who's curious about your new platform. Before last week, I'd never even heard the phrase, but as of this moment, a search of the words *clone citizenship* yields more than"—she glances at her tablet—"three point two million results, with very little actual information to be found. You've started something!" Her smile looks more nervous than sincere, which echoes the curious but wary responses I've been getting from my followers. "You've gotten people talking, but your announcement seems to have come out of nowhere. Can you tell us what led you to take on this particular issue?"

I pause and give the camera a thoughtful look, as if I'm coming up with my response in real time. Hennessy takes my hand, a visible sign of encouragement that—according to the network's behavior analysts—paints me in a sympathetic light. "Humanity."

Deena blinks into the camera aimed at her and cocks her head to the side. "Humanity?"

"Yes." I shift in my seat, getting comfortable as I launch into my answer. "Hennessy and I were born into good fortune, and we were taught to give back. We raise money. We build houses. We donate toys and clothes. And we come to places like this"—I gesture to the kitchen around me—"to give of our time. But in all that giving, and building, and raising, for orphans, and the homeless, and the jobless, we've been overlooking the largest disenfranchised population there is. Clones."

"You're saying that clones are . . . what? Being denied basic rights?" Deena frowns. "But they're provided with everything they need in exchange for their work."

"Yet I bet you'd have a hard time finding any citizen willing to work under the same terms. Clones don't get time off. They can't own property. They don't earn wages. They can't decide what to wear. They don't get to choose what kind of work they do."

"They don't even get to choose what to eat," Hennessy adds.

"Clones work alongside us every day, doing jobs many people aren't willing to do for themselves, yet most of the time we don't even notice they're there," I continue. "They're practically invisible. They can't speak up for themselves. So someone has to speak for them."

Hennessy squeezes my hand.

Deena shifts in her seat and crosses her legs at the knee. She leans forward and glances at her notes. Then she sets her tablet in her lap and looks right at me.

Uh-oh. She's going off-script. I can see that before she even opens her mouth.

"Ms. Whitmore, with all due respect, there's a reason clones can't speak for themselves. While many of them are obviously highly skilled in their service areas, they don't operate on a cognitive level that would allow them to use most of the rights that come with citizenship. Not to mention the responsibilities. Clones are incapable of managing a bank account. Or operating a tablet. Or understanding political issues in order to cast a vote. Or making more than the basic daily decisions. Wouldn't giving the rights and responsibilities of citizenship to a populace that isn't capable of understanding them actually be doing them a disservice?"

"No!" She's veered from the questions we agreed on, but that's given me an unexpected opening. Hennessy squeezes my hand again, but I'm too caught up in this to smile at him and appreciate his support for the camera. "They *are* capable. That's what people don't understand. Clones aren't born staring at their feet. They don't toddle around their nurseries in a mental fog. They're normal until they get here. Until they start working for us. Until they start—" I nearly bite my own tongue to keep the rest of the words from forming. But I've already said too much.

And now I realize that Hennessy wasn't squeezing my hand in support. He was warning me to *shut up*.

"Until they start what?" Deena asks.

"Um . . . the details don't matter." I stare at the camera for a moment, grasping for a way to recover. "My point is that clones are capable of much more than we give them credit for."

Deena leans back in her chair. "Ms. Whitmore, I think

the details *do* matter, and I suspect our viewers would agree. What makes you think clones are capable of operating on the same level as the rest of us?"

Hennessy shifts uncomfortably beside me.

"I . . ." I can't tell her how I know what I know about clones. And if I lie, there will be millions of viewers waiting to dig up proof to discredit me.

"Ms. Whitmore, you just told us that clones are born normal. That something happens to them to make them the way they are when they're bought. That's an *extraordinary* claim. I certainly hope you have evidence to back it up."

"I just . . . get that feeling sometimes, when I talk to them."

Deena's eyebrows arch comically high. "Are you saying you carry on *conversations* with *clones?*" She laughs as if I've just told her I share my deepest secrets with the birds in the park. "Ms. Whitmore, is it possible that this whole thing was a publicity stunt? An artificial controversy intended to create higher ratings for your show, with the wedding episode coming up?"

"No! I would never—" But that's not true. I *have* participated in publicity stunts, but they were all orchestrated by Network 4. As a network employee, Deena Philips probably knows that. Which is how she knows I can't entirely deny the accusation.

She set a trap, probably to improve her own ratings, and I walked right into it.

"Dahlia?" my mother says when I sit next to her in the back-seat of the car.

I scowl at her.

"Just checking." My mother's frown feels like ice as she holds up her tablet to show me a still shot from the interview. "Because you sounded like someone who's never been on camera."

"I *know*! Deena went off-script, and I followed her."

"Right over a cliff. Waverly, I'm trying to save your life. That'd be a lot easier if you stop giving the Administrator reasons to have you killed. Let's go!" my mother snaps at the driver, and the car begins to roll forward. I wish Hennessy were coming with us. But it's his father's birthday. This morning, I was worried about coming up with a believable excuse for missing the party, but now I'm pretty sure his dad would rather I stay away.

"Do I even want to know about the optics?"

"People seem to be buying the publicity stunt angle."

I groan. I resented being forced to go along with Dahlia's announcement, but for the first time since I'd found out about my five thousand identicals, I'd felt like I was doing the right thing. Even if it wasn't my idea. But if no one takes the new platform seriously . . .

"Consider yourself lucky," my mother snaps. "If that's the public consensus, the Administrator might not feel threatened enough to back out of our agreement."

"Do I have any other option?"

She drops her tablet onto her lap and turns away from me to stare out the window. "Let's just say that leaking a story about your complete mental breakdown is starting to look like a viable option."

TWENTY-TWO

DAHLIA

On my wall screen, Trigger looks up at the camera again, and I wonder if he knows I can see him. That Lorna is letting me watch him as a constant reminder of what she'll do if I don't cooperate.

My tablet beeps with a message from Waverly asking—no, *telling* me to come to her room for another prep session. I slide the tablet back into my pocket without replying. I'll go. I have no choice. But I'm going to take my time, to remind her that I am not a servant.

In his basement cell, Trigger begins a set of sit-ups with his toes anchored beneath the bathroom door. He's been given a change of clothes, but he's only wearing the exercise shorts, and even through the low-quality security feed I can see sweat building up on his chest and shoulders as he exercises.

His physique is . . . pleasing. I miss feeling the firm breadth of his back beneath my palms when I hug him. I miss his hand in mine. I miss the way he used to smile at me over our lunch trays. But as miserable as I am here alone, it must be much worse for him.

His cell has no window. He hasn't seen daylight in nearly a week, nor has he spoken to another human being, except for the clones assigned to slide his meal tray through a slot in his door. And they're not allowed to reply, no matter what he says or does.

I wish there were something I could do for him. But even if I knew how to open his door—even if I could sneak him out and run away with him—Lorna would only take her fury out on my identicals.

I *hate* her.

When I knock, Waverly opens her door, and I find her staring at the wall screen. It's covered in a grid of twelve windows, each showing a headline or an article about the "ratings stunt" Waverly Whitmore was accused of pulling during an interview yesterday.

"What's a stunt?" I ask as the door whispers closed behind me.

"That means everyone thinks your announcement at the engagement party was insincere. That it was only intended to draw more viewers to the wedding episode of my show."

"They think I was *lying*?"

"No, they think *I* was lying. Well, saying something I didn't really mean, anyway. But forget about that." She swipes the windows closed, leaving the screen transparent. "Today, I think we both need a little fun."

I frown. Waverly's been angry with me all week, snapping at me in every prep session and kicking me out so she can eat meals alone in her room, even though I'm not allowed to eat with Trigger now. I don't understand why she's suddenly being so nice. "I thought we were going to prepare for the bridal shower."

She tilts her head to the left. "You're saying that can't be fun?"

I nod, but that only makes her laugh.

"Shopping always makes me feel better. You're going to love this."

By now, I know that shopping means buying things with credits, but I've never done it, because I don't have any credits.

Waverly pulls open one of her drawers. "Dressing room," she says in a commanding tone, and a new box opens on her wall screen. "One hundred percent."

The box grows to take up the entire wall, and it's like looking through a window into another place. Into a room with thick white carpet and cloth-covered walls embroidered with intricate, repeating patterns, in several rich shades of gold and red. On the left stands a rolling rack, from which hangs a series of shirts, pants, and dresses.

Waverly returns from her dresser carrying a tiny black leotard. "Here. Go put this on."

"What is it?" I take the garment from her. It feels . . . slick. And thicker than I expected. "It's too small."

"It's a VirtuFit. Sensors in the screen get your measurements from it, and the screen will show you what you look like with the clothes on."

I can only frown, waiting for her words to make sense.

"Just go change." She points to the closet. "You'll see."

I open the closet door, and though I was in here once before, I was too nervous to really process what I saw. Now that I have time, I can only stare around the space in amazement. Unlike the narrow cupboard where my roommates and I hung our workforce uniforms, this is an entire *room* lined in rods packed with hanging clothes.

Beneath the clothes, in little cubes lined up three high all the way across the room, are *hundreds* of pairs of shoes. Some of them are rubber-soled athletic shoes in an assortment of bright colors. Some are flat-soled sandals, and yet others have heels higher than anything I've worn since I got here. The heels of one pair are carved into tiny silver statues of a lady. The thick, wedge-shaped soles of another are little cages with vine-wrapped golden bars imprisoning a tiny, beautiful, snow-white bird. Another pair is shaped like a set of bananas, with the peels folded back to make room for feet, where the fruit should be.

"Those are from a costume," Waverly says when she sees what I'm staring at. "Don't ask." Then she backs out of the closet and closes the door, leaving me alone.

In the center of the room, standing on a plush rug, is the long, upholstered bench where I got dressed the night of the engagement party. I take off my tank top and soft, stretchy pants—clothes I borrowed from Waverly—and set them in a folded stack on the bench. Then I step into the VirtuFit.

The leotard stretches to fit my body from my ankles to my neck, and down my arms to my wrists. I feel strangely apprehensive when I turn to look at myself in the wall-length mirror at one end of the huge closet. I can see every dip and curve I'm made of.

"Did you get lost?" Waverly calls from the bedroom, so I emerge reluctantly.

She studies me from head to foot, and after a minute spent awkwardly fidgeting, I realize she's not trying to make me uncomfortable. Not entirely, anyway. She's looking for differences between us. Or maybe for similarities.

Her gaze lingers on my chest, and she frowns. "Yours are bigger than mine."

I glance down at myself, then over at her, but I can't see the difference. Unlike her mother and most of the women here in Mountainside, she and I have very little to notice, as do all the female clones I've ever known. Evidently that's due to the hormone deficiency and suppression.

"It's subtle, but it's there." She looks distinctly displeased. "Were your sisters' as big as yours are?"

"I don't . . ." I frown, trying to remember. "I never noticed any physical differences between any of us. But I don't see a difference between you and me either."

She looks skeptical. But then she pastes on a fresh smile, clearly determined that we will both enjoy ourselves today. "Come over here."

I head toward the wall, and when I'm about five feet away, my image appears on the screen, facing me as if I'm looking at a mirror. Waverly steps up to my side, and her image appears next to mine.

"Okay, I guess you just need the basics, for now. Tops and bottoms." She glances from my torso down over my legs. Which is when what we're doing finally sinks in. We're shopping for clothes for *me*.

"Is this another gift?" I have to admit, I like the tablet, even if it doesn't connect to the house system. I like that it is *mine*.

"Kind of." Waverly frowns. "Not really."

Oh. "You don't want to share your clothes with me anymore." After hearing her complain about everything I've taken from her, I probably should have anticipated that.

"No! I just think you should have some clothes of your own. Everyone should."

"Even clones?"

Waverly looks frustrated. "Yes," she says at last. "Even clones. You know . . . I mean, you *do* know I don't disagree with what you were saying that night. Right?"

"At the engagement party?"

"Yes. I don't disagree," she insists again. "I just . . . you can't go around putting words like that in my mouth, because you don't understand the repercussions. You don't understand my life."

I glance around her room full of fine furniture and hundreds of articles of clothing. "I think I understand enough."

She exhales slowly. "I'm trying to spread the wealth here, if you'll let me. If I could, I would do the same for . . . other clones. But for now, at least I can start with you." She gestures at the screen, where we both still stand in a dressing room. I nod, and she scrounges up another determined smile. "Good. Let's start with pants."

The rack of clothes on the screen blurs, and when it comes back into focus, it holds two dozen pairs, in a stunning array of colors and fabrics.

"How does the screen know when you're talking to me and when you're talking to it?" I ask.

"It's programmed to recognize certain key words and phrases. Narrow selection to the last twenty pairs I ordered," Waverly says, and the rack blurs again, then comes into focus to reveal another selection of pants. "Okay, pick one." She shrugs and takes a step back. "Just . . . point to the one you want to try and lift one leg, as if you're going to pull them on."

I select a pair of simple black pants with prominent white stitching. When I lift my left foot, my image on the screen grabs the pants and bends to pull them on one leg at a time. Dressing-room-me laughs and stumbles to the side a little, then straightens, pulls the pants up, and buttons them at her waist.

Waverly laughs at my surprise. "It plays a different simulation every time. They're from videos of me actually getting dressed."

"Video from your show?"

"No. From the cameras in the room." She turns and points at cameras I can*not* pinpoint. "They're always recording. So, what do you think?"

I think I never want to take my clothes off again. I knew the cameras were there, but I never really *thought* about that.

I turn, and dressing-room-me turns, showing off the pants. They reveal . . . everything.

"Trifold mirror," Waverly says, and a framed set of three mirrors appears on-screen behind my image, reflecting my backside from all different angles. "So?" she asks.

I shrug. "They're pants."

She rolls her eyes. "There is *no way* we come from the same genes." But she's smiling as she says it.

We spend the next hour picking out simple, comfortable tops and pairs of pants; then a box opens in the middle of the dressing room. In it is the silhouette of a woman's head. "Are you ready to consult with your personal designer?" a voice asks.

"No!" Waverly jabs at the box, and it disappears.

I lift both brows at her in question.

"If I'd said yes, my designer would have come online for a consultation. But obviously we can't let her see you." Waverly scowls at the screen, her shopping joy eclipsed by the near-miss. "I think that's enough for now."

In the training ward, clean clothes were issued to us from a shared supply of thousands of articles, all in the same shade of green. Here, I've borrowed clothes Waverly intended to donate to a homeless shelter, except for some unused underwear she instructed me to "just keep." But I've never really owned my own clothing. Until now.

"Purchase: everything on the 'definitely' rack," Waverly says. "Add a dozen basic socks, underwear, and bras, in the eight basic colors."

"Order prepared," the screen says. "Please confirm."

"Confirm."

"Your purchases will be delivered within the hour."

Waverly swipes at the screen, and the dressing room shrinks until it's the size of an icon, which then slides into the upper right corner of the wall. "Okay, why don't—"

A sudden cramp low in my stomach doubles me over.

"You okay?" Waverly asks.

"May I use your restroom?"

"Of course," she says, and I duck into the closet to grab my clothes on the way.

In the bathroom, I strip out of the black dressing-room suit, fold it, and set it on the counter. Then I use the restroom.

The toilet paper has a bright red spot on it.

Puzzled, I stand. The water in the bowl is a pale, uneven shade of pink.

My heart slams in my chest. I'm bleeding. Something is *wrong*.

Pulse racing, I get dressed and stuff a handful of toilet paper into my underwear.

"You okay in there?" Waverly calls.

"Um . . ." Maybe I should tell her. Maybe I need a doctor.

"What's wrong?" The door slides open, and she finds me stuffing another wad of toilet paper into the pocket of my pants, just in case. "What are you . . . ?" Her gaze falls to the toilet and her eyes widen. "Oh. I guess your system has flushed the hormone suppressers."

"What does that mean?" I don't see the connection between hormones and . . . this.

Waverly frowns. "Do they seriously not even teach you guys this stuff? I mean, I know the rest of them will never need to know, but it's still basic biology." Then her expression softens, and she looks almost sympathetic. "This is normal. It's called menstruation. Though most people call it 'getting your period.' If I weren't a clone and you hadn't been eating hormone suppressors all your life, we both would have gotten it already."

"What? Why?"

"It's your body getting ready to make a baby. That's what your hormones will help my body do." She studies the confusion that must be written all over my face. "You don't know how that happens either, do you?"

"I know how embryos are created in Lakeview. And I know that here that's done the ancient way." Like animal husbandry, in the livestock classes.

Waverly laughs. "Yeah, I guess you could call it ancient. People have been doing that as long as they've been harvesting plants and hunting animals."

"We didn't do any of that in Lakeview." Except harvest plants.

"*You* may not have, but my mom says soldiers aren't denied hormones like the rest of you. They need testosterone and aggression, or something like that, in order to develop muscle mass. You better bet your toy soldier has played a couple games of 'ancient doctor' with the girl soldiers. And maybe with the boys."

Stunned, I can only stare at the floor, trying not to think about Trigger . . . touching someone else. I know he's kissed other girls, but it never occurred to me that he might have done anything more. Or that there was anything more to do.

I feel oddly achy at the thought.

Is this how he felt when Hennessy kissed me?

Waverly bends to open the cabinet beneath her bathroom sink and takes out two unopened cardboard boxes. "My mom brought me these years ago, but I never got to use them." She lifts the first box. "These stick into your underwear. The other ones . . . well, you can read the directions for yourself."

As she swipes the door, leaving me mystified and humiliated in her bathroom, Waverly glances at me one more time, and the sympathy in her gaze is gone.

All I see in her eyes now is envy.

TWENTY-THREE

WAVERLY

Dr. Foster sets his supply bag on the exam room counter. "How are you today, girls?"

"Fine," Dahlia says as I hop onto the padded table next to her. Though this is his third visit to take blood samples, this is the first time she's spoken directly to the doctor.

"Better than fine." My mother beams a smile like the sun, as if she were personally responsible for the good news. "Dahlia has begun menstruating."

I flinch over her causal announcement of something so personal, but Dahlia doesn't seem embarrassed. I told her this is a normal biological function, and she took me at my word. I probably should tell her it's not an appropriate topic of conversation on camera at the bridal shower.

"Well, that *is* good news!" Dr. Foster declares. "That means her hormone production must be at or near normal

239

levels." He turns to me with a smile. "Which means we're ready to create some custom hormone therapy."

"How long will that take?" my mother asks.

"Not long at all. We've already designed a preliminary version from the sample I took last week, just to work on the technique. I'm pleased with what we came up with and we should be able to repeat the process pretty quickly with the samples I'm about to take." He opens his bag and pulls out the sterile phlebotomy supplies. "I hope to be back with something to try out on Waverly within a couple of days."

"Excellent," my mother says, and despite the week I've had, this feels like lighting a candle in a dark room. This could change my life. This could give me children. This could make me . . . normal.

The fact that I want "normal" so badly feels like a bitter irony after a lifetime of fighting to stand out. But no one wants to be known for infertility and small breasts.

Dr. Foster reaches for Dahlia's left arm, holding a rubber tourniquet.

"No," she says quietly. Then she crosses her arms over her chest.

I blink at her. "*What?*"

Dahlia turns to my mother, anger burning behind her eyes, despite the soft, calm quality of her voice. "You broke your word, so I see no reason I should stand by mine."

I can only stare at her. In three weeks, the meek little gardener has become a rebellious saboteur, and now she's holding my reproductive health hostage! After I took her shopping!

"Doctor, will you please excuse us for a moment?" My mother's request is actually an order. "If you'll head up to the kitchen, Julienne will offer you some tea or coffee. We'll only be a minute."

"Of course." He glances at the three of us in confusion. Then he grabs his bag and steps out of the exam room.

"This is not a game," my mom snaps the moment the door closes behind him.

"I know." Dahlia sits straighter, her hands clutched in her lap, and she holds my mother's gaze boldly. "You said I could take my meals with Trigger, but I haven't seen him in a week, except on the screen in my room. It isn't good for him to be alone for so long."

My mother's eyes narrow. "You're not in any position to make demands."

Dahlia takes a deep breath. "Actually, I believe I am. You can probably take my blood by force, but you can't make me play Waverly in public. At least, not the way you *want* me to play her."

"Are you seriously blackmailing us?" I demand. "After you threw me under the bus at my own engagement party?"

"What bus?" she says with a frown.

"Mom!" I turn to my mother, trying to control the panic threatening to overwhelm me.

"Dahlia, I hope you haven't forgotten about the thousands

of identicals who're waiting on you to earn their release. . . ." My mother's voice is as cold as I've ever heard it.

"I haven't forgotten that you don't have access to them yet," Dahlia says slowly, and I can practically see her thinking through each word. "Which means you can't hurt them."

My mother's scowl feels like a bolt of thunder. "I can tell the Administrator that I've changed my mind. That she's free to have them 'recalled.'"

My clone thinks about that for a second. "If she were willing to do that, she already would have. I think she's keeping them alive as a threat against you. Against Waverly. I think she gave you access to the Valleybrook security feed for the same reason you gave it to me."

"Oh my God!" I shout, astonished by how much she's come to understand in three short weeks. Terrified by how far she's obviously willing to take this. "Mom! Let her have lunch with Trigger!"

"I want him back in his room." Dahlia sits straighter, and I can practically see her confidence growing as my panic swells. "You're being cruel to him because you're mad at me, and he doesn't deserve that. Treat him like a guest, rather than a prisoner, and I'll do everything I can to help Waverly."

My mother presses her lips together, her eyes narrowed as she considers.

"Mom!"

She shoots me an angry glance, then turns back to Dahlia. "Fine. I'm going to assume you've learned your lesson. But if you don't participate fully for Dr. Foster and deliver a *flawless* performance at the shower tonight, I will have Trigger euthanized *myself.* Do you understand?"

Color drains from Dahlia's face, and I have to swallow my own shock.

Dahlia's jaw tightens, and her gaze goes hard. "I understand *exactly* what you're telling me."

As soon as a week. As long as a month.

Dr. Foster wasn't sure how long it would take the hormone therapy to begin affecting my body, but he seemed to think that four weeks would be on the long end.

I stop pacing across my rug and turn to eye my wedding dress on the e-glass. If the hormones kick in sooner rather than later, will I have to get the bust let out?

I mentally cross my fingers. . . .

My mother knocks once, then comes in. "So?" I demand the moment the door closes behind her. "Did you pick a gene therapist?" Over the past three weeks, she's narrowed it down to the top two doctors in the field, and after Dahlia's little rebellion this morning, she decided today was the day to pick one. That the sooner we moved beyond dependence upon my clone, the better.

I was starting to feel guilty about keeping Dahlia in the dark about the expiration date, considering that it might affect Trigger and definitely *will* affect her identicals—until she threatened to let me die flat-chested and childless. Now I'm leaning back toward "what she doesn't know won't hurt her."

"I dug into their finances to see which of them might be most in need of a large infusion of credits, in exchange for working in complete confidence, and it turns out neither of them does," my mother says. "The top two gene therapists are both being bankrolled by Amelia Locke."

"Huh? What does that mean?"

"For the past decade, Lakeview has provided the funding for their research—to the tune of nearly a billion credits, total—in exchange for majority ownership of the results. It looks like that's how she stays ahead of the technology curve on proprietary cloning methods. Which means that neither of them is likely to choose confidentiality to us over the continued research and revenue stream."

I sink onto the end of my bed. "We can't hire the best geneticists in the world because they already work for the Administrator?"

"Basically."

"So I'm screwed!"

"No!" My mother settles onto the comforter next to me. "Your father's looking into several other geneticists—"

"But you said those two were the best."

"Yes, but that doesn't mean the others can't help us. However, there's a possibility that if she's funding two of the top geneticists, she could be funding more."

I fall backward on the bed with a groan.

"I don't want you to worry about this right now. Dahlia will be here any minute to prep for the shower, and I want you to focus on that. I'll take care of everything else."

I nod, and my hair snags on the comforter beneath my head. But I'm lying. I don't think I *can* think about anything other than my "expiration date" now that I know we might not be able to change it.

"Hey." My mom pats my leg. "Get up. Put your game face on, or Dahlia will know something's wrong the moment she walks into the room. After that stunt she pulled this morning, I'm pretty sure *both* of you take after me more than after your father."

I sit up and brush my hair back from my face. "You have only yourself to blame for that."

My mother actually laughs, and though the sound is more bitter than amused, I find myself laughing along, because my only other option seems to be crying. And I'm *done* crying over this.

Dahlia arrives minutes after my mom leaves, and I wonder for a second if she timed that. She looks beautiful in my dress, and though her hair could use a little help, she's clearly mastered the automatic makeup applicator I had installed in her bathroom last week.

"Trigger's back in the gray room?" I ask.

She nods. "Waverly . . . I feel like I—"

"Don't." I wave her apology off. "You did what you had to do."

She seems surprised that I understand that. "I . . . I think I love him. I *know* I miss him. And I had no other way to—"

"I know. How is he?"

"I haven't spoken to him yet, but your mom gave me access to the feed from his room. He looks much more comfortable. And he won't stop staring out the window."

I feel bad about that. I can't imagine being locked in the basement for a week. "If this goes well, Mom said she'd let you have a late dinner with him tonight after the shower. Speaking of which . . ." I mentally shake off gloom and wave to wake up my wall screen, where I've already loaded head shots of the most important bridal shower attendees. "Okay, the theme of the shower is 'Pink Champagne.' You won't have to sit down to a formal dinner, but when it's time to open the presents, all eyes will be on you."

Thank goodness the network vetoed the intimates-themed shower; I can't imagine trying to explain the purpose of sheer lingerie to Dahlia.

"Just like at the engagement party, eat nothing with onion, garlic, or anything leafy that might stick in your teeth. This is a smaller, more intimate function, which means the cameras will be watching you more closely. So after you've tried the food, sneak out to the bathroom and do a teeth-and-breath check. There's a mini bottle of mouthwash in your clutch."

I pick up the small, pink sequined bag from the edge of the table and hand it to her. "Do *not* lose that."

Dahlia peeks inside, then sets the purse in her lap.

"Pick one cocktail and sip from it. Drink it slowly—you only get one; I'm serious—but make sure you're always holding it. That way it looks like you're having fun without actually compromising coordination or doing anything stupid."

"One drink," Dahlia repeats.

"And make it something pretty. Something colorful. But *do not spill*." I look down at the lacy white bodice of her dress and suddenly wonder if I should have put her in something darker. But I had that dress, with its pale pink skirt, designed specifically to coordinate with the theme of my shower, and I'm not going to let it go to waste. Even if I can't be the one wearing it.

"What if I do?"

"Don't," I repeat. "But if you do, head straight to the restroom. My mom will follow you with her cleanup kit. Worst case scenario, you're traveling with a change of clothes. But if that happens, we'll have to let the network broadcast the spill and make a big drama moment out of it."

Dahlia looks like she might object, but I move on. "Sofia and Margo both think they're your best friend, and since this is a girls-only party, Hennessy won't be there to act as a buffer."

"Really? But they were mean to you—to *me*—at Seren's party."

"Friendship is complicated here. It's a little bit like dancing

247

with an alligator. You know that at some point it's going to snap at you, but until then, it's taking bites out of your enemies."

"Do you have enemies?"

I shrug. "Everyone has enemies. Most of the time, they look just like your friends."

That, she seems to understand. Is she remembering some identical gardener from the training ward? Or is she thinking of me?

"Anyway, you have to spend equal amounts of time with each of them. Both of them together, if possible. But don't compliment Margo's lipstick in front of Sofia."

"Why not?"

"Because Margo had her lips done last year, and the Administrator won't let Sofia get hers done. And if you compliment Margo's lipstick, Sofia will think that you're pointing out that Margo has the prettier mouth."

"Why would she think that?"

I roll my eyes again. "Because when I compliment Margo's lipstick, I'm actually pointing out that she has the prettier mouth."

Dahlia shakes her head slowly. "Friendships are much simpler in the training ward. Where there is no lipstick."

"Yeah, well, simpler doesn't always mean better."

The door slides open and my mother steps into my room wearing a knee-length, off-the-shoulder dress in pale blue. She looks like an only slightly older version of Dahlia. I hope I look that good when I'm forty-three.

I hope I live to be forty-three.

"We need to go." She studies Dahlia for a moment as if she's looking for something to criticize. When she can't find anything, she turns back to me. "Waverly, they're hooking up the live feed from the garden, and as soon as it's ready, I'll have it fed directly to your screen. Obviously, just like last time, you need to stay in your room until we're back from the event, just in case."

"In case of what?" Dahlia asks me. She hasn't looked at my mother since she walked into the room.

"Rogue photographers," I explain. "Stalkers. Whoever. Sometimes if they think no one's home, they try to break in, and if they find me here, the headline goes from 'Stalker Breaks into Waverly Whitmore's House' to 'Concerned Citizen Finds the Real Waverly Whitmore in Hiding While Her Secret Clone Parties.'"

"This is a very strange place," Dahlia says. And for once, I agree.

TWENTY-FOUR

DAHLIA

Being in a car alone with Lorna feels like sitting inside a refrigerator. I give her my best cold shoulder, hoping she feels the same way.

The car begins to slow, and my gaze catches on the crowd of people gathered at the entrance of the large hotel—a building where people with enough credits can rent a bedroom for the night. Just like last time, they're all holding tablets or professional cameras, eager for a glimpse of Waverly Whitmore or—if they're lucky—a personal greeting. A smile. A handshake. A picture taken with the people's princess.

I've done this before, but last time I had Trigger and Hennessy for support. This time I have only Lorna Whitmore.

I'd rather be wearing a python as a necklace.

As the car rolls to a stop, people from the crowd lift their tablets, which come in as many sizes and styles as the clothes they wear, and though we haven't opened the door yet, they begin taking pictures. The car windows hum with vibrations from the buzz of their excited chatter.

"They've been here for hours, waiting," Lorna says.

I ignore her.

"You got what you wanted. It's counterproductive to act like a child when you could be asking for last-minute advice."

I want to hurt her. I want her to understand what it feels like to know that your life is worth nothing more than the lie you are about to tell. Than the chemicals your body produces. I want to lock her in a windowless room for a week with no human contact so that she feels like a possession held for ransom. I want her to understand what it's like to be someone else. Anyone who wasn't born with an account full of credits and a unique, beautiful face.

But Waverly's right. This world is too broken to be fixed by one person. This place is a cruel game people in my position have no choice but to play, even though we know people like Lorna will win every time. People like Waverly herself.

What I don't understand is why everyone keeps *letting* them win.

"Why would so many people who've never even met Waverly want to stand out here for hours, just to get a glimpse of her?" I meet Lorna's gaze without bothering to hide my anger, hoping for *one honest moment* from a woman whose life is a tower of lies.

"Because she's the people's princess." Lorna turns to me,

her hands folded in her lap over a sparkly silver purse. "The most common network search the year I was pregnant with Waverly was 'Lorna Whitmore baby bump.' The picture we released from the hospital was of me holding her, wrapped in a white blanket. It became the single most viewed image of the *decade*. The world watched her grow up, and Dane and I let that happen because if you don't throw crumbs out for hungry birds, eventually they'll swoop down and take the whole loaf right out of your hands."

I nod as the picture starts to come into focus. From her perspective, the problem is everyone else—all those people who *don't* have everything they could possibly need or want. "Give them a little to keep them from taking a lot. The same reason she does the show."

"Exactly. For most people, the life Waverly and Hennessy and their friends lead is a fantasy. A reality so far out of their reach that when they watch her, they are, in essence, living that life through her. Vicariously. In a way, that makes this their wedding too. They are *deeply* invested in every little detail of the planning. And when they watch the wedding episode on their wall screens and tablets—when they see Waverly peek through a crack in the door and giggle when she spots Hennessy waiting for her at the front of the chapel— they will feel like they're actually there."

Lorna taps the e-glass window, and suddenly I hear the excited buzz from the crowd outside the car. "Those people love Waverly. They think they know her. Your job is to maintain their fantasy. To get out of the car and be gracious and beautiful and kind and generous. To maintain that image on behalf of the nobility, so the people know that their belief in us has not been misplaced. So that they know we care about the problems that plague common citizens and we are working to fix them."

"That feels like a lot of pressure." It also sounds like a lie. "Wouldn't it be easier to give some of the credits you don't need to people who need them, so they can pay rent and buy food?"

Lorna's gaze ices over. "That's not how the world works." Before I can ask her to explain, she taps the back of the driver's seat. "Let's go."

The driver circles the car and opens the door. Lorna steps out, and the crowd goes wild, shouting her name. I watch as she waves and smiles. People love her, just like they love Waverly. Because they don't really know her.

When she steps out of the way, a clone in a security uniform reaches down to help me out. I take his hand and step out onto the sidewalk. The excitement from the crowd explodes into a cheerful cacophony.

I can do this.

"Waverly!" Shouts echo at me from all sides. "Waverly, over here!"

I glance at Lorna, and she gives me an encouraging smile so sincere-looking that if I didn't already know she hates me, I would never guess.

I take my clutch in my right hand and lift my left into the air, showing off the union ink as I wave. Then I smile and start walking.

"Waverly! Waverly! Over here!" They're all calling for me—for her. They're desperate for eye contact. For acknowledgment. For a smile. For a word. And now, seeing their faces, seeing their unwavering support, I want desperately to give them what they want. To let them know that I *see* them, even if they don't truly see me.

Suddenly this feels every bit like the responsibility Waverly insisted it was.

"Hi!" I call out, thinking back to the hours and hours of footage I've seen. Trying to pitch my voice exactly like Waverly's when she greets the crowds. "What a beautiful evening! I'm so glad you all came!"

"Waverly!" A little girl's high-pitched squeal catches my ear and I bend to take her hand.

"Hello, what's your name?"

"Morgan." She smiles at me shyly. "I want to be as beautiful as you when I grow up."

"You already are, Morgan."

The little girl beams at me, and her mother mouths a silent "thank you."

I smile at her, then continue down the line of people being held back by a black velvet rope, as well as a line of the hotel's security staff. I shake hands and smile, and give well-wishes and smile, and accept compliments and smile.

Halfway down the line, Lorna touches my shoulder and I

turn to realize I've been neglecting the crowd on the other side. So I adjust my attentions to include everyone.

By the time we make it to the door, I'm exhausted. I feel like I've just fought my way through a crowd of hundreds, when I've only walked twelve feet.

"Turn around," Lorna says into my ear as one of the security guards pulls open the door to the hotel.

"What?"

"Turn and say goodbye."

"Oh." I spin around and lift my left arm in a wave again, slowly scanning the entire crowd. Taking my time. Just like Waverly does. Then I pivot and walk into the building.

The door closes behind us, and I exhale.

"Thank you," Lorna says to the hotel's security detail. "We'll be fine from here."

They nod and head off to whatever other duties they have to perform.

"Okay, we're going out to the garden in back," Lorna says, too low for anyone else to hear. "It's an exclusive party, so it'll just be you and your guests. And the production crew, of course."

I can already see them. Audra is stationed by an exterior door on the other side of the huge, three-story lobby, whispering something to someone connected to her through the tiny headset stuck in her ear.

"Let's go." Lorna heads for the producer without waiting to see if I will follow.

I can feel everyone watching us as we cross the lobby, heels clicking on the slick, shiny floor, and I'm suddenly grateful for hours spent practicing walking on these stilts. I smile at two pairs of guests staring from a cluster of fancy couches on the left, but a group of identicals in hotel uniforms never even glances at me. They just stare at their shoes as they push brooms across the lobby floor.

A family of four emerges from an elevator in a well-lit alcove, and the little girl stops to stare until her parents notice us. Then they stop and stare too.

I wave. I smile.

Always, I smile.

"Waverly, are you excited?" Audra demands, her eyes sparkling as we come to a stop in front of the door to the garden. Based on her expression, I'd guess she's several times more excited than I am.

"Thrilled!" I clutch my purse in both hands, as I've seen Waverly do on-screen, but when her smile slips, I'm afraid I might have sounded less than genuine. "Actually, I'm a little nervous," I confess.

Lorna frowns, but Audra tilts her head. "Why?"

Good question. Waverly has lived her entire life in front of this crowd. Why would she be . . .

"Wedding," I blurt out. Though in my head, I'm not talking about Waverly's ceremony. I'm talking about exposing Lakeview for what it really is, to all those living under the Administrator's lie. "I've been waiting all my life for this, since before I even knew what I was waiting for, and it's finally about to happen. I'm excited, but I'm also nervous. This is going to change everything. Right?"

Audra's smile blooms bright and big. "Great. Say it *just* like that in the voice-over."

I frown, uncomprehending for a moment. Then I understand. She's turned one of the very few genuine moments I've had in Waverly's skin into a soundbite for the cameras. That makes me feel a little . . . used.

"Okay!" Audra touches her earpiece and seems to be listening to something. "They're ready for you!" Then she throws open the door.

Lights flash in my face, and I blink from the glare. It's one in the afternoon, but at a glance, this winter-season garden looks and feels like the surface of the sun.

"Waverly!" a familiar voice calls as light, polite applause breaks out from the guests.

My eyes adjust, and I step into the garden smiling, clutching my purse. Wishing it were Trigger's hand. From near the back of the space, next to a tall wall of shrubbery, a string quartet begins a beautiful song full of rippling harmonies. All four uniformed musicians are pale-haired male identicals who couldn't have graduated from the Arts Bureau more than a few years before.

I'm sad to see them here, working, while forty women with the wealth and power to literally buy them stand around sipping drinks in varying shades of pink and chatting softly with each other.

The garden is a broad, mostly open lawn, divided into symmetrical sections by formal lines of shrubbery. On one end stands a three-tiered white stone fountain, gurgling as arcs of water flow and splash. Lights have been strung overhead, illuminating the space for no purpose I can understand, considering that it's broad daylight. Then I realize that the lights are actually radiating heat down at the party—the only reason we can all stand comfortably outside in short, sleeveless dresses.

There are almost as many cameramen here as there are guests.

Sofia and Margo are the only people I recognize immediately, and though their smiles seem welcoming, after hearing Waverly talk about their contentious friendship, I can't help thinking of them as wolves descending upon a fresh carcass.

Sofia loops her arm around mine, and for the first time, I realize she has the Administrator's eyes. "Margo and I were just taking bets on whether you'd actually show up. We've hardly seen you in ages!"

"I get hiding from the press, after that social media spanking you took over your new 'platform,'" Margo says. "But are you hiding from *us* too?"

"Of course not." I smile, even though my cheeks are starting to ache. "I was just feeling run-down. I'm still a little tired." But the moment the words are out of my mouth, I realize they don't sound like Waverly. She would make a joke at her own expense. And speak with more confidence.

I *know* what to do. But actually doing it is another story.

"Speaking of the engagement party," Sofia adds. "My mother was *pissed* about what you said."

"Oh, I . . ." It never occurred to me that my statement on clones' rights could affect Waverly's relationship with the Administrator's daughter. Not that that would have stopped me from making it.

"It was *awesome!*" she leans in to whisper, squeezing my arm. "Next time give me a little warning so I can livecast it!"

She's happy that her mother was angry?

"It was spontaneous, right?" Margo asks. "That's what my brother said."

"*Hell* of a publicity stunt," Sofia leans closer to whisper.

"It wasn't—" But before I can insist that my speech was sincere, Lorna catches up with us, with three other women following her like ducklings behind their mother. For the next half hour, while Sofia and Margo sample hors d'oeuvres and sip champagne, I smile and make small talk with women whose faces look familiar from the engagement party, but whose names I can't remember, because Waverly didn't deem them important enough to include in our prep work.

I don't know how anyone can keep all these different faces straight, and their names tell me nothing about what function they serve in society.

Lorna leads her friends away to find fresh drinks, and Waverly's friends flock back to my side. "I can't believe you're getting married!" Sofia gushes as she stares at a stack of elegantly wrapped gifts standing on a table across from the buffet. "I'm *so* jealous."

She is? That's not something anyone in Lakeview would have admitted to, and I don't know how to respond. When I look to Lorna for a silent prompt, she makes a circular gesture, telling me to circulate. Go talk to more people.

For the next hour, I make my way around the garden with Sofia and Margo, thanking people for coming, challenging my memory with names and personal facts I'd never even heard until two days ago. My goal is to disappoint Network 4 with the most uneventful shoot they've ever filmed. I know from the episodes I've watched that Audra can turn a broken fingernail into a full-scale crisis, and they're going to have to do just that if they expect any drama from me tonight.

Margo, Sofia, and I have gotten through about half the guests when a clone waiter approaches carrying a tray of very tall cone-shaped stemmed glasses half-filled with what looks like a scoop of pink ice cream floating in a bubbly liquid. "Raspberry sorbet cocktail?" he asks.

"Yum!" Sofia takes one, but Margo turns her nose up with a muttered comment, calling the drink juvenile.

Mindful of Waverly's instructions, I thank the waiter and take a glass, then sip from it as I continue mingling with people who think they know me. The cocktail is much sweeter than champagne, and the bubbles still tickle the back of my throat. But I like this drink. Though I'd rather be eating the sorbet than letting it melt in my glass.

When I've spoken to everyone and shown off the ink on my arm about a thousand times, I head for the buffet table.

I'm tired of making conversation with strangers, and I can't be expected to talk with a full mouth, can I?

Sofia and Margo trail after me, but I hardly hear anything they're saying because I'm captivated by the display of food. At the center of the table is a tall white tiered cake stand, crowned with a gorgeous white cake—like a miniature version of the one being made for the wedding. It's covered in smooth rolls of cream-colored frosting, decorated with dozens and dozens of intricate cream swirls and hearts, topped with a real ribbon.

On the tiers below is a series of tiny cakes decorated like the larger one, in alternating shades of cream and "pink champagne," each topped with a stunning, delicate flower made of frosting.

I'm dying to try one of them, but I don't know how to eat it without making a mess of such a beautiful cake. So I grab a tiny, flaky piece of puff pastry instead. It crumbles in my mouth and chocolate melts on my tongue. I select another one and take a bite. Then I turn to find Margo and Sofia staring at me.

"Run-down, huh?" Sofia's smiling. "Hungry too, I guess. Any nausea yet?"

Margo rolls her eyes. "I told you. She's not pregnant."

"Definitely not pregnant," I confirm, and for once I'm glad that I'm the one here in Waverly's place—that question would have been like a slap to the face for her.

As nervous as I am about the party games, it's almost a

relief when they begin. Margo and Sofia are the people most likely to notice that their best friend is acting strange, so the less time I have to spend alone with them the better.

Waverly prepared me for the games during our shortened prep sessions all week. Fortunately, as the bride, I only have to play judge for most of the silly contests, and when I realize my role is actually kind of fun, I can't help but wonder if the raspberry sorbet cocktail I've almost finished is as much to blame as the games themselves.

By the time the trivia contest begins, I'm truly enjoying myself. I've never heard most of the stories about Waverly and Hennessy that the women read from their score pads, and they show a side of my clone I wish I could see in person. A fun-loving, humorous side.

After the games, Lorna leads me to the bride's chair in the gazebo, and the guests file in to sit around me on the built-in benches. Cameras peer into the gazebo from all angles, and the light is so bright it's giving me a headache.

Lorna hands me gift after gift wrapped in shiny paper and beautiful ribbons, and I open and exclaim over them, though I have no idea what half of them are.

As soon as the last one is opened, I thank everyone, then excuse myself to use the restroom. But really I just need a moment to myself. As I walk alone—faster than Waverly probably would—through the garden, then into the lobby of the hotel and down a back hall toward the restroom, my gaze catches on all the clones. Working.

Were there this many when we came in? How could I have missed them?

Their uniforms are drab and nondescript, their mannerisms quiet, their gestures small. Their voices, when they're actually used, are soft, as if to avoid being heard unless it's absolutely necessary.

Every motion they make is designed to fade into the background. To be overlooked. But *I* should see them.

By the time I get to the restroom, I feel sick.

A woman stands by the bank of sinks set into a marble countertop, waiting to give me a towel after I've washed my hands. A name tag reading *Aida 27* is pinned to the front of her gray uniform.

When I'm done, she takes the towel from me and drops it into a hole cut into the countertop. She never once looks at my face.

My heart aches as I leave the restroom. Aida 27 and Julienne 20—and *all* the Aidas, and Juliennes, and Stewards, and Lances, and Triggers, and Dahlias—we're worth more than a nearly mute existence, wandering around in a mental fog, making people's meals and handing them towels. We're worth what we were promised. What we were told we were working for—ourselves and our own lives.

I have a platform. The crowd isn't as big here as the one at the engagement party was, but there are still plenty of cameras, and if I give another speech, *someone* will livecast it. Sofia, probably.

But Trigger will suffer. Lorna will have him killed. And for what? So that some interviewer can speak to Waverly again next week and tell the world that this is another stunt?

That's not the way. People in Mountainside can't see the problem because they don't want to know it exists. They don't want to *admit* that it exists.

The way to fix this is to open eyes, but not these eyes. I have to open eyes in Lakeview. There will be nothing the Administrator and her soldiers can do against several hundred thousand angry and enlightened clones, half of whom are old enough to put up a fight. Especially once the clone soldiers realize they're fighting on the wrong side.

Trigger can help me show them that.

I head across the foyer with renewed purpose, but when I see Audra looking for me, I duck into a hallway behind the elevator bank. I'm too angry to fool her at the moment, and I will *not* be roped into doing voice-overs for Waverly's show.

I walk down the narrow, dim hallway as fast as my high heels will let me, and the farther I go, the louder the sound of running water and the clang of metal pots becomes. I'm near the kitchen, in the employee-only section of the hotel, and if I'm caught, I'll have to pretend to be lost.

I pass a set of double swinging doors and glimpse a massive stainless-steel kitchen bustling with activity, and I've almost decided to turn back the way I came when a sharp voice at the end of the hall draws my attention.

"Yes, round up all the 27s tonight, as soon as they've finished cleaning up after the Whitmore party."

I freeze at the sound of Waverly's surname. Then I inch closer to the open door, on my toes to keep my heels from clacking on the tile.

"All of them, boss?" a second voice says.

Chair springs squeal as someone inside the office sits. "Of course all of them. The vouchers came through last week, and our batch will be out of transition tomorrow. We're getting forty brand-new year-eighteen manual laborers at a discount, to replace the forty who're being retired."

"You ever seen it happen?" the second voice asks, and I realize from the slightly distant quality that he's speaking from a tablet or a wall screen. "You ever seen them . . . retired?"

"Hell no. That's why we return them before they hit their expiration date—so I don't have to see forty identical hotel maids drop dead at once."

I gasp, then slap a hand over my mouth. My legs shake, and I lean against the wall for support as what I'm hearing zooms into crystal, brutal clarity.

This is the other anomaly. The bridge Lorna said I wouldn't have to cross for more than a decade.

This is why none of the clones in Mountainside is older than year twenty-seven.

When clones turn twenty-eight, they die.

TWENTY-FIVE

WAVERLY

My dad's working late and my mom's with Dahlia at the bridal shower, so there's no one home to catch Julienne 20 and me having a late lunch together. Yet when she steps into my room carrying the tray, she looks ready to cry.

"What's wrong?" I take the tray and set it on the table as the door closes behind her.

"I don't understand what's happening—" She slaps one hand over her mouth and stares at me with wide, horrified eyes. Then she drops her gaze to the floor. Her hands are shaking. Her eyes are damp.

"Sit." I pull out a chair for her. "Tell me what's wrong."

Julienne looks up again, and the conflict behind her eyes appears excruciating. She doesn't sit. "I'm not supposed to do this. I'm breaking all the directives, but I don't know what else to do!"

"What directives?"

"*The* directives. The rules. I'm not even supposed to be talking to you, except to ask how I can serve you or what I can cook for you. I'm not supposed to be looking at you unless you tell me to."

My pulse races. The strange sedatives have finally been flushed from her system. She's truly awake and able to answer questions, but she is terrified, and I can't blame her. "You can trust me, Julienne. I want you to talk to me, and I'm not going to tell anyone else. I'm not going to get you in trouble. Okay?"

She hesitates. Then she nods. "Okay."

"Who gave you these directives?"

"I—I don't know," she says at last. "I remember the voice saying them over and over, but I can't see the face. There's just . . . darkness and directives. And that *voice*."

"Where were you when you heard the voice?"

"I don't know! I was at graduation, and they gave us cake to celebrate. Then there was the voice and the darkness. Then I was here, and everything was different."

"They drugged you," I tell her. "It was in the cake." That's the only thing that makes sense.

She nods, but her eyes are unfocused. Whatever she's seeing, it isn't happening here and now. "There were directives in the training ward, and there are new directives here, and I'm not following them now. Someone's going to notice, and I'm going to be recalled." She meets my gaze again, her eyes wide and panicked. "My whole genome will be recalled!"

"Julienne. Sit. Please." I point to her chair at the table, and she sits. But I start pacing. I've done this to her. I was trying to understand what made her the way she is, but instead I've scared the crap out of her.

Recalled. Euthanized. Murdered. That's what she thinks is going to happen, because I broke her.

Only I didn't break her. I fixed her.

Right?

"No one's going to be recalled," I assure her. "We don't do that here." But don't we? At twenty-eight, don't we send clones back to the Administrator to be euthanized? And isn't my mom planning to send Dahlia and Trigger back as soon as we're . . . done with them?

I can't let that happen.

"I don't feel right," Julienne mumbles, staring at nothing, though her gaze remains fixed on the thick white rug.

I sit in the chair across from her and study her face. "Does something hurt?"

"No. I feel . . . *good*. But that's not right. Everything is too bright. Too focused. Everything sounds too . . . clear. There's too much . . ." She glances around my room as if she'll find the answer there, among my posters and pictures and hologram planters. "There's too much of everything."

Her gaze strays to the tray, where our plates still sit covered by silver domes. "Is it the food? Did you put something in the food?"

"*You* made the food," I remind her. "There's nothing bad

in what you make, but the food they've been giving you for years—the food from Lakeview—is drugged, like the cake you ate at graduation. Contaminated with something that keeps you in a mental fog. When I threw away your food and started giving you mine, you began to . . . wake up." I don't know how else to describe it. Or how much of it she remembers. "Before, you hardly spoke and never looked anyone in the eye. You just worked and kind of shuffled through the halls."

"Those are the directives," she says. "Speak only to offer assistance or answer questions. Keep your gaze downcast. Do your work quickly and efficiently. Don't draw attention. Don't ask questions."

"But it wasn't like that in the training ward, was it? You were normal back then, right? You felt like . . . this?"

She nods slowly. "Everything was bright then. Everything was clear. Food tasted good and running felt good, and talking was . . . allowed. With our identicals, anyway. I had friends. I had sisters. . . ."

"I—" The screen on my wall plays a happy little melody, then fogs over as it wakes itself up.

"What's that?" Julienne asks.

"My bridal shower. It's starting." I look up as a new camera feed opens on my e-glass.

"Bridal shower?"

"It's a party where people bring gifts to the bride. A woman who's about to get married," I explain when Julienne's expression remains blank. "Like how my parents are married."

A light goes on behind her eyes. "Like before the world changed."

"Yes. Only the world didn't change that much anywhere except for Lakeview. People everywhere else still get married and have babies. The 'archaic' way." That's the term Dahlia uses.

Julienne looks confused, but not as surprised as Dahlia was when she got her period. "I . . . I think I knew that." She frowns at the hands she's wringing in her lap. "It feels like remembering something I didn't know I'd forgotten."

"It's the drugs. In your food." It has to be. "I think you've seen and heard everything around you in Mountainside for the past two years, but the drugs kept you from truly processing anything." From understanding what she was seeing and hearing.

In the window in the middle of my screen, my closest friends—and several of my mother's business associates—are standing in small groups in the garden at Ridgecrest, the nicest, most expensive hotel in Mountainside.

The garden looks *beautiful.* Real pink tulip arrangements are scattered all over the place, and stunning champagne-colored flowering vines climb the sides of the gazebo. We had to order them three months in advance to train them to climb as they grew, which meant reserving the gazebo for that entire time, to keep anyone else from renting it for another event and ruining my flowers.

It breaks my heart that I can't see them in person.

"Audio on," I say, and string music fills my room. The buffet is covered in tiny cakes and bite-sized appetizers, centered around a gorgeous champagne fountain.

"Wow." Julienne stares at the screen. "I've seen these a million times, but never really stopped to look before. It's like a giant tablet." She squints at the figures milling around the garden. "Is that happening now?"

"Yes." I spot Dahlia talking to one of my mother's associates, flanked by Margo and Sofia. She's holding a half-empty champagne cocktail, which means she's drinking too fast. And there must have been a delay in setting up the feed. Dahlia's already mingled her way halfway around the garden.

"If that's your bridal shower, shouldn't you be there?" Julienne says.

"I am there. In a way." I point at Dahlia on the screen.

Julienne's eyes widen, but rather than looking confused, she seems relieved to finally understand something. "You have an identical." Then she frowns. "I thought you were an individual."

"So did I, until a few weeks ago," I mumble as my identical stuffs her face with a fourth hors d'oeuvre. Which I would *never* do. Which I *told her* not to do. "That's Dahlia 16. You've cooked for her every day for the past month. She's staying in the blue room."

Julienne slaps one hand over her mouth, then speaks through it. "I thought that was you . . ."

271

I turn to her, surprised. "You thought you were feeding me six meals a day in two different rooms?"

"I don't . . ." She stares at her hands again while she visibly tries to sort out her memories. "I don't know. I didn't realize that made no sense. Or, maybe it didn't matter that it made no sense. I couldn't . . . I couldn't think. Trying to figure things out felt like an enormous effort. It was easier just to follow the directives and do what I was told."

A cold current surges through my veins, chilling me all over. "That is terrifying." What kind of drug can sap someone's will to think?

"Yes, it is. Now," Julienne murmurs, her gaze unfocused, as if whatever she's seeing has already happened. "But while I was in that moment, it felt . . . *right*. I felt good. Satisfied. I felt like everything was okay, and nothing really mattered, as long as I followed the directives." She looks up at me, her gaze now sharply focused. "Is that how I'm *supposed* to feel?"

"There is no 'supposed to,'" I tell her.

"Then why was I eating that food in the first place? Who gave it to me?"

"It's sent from Lakeview. People here think clones have to eat special food to maintain their hormone levels." But I can see from her frown that she doesn't understand hormones. She turns to the food she brought, as if it suddenly puzzles her. "Are you hungry?" I ask.

"Will I be in trouble for this?" She waves one hand at the lunch neither of us has touched.

"I . . ." *Yes.* She and I will both be in trouble for this. "Um, if anyone figures out that you're . . . awake. For now, when we're not alone, can you just pretend? Just stare at the floor and stay quiet. I don't think anyone will notice." No one really ever notices clones anyway, and clearly the drugged food is intended to make sure of that. "I'll figure out what to do in the long term, I promise."

Though the truth is that I have no idea what a long-term solution might look like. I didn't think beyond figuring out why our servants acted so differently than Dahlia and I do.

Now that I've "fixed" Julienne, what am I going to do with her?

On-screen, the string quartet finishes its song, and I turn to see the shower guests head toward the gazebo, where Dahlia sits in the chair of honor.

"Why do you only have one identical?" Julienne asks.

"The Administrator had the others recalled," I mumble as I watch Dahlia take her—*my*—seat at the front of the gazebo.

Julienne's gasp startles me and I turn away from the screen to see her staring at me in horror. "You said they don't do that here."

"Do what? Oh, recall clones? It happened in Lakeview, but they're not dead. The Administrator lied about that, but Trigger 17 and Dahlia 16 didn't know that when they escaped."

"Dahlia 16," Julienne murmurs, walking around my room. Her gaze fixes on me and her eyes widen. "That's where I've

273

seen you. Your class is four years behind mine." She studies my face. "You look older now, but I saw you on the training grounds all the time."

"That wasn't me," I tell her. "I grew up here, as an individual." I block her path to recapture her attention. "You had classes with Dahlia 16 in the training ward? Or . . . meals? Your class knew her class?" I don't really understand how daily life works in Lakeview.

"No, but I saw her class on the grounds all the time."

"And there are five thousand of you, right? And five thousand from the boys' year-twenty class?"

Julienne nods. "Why?"

"And there are ten thousand nineteen-year-old clones out there somewhere, working in cities all over the world? And ten thousand eighteen-year-olds?"

She nods again. "And the year-seventeen class will graduate soon, when they're all promoted."

"Promotion" is the clone equivalent of a birthday. When the numbers behind their names increase.

Horror washes over me and I sink onto the sofa while the room spins around me. "That's *thirty thousand* clones already out in the world who should recognize my face whenever they see it." Because they grew up seeing Dahlia and the rest of my identicals on a daily basis. "And that's just in the manual-labor category. So why haven't they recognized me?"

"How would they have seen your face?" Julienne asks.

I look up at her in surprise. "On the wall screens. On

their . . ." Finally, I understand. "Clones don't have tablets. And they don't use wall screens." And the mental fog from their medicated food keeps them from truly noticing the people they serve, much less anyone else who appears on-screen in a room they happen to be working in.

For one blissful second, relief washes over me. If none of the other working clones has recognized me so far, surely the chances that they ever will are slim. Especially since Dahlia's class will never be put into the workforce.

But I feel guilty the moment I've had that thought. They won't be put into the workforce because my mother's going to have them *killed*. And the only reason none of the rest of them recognize me is because they're kept drugged out of their minds.

That shouldn't be happening. But I don't know how I could stop it, even if I were willing to expose myself as a clone. All that would do is humiliate my family, and possibly get me—and Dahlia—"recalled."

Who would that help?

I need to talk to Dahlia. And to Hennessy. If I'm going to do something, I need to make sure my fiancé is on board, and that Dahlia, Trigger, and even Julienne are all on the same page with us.

This is too big for me to tackle alone.

TWENTY-SIX

DAHLIA

"Pack up all the gifts and have them stored in the guesthouse for now," Lorna says to a clone named Marshal 24, who's stood beside the car listening to her instructions for at least five minutes. "Double-check the inventory and make sure they're all accounted for. Dismissed."

"Happy to serve, ma'am." Then he heads back into the hotel as she sits in the backseat next to me.

"Well done," Lorna says as the car pulls away from the curb. "I'm glad to see you can behave when you're properly motivated. Although your goodbyes could certainly have sounded a little more sincere."

We're lucky I remembered to say goodbye to anyone at all. The only thing I could think about when I made it back to the garden was that Aida 27, the bathroom attendant, might have only hours left to live.

Lorna must know that clones die at twenty-eight. Which makes her offer to build a clone town in the wild for my identicals sound even less believable than it did before.

"Does that mean I may have dinner with Trigger?"

I can feel her watching me, but I don't look up because I can't shield my thoughts right now. They're too fresh. Too terrifying.

"Yes," Lorna says as the car winds its way up the mountain toward the Whitmore estate, driven by a clone named Lance 26. "If you behave, you will be rewarded." Her magnanimous tone grates on me like sandpaper, slowly grinding me down to nothing.

We spend the rest of the ride in silence, while Lorna checks the public feeds on her tablet. She seems pleased with whatever she's reading, and she doesn't look up again until we pull through the gate. "You can go to Trigger's room now," she says, tapping through a menu on her tablet. "Your dinner will be there in half an hour." When the car stops, she follows me inside, then disappears into her suite without another word.

I knock once on Trigger's door, and when I open it, he stands up from the chair by the window, where he's clearly spent most of the day.

"Dahlia!" He races across the room and I meet him halfway, where we collide in an embrace that quickly becomes a meeting of lips and tongues and hands. It's only been a few days, but Lorna could take this away from us again at any moment, so I can't stop until I've kissed him so long and so hard I can barely feel my lips.

And even then I don't really let him go. I just pull him into a hug, still standing on my toes.

"I missed you so much," he whispers into my hair. "More than I missed the sun." His neck is warm and scruffy against my face, and every word he says vibrates against my cheek. "Do you know why they let me out?"

"Because I refused to help Waverly."

"Why would you do that?" He murmurs the words against my skin so they can't be overheard. "She could have hurt your identicals."

"She doesn't have access to them yet. I only had one move, so I made it. And it worked. This time, anyway." I hold him even tighter and whisper into his ear. "We have to go. Now. Tonight."

He nods without question. Without objection. "You have door access?"

"Yes, but our dinner will be here in a few minutes. If we run before that, Julienne will raise an alarm."

"Okay." He leads me toward the small table and chairs Lorna had set up for us when we first started eating in the gray room, with its disabled wall screen. "Do you still have a tablet?"

I pull it from my clutch and set them both on the table between us.

"Good." He lays his hand casually on the table, covering

my translucent tablet, and when he stands, he palms it and casually slides it into his pocket. Then he leans down as if for a kiss and whispers into my ear. "I'm going to go in the bathroom, where there are fewer cameras, and disable the audio in this room."

"My tablet isn't connected to the system," I whisper back.

"It will be in a minute."

While he's gone, I wave one arm at the wall screen, just in case it's somehow been reactivated.

"That doesn't work," Waverly says.

I whirl around to find her standing behind me. I never even heard the door open. "I was just checking."

She glances at the closed bathroom door, then aims a look up at the ceiling. "Dahlia, I've ordered dessert from the kitchen. Come have some with me and tell me about the shower. In my room."

"Your mom said I could have dinner with Trigger."

"*Please.*" She glances at the ceiling again. Where there are cameras. *Oh.* She wants to talk about something she doesn't want overheard.

This is new.

"Okay, we're all . . . ," Trigger says as he steps out of the bathroom, but he bites off the rest when he sees Waverly standing in the middle of his room. "Hi."

"We're muted?" I ask, and he nods, one brow raised to ask me why I would say that in front of my clone. I turn back to Waverly. "Say whatever you have to say. And if you really ordered dessert, you can have it sent here," I add. "Because I'm not going to your room without Trigger."

"How did . . . ?" She frowns at him, until he hands me back my tablet. "Oh." For a second, I'm afraid she'll turn him in. Then she nods. "Okay, I'll update the dessert order." She taps a few times on her tablet, then pockets it. "It's not something I have to say so much as something I want to show you. But that'll have to wait until the food gets here."

"Then I'll go first. Waverly, I overheard something at the shower. You might want to sit." I pull out a chair at the table for her, but she only frowns at it.

"Just spit it out, whatever it is."

I take a deep breath. Then I take Trigger's hand. "I think we're all going to die at twenty-eight."

"What?" Trigger says. "What are you talking about, Dahlia?"

But Waverly leans with one hip against the dresser and exhales heavily. "She's talking about the expiration date. All clones have one. Most of them are ten years after the date of maturation—which is age twenty-eight."

"You already knew about this?" How could she not tell us?

"Yes. And I also know you don't have one. That was the other anomalous thing they found in your genome. Trigger may not have one either—soldiers are an exception to a lot of rules. But *I* have one."

I sink onto the end of Trigger's bed and he sits next to me, clearly trying to absorb the news.

"My mom's trying to find a geneticist we can trust to develop a gene therapy for me, using your DNA. To see if that'll help. But finding a doctor has become complicated," Waverly says, her voice cracking.

She's scared.

"Why didn't you tell me?"

"In part because my mom told me not to." She holds my gaze. "But also . . . you already lost your identicals once. It felt cruel to tell you that you're going to lose them again. For real this time." She shrugs. "I mean, ten years seems like forever until you truly start thinking about it. College is four years. If I go, that'll only leave me six years, really, to live my life. Even if I manage to have kids, I'll die while they're still young."

"Waverly . . ." I feel like I should do something. Hug her.

"I know kids and college aren't really relevant to your identicals, but ten years is still a really—"

I'm already across the room with my arms open as she bursts into tears. I pull her into a hug, and for the first time since we met, she feels like my sister. Because for the first time since we met, she seems to truly understand what it's like to be a clone.

Slowly, her arms wrap around me until she's hugging me back. Crying on my shoulder.

I sniff back tears of my own and when her soft sobs ease, I loosen my hold on her. But instead of letting me go, she holds me tighter, just for a minute. "Dahlia, there's something else I have to tell you. About your identicals."

But then the door slides open and Julienne 20 comes in pushing a small cart carrying three silver domed plates. As she begins setting our food out on the table, her eyes downcast, Waverly sniffles and lets me go. Then she pulls up a series of camera feeds on her tablet until she finds her mother, who's neck-deep in a bubble bath in her own suite. With a green mask over her eyes.

Apparently satisfied, Waverly pockets her tablet. "Julienne. It's okay. You can show them."

Trigger arches one brow at her. "Show us—?"

Julienne 20 stands up straight and slowly raises her gaze until she's looking me right in the eye. Then she gives me a small smile. "I'm . . . um . . . awake."

It takes me a second to understand. "Oh!" I pull her into a hug, even though we're really just now meeting. I'm so thrilled to see another clone acting normal that I don't know what else to do. "How did this happen?"

"There were sedatives in the food," Waverly says. "The boxed food Lakeview sends. For the past week, I've been splitting my meals with Julienne and the drugs finally wore off."

"You did this? For her?" I can't stop smiling.

"And for answers," Waverly admits.

But now Julienne looks worried. "Are you sure this is okay?" she asks.

Waverly nods. "Only when it's just the three of us, and I'm sure no one's watching."

"Welcome back," Trigger says with a smile. "I wish I could

say I'm happy for you, but this isn't a very good place for clones to be." He frowns. "Not that there's a good alternative."

For a moment, we stare at each other in silence, sharing a problem that is bigger than any of us. Than all of us. Finally, Waverly bursts into motion. "Come on. Julienne made this food; the least we can do is eat it. And eat *this*." She pulls the cover from the last large platter, and I can't help but smile, in spite of the circumstances.

The dish holds a dozen of the pink-and-white miniature cakes from the bridal shower, each small enough to fit into my palm.

"I asked my mom to have an assortment of leftovers brought home so I can at least try the food from my own shower."

There are only two seats at the table, so I set a couple of the tiny cakes on the edge of my dinner plate and join Trigger on the end of his bed, where we eat with our warm plates on our laps. Waverly insists that Julienne join her at the table. Like a guest.

I watch them for a few minutes and realize that they look pretty comfortable with each other. That Julienne seems to trust my clone. *I* want to trust her. I want to tell her what Trigger and I are planning. I want to ask her for help. Or at least for advice.

But if our trust is misplaced . . . If she tells her mother . . .

Waverly looks up, as if she can feel me watching her, and her expression sobers as she sets a half-eaten little cake on the napkin in front of her on the table. "Dahlia. Your identicals . . ."

I'm pretty sure I know what she's going to say, but I need to hear her say it.

"My mom's not going to build a town for them. She's planning to have them recalled. Once we're done with the hormone and gene therapy." Though it can't be easy, she holds my gaze, waiting for my reaction. But Trigger beats me to it.

"We assumed that was her plan," he says with a shrug. "But obviously we can't let her do that."

"I'm not going to let her have anyone killed," Waverly says with a glance at Julienne, who has a smear of pink frosting on her upper lip. "I swear on my life—what's left of it. On my marriage," she amends. "On the kids I still hope to have someday. Even if she's doing it to protect me."

I believe her.

Finally, I believe her.

I look over at Trigger, and he nods.

"Waverly, we're leaving," I say. "Trigger and me. Tonight. We have to go back to Lakeview and find a way to tell them what the Administrator is really doing."

My clone frowns. "There are, like, a million reasons that won't work. She'll kill you. And even if she doesn't . . . there are *hundreds of thousands* of clones spread all over the compound, right?" I nod, trying to follow her thoughts. "And none of them have tablets or wall screens?"

This time Trigger and I both nod.

"So you'll have to tell them all in person. How are you

284

possibly going to get to them all and convince them that this is real"—she opens her arms to indicate the entire world, outside of Lakeview—"before the Administrator sics her clone army on you?"

"I . . ." I frown.

"Do you have a suggestion?" Trigger asks.

Slowly, Waverly smiles. "I might." She shoves the last half of her tiny cake into her mouth and makes us wait while she chews. "The problem isn't just that clones don't understand the true nature of the rest of the world. It's that the rest of the world doesn't understand the true nature of clones. Julienne's living proof that they're normal people. That the Administrator is lying." She sucks in a deep breath. "So am I."

"You'd do that?" I feel like I'm meeting Waverly for the first time. "You'd expose yourself?"

She shrugs. "I think the Administrator's going to do it anyway, eventually. I think that's why she's been keeping our identicals alive. So we may as well use that to our advantage. Maybe if people here knew the truth, they wouldn't be able to justify buying other human beings."

Trigger stands and sets his nearly untouched plate on the comforter. His frame is tense. He looks . . . excited. "So let's tell them."

"No." A smile blooms across my face. "Let's *show* them."

"A livecast?" Waverly says.

"Mm-hmm. For when you want to tell the world something that can't wait for editing. You taught me that, remember?" I frown, remembering something else Waverly taught

285

me. "Wait. Lakeview has a cyber-blackout. They're run on a . . . um . . . closed network system."

"That's not entirely true," Trigger says. "If it were, the Administrator wouldn't be able to communicate with anyone outside the compound. Which means the necessary infrastructure is in place to open things up in Lakeview; it's just an issue of flipping the right switch, so to speak. I might be able to help with that, if I can get hold of a tablet connected to the Lakeview system."

"Any instructor would have one," I say. "Or just about any adult."

"Wait." Waverly shakes her head, as if to clear it. "You want to go to Lakeview?"

"Well . . . yeah." I shrug. "We'd have to, in order to record the livecast."

She frowns. "I thought you wanted to do that here, with me. We could show the world that we're clones, and that clones aren't any different from anyone else. We could answer questions side by side, to prove to the world that what they're seeing is real. And live. The ratings would be *unreal*."

"But the Administrator could always claim you're normal because you were designed and cloned using your parents' normal DNA," Trigger says. "This would have a much greater impact if we could prove that you two aren't the exception. That thousands and thousands of clones are being produced every year, and that all of them—of us—are normal people, until the Administrator lobotomizes us with that drugged, prepackaged food."

"People won't want to hear that," I say. They won't want to believe they've been complicit. That's become clear during my weeks in Mountainside.

Waverly shrugs. "It doesn't matter what they want. This is going to change the world. Again." She nods slowly, thinking it through as she speaks. "A livecast, breaching the Lakeview blackout. Featuring hundreds, maybe *thousands*, of clones acting like normal people." Another nod. Firmer this time. "I can do that." She glances around the gray room, as if she's just woken up and isn't sure where she is. "This will be *huge*."

I glance from Waverly to Trigger, to Julienne, and back to Waverly. "When should we . . . ?"

"The sooner the better," Trigger says. "We were going to leave tonight. I see no reason not to."

"No!" Waverly frowns. "Hennessy will want in on this. And we should plan it for sometime when the Administrator is off the compound. It'll be harder for her to react if she's not on-site."

I frown, thinking over my conversations with the Administrator's daughter. "But Sofia says she never leaves. . . ."

"Well, she *will* be leaving next week, for three days." Waverly smiles. "She's coming to my wedding."

TWENTY-SEVEN

WAVERLY

"You look beautiful, sweetheart." My mother brushes my freshly curled hair over my shoulder and smiles at my reflection in the e-glass. "I'm sorry it has to be this way. But at least you get to wear the dress."

My gaze wanders over the strapless sweetheart neckline of the satin bodice, cinched with a diamond-studded silver satin belt. Layers and layers of white starched organza bell out from my waist, over the full satin skirt. This is exactly how I always pictured myself on my wedding day.

But this is not my wedding day.

Tonight is the rehearsal and the rehearsal dinner, but before that . . .

"Are you ready?" My father knocks on the door, though it's already open, and I turn to him with my arms outstretched. Showing off my dress. Tears shine in his eyes as he folds me into a careful hug. "You look stunning, honey. It looks even better on the real you than it looked on virtual you."

Which is a miracle, considering that Dahlia had to stand in for me during the final fitting because of the ink on her arm.

"Thank you." I sniffle back tears of my own, because we're minutes away, and I will not walk down the makeshift aisle with red eyes.

Finally, my dad lets me go. "They're ready for you."

My mother adjusts my hair again, and there are tears in her eyes now. "I'll see you in there," she says. Then she and my father walk out, hand in hand.

The closer we've gotten to the wedding, the nicer she's been, until—during moments like this—it's hard to keep in mind that while she's throwing me the best secret wedding ever, she's also planning to execute five thousand girls who share my DNA. I can't let that happen. Which is why this may be the last normal day of my life.

Alone, I walk down the hall and continue carefully down the curving front stairs, because there are no wedding planners or bridesmaids here to help. I can hear the wedding march playing from the house system, since secret weddings don't warrant live music, but the whole thing doesn't truly feel real until I see my father waiting for me at the foot of the stairs.

I take his arm, and he pats my hand with a smile. He swallows thickly, as if he's holding back more tears. Then he walks me slowly down the center hallway and into the formal dining room. *This* part is just as it should be.

I have to give my mother credit—she made amazing things happen with no one to help her but our household staff.

The table is gone. The room is covered in flowers—tulips of every color, since she couldn't find enough red and white ones without placing a conspicuous order.

Hennessy stands at the end of the room in his tuxedo, wearing a red rose boutonnière. A wealth of emotions flickers behind his eyes when he sees me, and for a moment, I can't believe how lucky I am that he was willing to do this, without his family and friends here. Without any of the food we chose or the guests we invited.

For me.

He's doing it all for me.

God, I love him.

Trigger stands at Hennessy's side, in place of Seren as the best man. Across from them, Dahlia stands as my maid of honor, in a red silk dress and matching shoes from my closet. I'm not entirely sure they understand this moment or what it means to me, but they're all in. They have been since that night in the gray room.

There are only two chairs set up for "guests," and my mother sits in one of them. When we enter the room, she turns in her seat and watches my father walk me down the makeshift aisle with fresh tears in her eyes.

We stop at the front of the room, beside Hennessy, in front of a table draped in a white silk cloth. The table holds only a single sheet of paper and a very expensive ink pen. There is no minister. My mother was right: you don't actually need one, outside of the ceremonial tradition.

All you need is a bride, a groom, two witnesses, and the official documentation.

My dad laughs a little when he takes my hand and places it in Hennessy's. "I know no one's asked, but I'm still going to deliver my line." He stands a little straighter and stares at the empty space where the minister should be. "Her mother and I do."

I give him a smile as he takes his seat.

No minister. No guests. No cameras. But we still have vows, though they're a little different from the ones we wrote for the official ceremony.

"Hennessy." My voice cracks on his name. Somehow, though I thought I'd feel cheated without all the details I spent so long planning, this moment feels more intimate and real without the crowd and the cameras. As if for once, an event in my life doesn't belong to the entire world. This moment is *ours*.

"Hennessy, I love you with every cell in my body. With every beat of my heart. And I promise to be there for you like you've been there for me from the beginning. I promise to try to deserve you. Though you make that pretty hard, because you're basically perfect."

He chuckles, and my laugh in response is half-choked with happy tears.

"Waverly Whitmore." Hennessy takes my other hand so

that he's holding them both. "I've loved you from the moment I met you. Every second with you is an adventure, and I have no reason to suspect that will stop once we're both wearing rings. I promise to love and cherish you. To stand by your side. To have your back. No matter where that adventure takes us."

My parents have no idea what he's really promising, or how soon he's going to get to keep that promise.

Hennessy turns to Trigger, who hands him the custom wedding band. It's our initials, cut from platinum, repeating around the width of the band, bound with thin rings of platinum at the top and the bottom. From a distance, it looks like platinum filigree, but up close the significance of the letters becomes obvious.

Hennessy slips the ring onto my finger, next to my engagement ring. "With this ring, I thee wed."

I stare at my hand for a second. Then I look up into his eyes. I'm floating in this moment, so caught up in it that I don't remember the rest of my part until Dahlia taps me on the shoulder and hands me Hennessy's matching band.

"With this ring, I thee wed," I echo as I slide it onto his left ring finger.

He squeezes my hand. Then he leans in for our first married kiss.

"Wait!" my mother cries out from her seat. "You have to sign."

"Oh yeah." Hennessy laughs as he picks up the pen and hands it to me.

I lean over to sign the marriage certificate. Then I give him the pen, and he signs. Next, Trigger and Dahlia sign as our witnesses. They leave the numbers off, at my request, but their signatures still look strange with no surnames.

"Now may I kiss my bride?" Hennessy asks.

My father nods. My mother smiles. I can practically feel Dahlia watching us as Hennessy leans in and kisses me, softly at first. Then his hands find the waist of my dress and his head tilts, deepening the kiss. Prolonging the moment.

I want to live in this second. This one perfect second, before we bring the world as we know it crashing down around us. I have no idea how this day will end for either of us. For *any* of us. Changing the world could make it worse, not better. But I have to take that chance. And Hennessy has sworn to take it with me. With us.

I let him end the kiss. But I can't stop staring at him.

I'm married. For better or for worse.

I just hope he understands how bad "worse" might get.

"It was beautiful, honey," my father says. "And no matter what happens tonight at the rehearsal or tomorrow at the ceremony, this is the one that counts. This one."

"I know. Thanks, Dad." I can't let go of Hennessy's hand. I don't want to. "You're both going over early?"

"Yes." My mother smooths one hand over her pale yellow dress. "We're going to meet with the minister and make sure everything is set up for tonight. Can you get Dahlia ready on your own?"

"Yes." I've been doing that for a month now. "I'll put her in the car with Hennessy in a couple of hours."

"Are you sure you don't want me to patch a feed through for you?"

I shake my head. "I can't watch." And if she tries to patch a feed through to my screen, she'll figure out what we're up to. "We're already married. That's all that matters."

"Okay. If you're sure." My father takes my mother's hand and tugs her toward the front door. They're running late.

"The kitchen staff made you a small wedding cake. You should feed each other a bite. It's tradition," my mother says as she walks backward through the foyer, careful in her heels. "But take the gown off first," she adds. "It still has to appear tomorrow."

When they're gone, Hennessy and I each cut a huge slice of cake, alone in the kitchen except for Julienne. Dahlia and Trigger are upstairs, disabling the entire house system, so the cameras won't see or hear us. So that even when my parents discover us missing, they won't know at first what happened.

"Mmm," Hennessy mumbles around the bite I feed him, and I laugh. "It's delicious. Julienne, you've outdone yourself."

She gives him a small smile from behind the counter.

"My turn!"

Hennessy uses his fingers to break off a chunk of white cake with raspberry filling, very similar to the one we ordered for tomorrow's ceremony. I open my mouth, and he places it on my tongue. For a second, I just let the sugar melt in my mouth. It's delicious.

"All done," Trigger announces as he follows Dahlia into the kitchen. "We can say and do whatever we want."

"We need to go." As I stand from my barstool, I brush cake crumbs from the organza on the front of my dress. I haven't changed out of it, because my mother's wrong: this dress doesn't have to appear tomorrow.

There will be no other ceremony. No wedding episode.

No one else will *ever* wear my wedding gown.

TWENTY-EIGHT

DAHLIA

Our car speeds down the road, driven by a clone with the number twenty-four behind his name who has no idea what we're up to. Who wouldn't be able to understand even if we told him, thanks to the sedatives he's been ingesting for six straight years.

Trigger turns away from the car window—from field after sunlit, empty field—to look at the rest of us. "We need a fail-safe."

"A what?" I ask.

"A backup plan, in case this doesn't work. In case I can't break through the Lakeview blackout. Or in case we get caught before I can even try. We need a way to make sure our message gets out there in some form, even if our plan doesn't succeed."

"A video," Waverly says from the bench seat across from

us. "We can record it now and schedule it to go up in a few hours. If we turn out not to need it, we just cancel it before it posts."

"Yes." Hennessy holds his hand out to her. "Give me your tablet. I'll record you two."

"Here?" I asked. "Now?"

Waverly shrugs. "We're only half an hour away from Lakeview."

My pulse leaps at that thought. Half an hour from my home. From the city that lied to me for my entire life, then ripped every friend I'd ever had away from me.

If the Administrator had caught me, would she have killed me? Would she have tried to "transition" and sell me, along with my identicals, even though I'm not a clone?

The fact that those seem to be the only possibilities only underlines how important what we're about to do is. Including the fail-safe. "Okay," I say. "How does this work?"

"Switch seats with Hennessy."

I climb past Waverly's new husband to sit next to her, while he sits next to Trigger. The ribbon-trimmed filmy layers of her white wedding dress fall over the comfortable pants I changed into, and I can't help reaching out to touch them. Coming down the center of the repurposed dining room, Waverly had looked like she was floating on a white cloud.

Now she looks happy to be back in the familiar territory of . . . videos. "Just look there and follow my lead." She points at her tablet, which Hennessy is now aiming at us from across the car. "Focus on me. Then zoom to show us both," she instructs. "Give us a countdown?"

He taps something on his side of the tablet. The number five appears on the side of the tablet facing us, and through it, I can see his shoulders and neck. The number flashes once, then becomes the number four and continues counting down.

At two, Waverly takes a deep breath and smiles.

One . . . Live.

"Hey, everyone, this is Waverly Whitmore with an exclusive for you. This is huge, guys, so pay attention. As you can see, I'm in my wedding dress. Because Hennessy and I just eloped. I know I promised you all could see the wedding, and I'm really sorry that didn't work out, but in a second, you'll understand why. I'm here in the car with Hennessy and a couple of very special friends, headed to the Lakeview clone compound to try to get some even better exclusive footage for you. If you're seeing this, something went wrong. We didn't make it out. So listen up.

"Last month, I met someone who changed my life. Someone who's about to change the whole world. I want you to meet her too. Okay, Hen, zoom out."

Hennessy touches his side of the tablet with his thumb and forefinger, then pushes them together on the screen, widening the camera's view. To include me.

I try to smile. It's not my first time on camera. But it *is* the first time I've been on camera when I wasn't pretending to be Waverly. When I wasn't shielded by the secret of my identity.

"This is Dahlia 16. Wow, right?" Waverly says to the tablet. "I thought the same thing when I met her. I promise that what you're seeing is real. There are no effects at play here. And it gets weirder than that. Dahlia is *not my clone*. I'm hers. Yeah." She nods dramatically. "Let that sink in.

"How that happened is a longer story than we have time for right now, but what I want you to know is that everything we've ever been taught about clones is a lie. Clones are not slow. They're not dim. They're not less than the rest of us in any way. What they are is drugged. They're bombed out of their minds on something that lets them work and keeps them happy, but stops them from truly thinking or feeling. Want proof? Meet Dahlia."

Waverly turns to me, but I can only blink at the camera. "What am I supposed to say?" I ask, and she laughs.

"Just tell them something about Lakeview. About how you grew up."

"Okay." I take a deep breath. "Lakeview isn't what you all think it is. It isn't even what *we* think it is, when we're growing up there. Clones grow up just like all of you do, in a lot of respects. Most of us go to class until we're eighteen, and we play sports for recreation, and we love cake and hot chocolate. But there's one big difference. We grow up thinking every other city in the world is like Lakeview. That everyone, everywhere, is a clone. That someday, we'll take jobs in Lakeview and work for the glory of the city.

"We don't find out we were actually designed, produced, and trained to work as unpaid servants until the day we

299

graduate and are taken to a facility in Valleybrook to be 'transitioned.' Drugged, to be made pliable and complacent, so we will work for you without complaint."

"Messed up, isn't it?" Waverly cuts in. "It's all true. Dahlia and I are proof. Clones are just like everyone else, and they don't deserve what's been happening to them—to us—for hundreds of years. We're on our way to Lakeview to blow the lid off this whole thing, and since that obviously didn't happen, if you're seeing this, I need you guys to do that for us. Share this video. Send it to everyone you know. Spread the truth like a disease and turn it into an epidemic. We're counting on *you* to change the world."

Hennessy hears the final note in her voice and taps the tablet to end the video. "Nice." He whistles as he stares at the image of the two of us, frozen on the transparent screen. "You're right. This is going to change everything."

"Thanks," Waverly says as she takes her tablet back. "Let me set this up. . . ." She taps a series of options and scrolls through a time wheel to schedule the video. "It'll drop on my main feed in five hours, unless we're still alive and free to cancel it."

"Just in time." Trigger points through the windshield, and Waverly and I turn to look. "There's Lakeview." He reaches across the car to take my hand. "Welcome home."

TWENTY-NINE

WAVERLY

"How are we going to get in?" Dahlia asks as the Lakeview city wall grows closer, and the breathless quality of her voice seems to echo the fear threaded through every beat of my heart. My mother and I have fought several times over her refusal to let me come here, and suddenly, despite the adrenaline firing through my veins, I'm starting to think she was right.

"If the guard sees Dahlia and me, he'll arrest us all," I say. "I feel like we should have given this part more thought."

"Relax," Hennessy says as sun flashes off the guard booth I can now see through the deeply tinted e-glass windows. "I've been here to see Seren a dozen times. The guards know me. Unless you think they'd know Seren's already in Mountainside, for the rehearsal."

Trigger shakes his head. "I doubt the Administrator keeps

them apprised of her personal schedule, or her family's. Most of the guards don't even know she has kids."

"Okay." Hennessy nods. "We just have to stop them from seeing you two twin princesses."

"How do we do that?" Trigger asks.

Hennessy winks, then stands hunched over in the fairly confined space, and I understand.

"We hide. Rise, soldier," I say with a smile. Trigger and Hennessy move and we fold down the back of the bench seat they've just vacated. "The trunk."

I crawl into the space and curl up on my side to make room for Dahlia, tucking the voluminous folds of my beautiful dress around me.

Dahlia crawls in after me and I wince when her hand slips on my hair and pulls several pieces out. She curls up in the other half of the trunk, her knees inches from my face, and Hennessy blows me a kiss, then folds the seat back into place.

For a second, it feels like Dahlia and I are true twins, sharing some kind of carpet-lined womb.

The seat groans as Hennessy sits on it, and dimly I hear the creak of leather as Trigger climbs into the front seat, assuming the same personal-guard role he played during their escape from Lakeview.

How could that have been just a month ago?

"Are you scared?" Dahlia whispers in the dark.

"Terrified," I confess. "You?"

"Yeah. I know this is the right thing to do—the only thing to do—but . . ."

"Exactly." I don't know how to put it into words either, but I understand how she feels.

The car slows to a stop, and my pulse races. Through the padded leather seat back, whatever Hennessy's saying to the guard is too muffled to be understood, but a second later, the car rolls forward again, and I release the breath I've been holding.

Surely if they were going to search the car, there would have been shouting.

A couple of minutes later, Hennessy says something. The car slows again; then the seat groans as he stands and folds it down. His face appears in the gap. "Come on out."

"But stay down," Trigger warns from the front seat.

Dahlia crawls out first, and I follow her, careful not to rip my dress. I practically collapse on the opposite bench seat, with my back to the clone driver, who sits in his mental fog, waiting for further instructions. I wish I had a way to rescue him from his drugged state. Something faster than taking away his Lakeview-issued food for a few days.

Out the window, I see nothing but sunlit fields of sheared winter-brown grass, but when I twist to look through the windshield, I find a cluster of tall buildings looming closer with every second.

"Okay, now what?" Hennessy asks as he pushes aside layers of my skirt to sit next to me, leaving Dahlia alone on the other bench seat. "I've pretty much expended my usefulness."

"Now we find a tablet," Trigger says. "And you're still plenty useful, because you're the only one of us who can walk into the Administrator's mansion without getting arrested."

Hennessy frowns. "Wait, you actually want me to go in there?"

"You told the guard that's where you're going, which means he's already called ahead to the mansion. Even though Seren wasn't there to take the call, the butler will be expecting to let you in, so we need you to show up, if for no other reason than to delay raising the alarm. No one can know that the rest of us are here until I punch a hole through the network blackout, which I can't do without a tablet. And that'll be just as easy to find at the mansion as anywhere else."

Hennessy's brows rise. "So I'm the distraction?"

"The very hot, very capable distraction," I say as I scoot closer to him, admiring the fit of his tux.

"Seren and Sofia send messages all the time, so they must have the same kind of bypass access their mother has," Hennessy says. "Do you want me to try to steal an extra tablet?"

"Have you ever stolen anything?" Trigger asks.

"Other than a bottle from the liquor cabinet? No."

"Then don't start now. You'll just get caught and blow the whole thing."

Hennessy looks insulted for a moment; then he shrugs it off. "Okay, so what? I just hang out with the butler while you steal a tablet?"

"Tell him Seren forgot something and you're there to pick it up."

Hennessy's brow rises. "You want me to tell him I left my own wedding rehearsal to pick up something several hours away for my best man?"

Trigger shrugs. "Even if he doesn't believe you, he won't question you. He's not allowed to."

"What about Dahlia and me?" I'm totally out of my element in clone central, an irony I am not unaware of.

"Stay in the car and keep your heads down," he says. "I'll be as fast as I can."

Dahlia's eyes widen; then she slides off the seat onto the floorboard. "We're here."

As I kneel next to her, pressing down puffy acres of organza, I glance out the window to see a large house looming in front of us, well ahead of the cluster of taller buildings beyond it.

"Pull around back, please," Hennessy says to the driver. "This isn't a formal occasion."

The car rounds the house and pulls to a stop beneath a covered portico next to the garage. I stare up at the building without rising from my crouch. I want to go in and see the infamous Administrator's mansion. I want to surprise Sofia and Seren, swipe whatever alcohol we can get our hands on, and order something to snack on from their kitchen, to make up for all the Lakeview parties I've missed.

But that will never happen. They're on their way to *my* party.

Even if they don't yet know about my strange connection to their mother's business—to the legacy they no doubt expect to inherit—they will by tonight. And I have no idea how they'll take that news.

"Wish me luck," Hennessy says.

"Good luck," I whisper, wishing I could give him a kiss instead.

He steps out onto the driveway, and just before the car door closes, I see the back door of the mansion open. A man in a butler's uniform speaks to Hennessy.

"Turn him around." Trigger whispers from the front seat, and I realize he's not talking to me—he's evidently trying to communicate telepathically with Hennessy. "I can't get out of the car while the butler's facing us. . . ." He must be watching through his peripheral vision, though, because like the driver, he's facing forward, wearing his professional guard face.

I hear a door close.

"Good," Trigger mumbles, and when he dares a glance toward the house, I understand that Hennessy has followed the butler inside. "Here goes everything." He silently eases his door open.

Trigger gets out of the car in a squat and drops below my line of sight. Then the door closes with a soft click.

"Don't worry," Dahlia whispers. "He knows what he's doing."

I know she's right. If she weren't, they would never have made it out of Lakeview in the first place. But there's a world of difference between hearing about dangerous escapes from the safety of the subsequent retelling and witnessing them firsthand.

I tap on the window and an opacity dial appears. I set the window to single-direction opacity so that we can see out but no one can see in; then I apply the setting to all the windows, as well as the rear windshield. Dahlia and I are now hidden from sight, unless someone glances through the front wind-shield, which can't be adjusted. I dare a peek to see what's going on.

"What do you see?" Dahlia asks.

"Trigger's rounding the car," I tell her. But he's so quiet that if I couldn't see the top of his head over the hood, I'd have no idea he was there. "I don't see anyone else, but—"

Trigger stands, then jogs toward the back door.

"I think he's going inside," I narrate. "No, wait. It looks like he hears something." Trigger flattens himself against the exterior wall of the house, right next to the back door, to the left of a set of simple concrete steps. A second later the back door opens. "There's someone—"

Trigger grabs the man emerging from the rear of the mansion and pulls him off the steps into a chokehold. In one fluid movement.

"A man in a black suit came out, and Trigger *took him down*. In, like, a second. In complete silence." I can hear the awe in my own voice, but Dahlia only nods from her crouch on the floorboard, pride shining in her eyes. "That guy's totally unconscious." If I couldn't see the rise and fall of his chest, I'd think he was dead.

"Trigger's *really* good." Dahlia shrugs. "Of course, the guy in the black suit is just Management. Not a soldier. But I've seen him take down soldiers too."

"He's taking him . . ." I watch as Trigger drags the unconscious man toward a door on the other side of the portico. "I don't know what's through that door." But it must be a storage room of some kind, because a second later, Trigger steps out alone, tucking something about the size of my hand into his pocket. He glances both ways, then jogs toward the car.

A second later, he opens the door and slides into the front seat again, as if he never left.

Dahlia exhales in relief, and I realize that though she was confident, she was also worried.

Trigger chuckles. "That was the easy part. *This* is the hard part." He pulls the tablet from his pocket and taps on it to wake up the screen. "Fortunately, they don't usually use screen locks, because they don't expect anyone in Lakeview to steal one. Or to hack one."

"Really?" I find that hard to imagine.

"They're really big on following the rules here," Dahlia

explains while Trigger taps his way through several menus. "Breaking rules means you're flawed, and flaws will get your entire genome recalled." She frowns. "Which, evidently, just means you'll be sold before you were scheduled to graduate. But everyone here thinks it means euthanasia, which is a pretty big deterrent."

"Do you think my instructors have changed their passwords?" Trigger mumbles, evidently to himself.

"You know their passwords?"

"He knows a *lot* of things," Dahlia says. "He once took down the entire communication system so he could come get me out of class himself, claiming Management wanted to see me but couldn't get a ping through." Her cheeks are adorably pink.

My clone is in *love*.

"I didn't think stuff like that happened in the training ward." Either the hacking or the hooking up.

Dahlia laughs. "It doesn't."

"We're not your average clones," Trigger adds. I peek over the seat to see that he's now navigating through a screen that contains only text. He's actually *typing* commands onto the screen, because there are no options to tap. No links to take. He's hacking the hard way. The way that only people trained in writing code—or in cyber warfare, evidently—know how to do. "Almost . . . there . . . ," he mumbles.

Then the back door of the mansion squeals open.

"Thank you." Hennessy glances anxiously at the car as

he comes onto the back steps, carrying something in his left hand, and I can practically see his relief when he realizes I've tinted the windows.

I drop out of sight again, just in case, and Hennessy rounds the car to get in from Dahlia's side so the butler can't see inside the car.

"Well?" he asks as he sinks onto the bench seat, holding one of Seren's neckties—evidently the ostensible reason for his trip to the mansion.

"Don't look down at me!" I whisper, and his head pops up immediately.

"Sorry." Hennessy's foot taps nervously against the floorboard, an inch from my hand. "Did you get what we need?"

"Yes," Trigger says. "But the butler's still watching."

"Head toward the front gate please," Hennessy says, and the driver gives a command to the car. Hennessy watches the rearview mirror as we pull away, and I know when tension melts from his frame that the butler has finally gone back inside. "Okay, take the next right and circle toward the training ward."

The driver does as he's asked, without question, and suddenly I realize what a travesty it is for anyone to be too drugged to question things. It seems to me that questioning authority should be considered a fundamental human right. That's the way I live my life, anyway, much to my mother's chagrin.

"That was fast," I say as I climb onto the seat next to Hennessy. Dahlia sits across from us, where she can look over the seat at whatever Trigger's doing on the stolen tablet.

"Yeah, I was afraid it was *too* fast for Trigger to—"

"Got it!" Trigger exclaims from the front seat. "The network block is down. At least until someone discovers that and puts it back up."

"How likely is that?" I ask.

"Not very. The instructors don't know the external network exists. Upper-level geneticists and Management must know, because they go off-site to take orders for clones for other cities. But they have no reason to try to connect, because they don't know they can."

"Won't their tablets automatically connect, like ours do?" Hennessy asks.

"There's no auto-connect on standard tablets here," I tell them. "DigiCore makes their tech specifically for Lakeview. That's why there's no e-glass." They use a cheaper, less advanced technology. "And they don't auto-connect because there's not supposed to be a signal for them to connect to." Or, more accurately, the signal is blocked, except on the Lockes' devices.

Hennessy nods. "Okay. So what's the plan from here?"

I shrug with a glance around the car at all three of them. "Find some clones and start streaming?"

Dahlia turns to Trigger, a sudden idea gleaming in her eyes. "We won't last long like that. The first instructors who see us will . . . Well, I don't know what they'll do. They think

311

I'm dead, and they've never seen e-glass or a livecast. But I'm sure they'll report us to Management. Can you get rid of them for us? Even just for a few minutes?"

"All of them?"

Dahlia glances out the car window at the sun, which is steadily sliding toward the horizon. "It's dinnertime. Why don't we stream from one of the secondary dormitory cafeterias? Secondary is years thirteen through seventeen," she explains. Then she turns back to Trigger. "We can use the cafeteria on the first floor so we won't have to wait for the elevator or waste time climbing stairs." She frowns as she thinks. "Which classes are on the first floor?"

"Um . . ." He types something on his stolen tablet, then taps and begins scrolling. "Assorted manual-labor classes. Years fifteen, sixteen, and seventeen."

"Perfect," my identical declares. "Can you send a ping to all the first-floor conservators telling them to meet somewhere and wait for an address from Management?" She shrugs. "I don't know how long they'll wait if Management doesn't show up, but if you disable their communications after you send the ping, they won't be able to ask about what's supposed to be happening without actually sending someone *to* Management."

Trigger beams at her. "That's a great idea." He speaks as he types on the tablet. "That should buy us some time for the livecast."

"Will the cafeteria work for this video?" Dahlia asks me.

"It's perfect. We want footage of clones doing something normal. Laughing, talking, arguing. Maybe even throwing some food around. The goal is for everyone to understand that we're just like everyone else."

"But how sure are we that this is going to shame the public into doing the right thing?" Hennessy asks. "History is full of evidence that that won't happen. My fear is that ultimately, business owners and wealthy private citizens—*our* people," he says with a pointed glance at me, "will always choose to buy clones rather than pay a fair wage for citizen labor."

"Okay . . ." I take Hennessy's hand in both of mine. "There's a possibility that as long as they *can* make and buy clones, they *will*. So we'll have to take that option away from them. For good."

"How?" he asks.

"By destroying their raw materials." Trigger smiles. He's caught on. "The central gene cache. Millions and millions of strands of DNA, stored and cataloged centuries ago, after the world changed. Most from casualties of the war, from all over the world. But if the Administrator loses that DNA, won't she just take more samples? Start mining DNA from . . . I don't know . . . citizens?"

"That's illegal," Hennessy says. "Living beings cannot be cloned without their permission because they own their own genes. So even if the Administrator started collecting new samples right now, she couldn't use any of them until the donors had all died."

"It would take decades, if not centuries, to amass a collection even *close* to the variety she has now," Dahlia says. "And that variety is what enables Lakeview's geneticists to design such healthy and efficient clones. We all learn that in school."

"So if we destroy the cache . . . ," I say.

Dahlia smiles. "We destroy the system."

THIRTY

DAHLIA

"Are you sure about this?" I ask as Trigger and I sneak through the shade of the Specialist Bureau. The sun hovers on the horizon, casting long shadows all over the grounds. It was only a month ago that we were here, doing this very thing behind this very building.

Back then, we'd been hoping to rescue my identicals from euthanasia at the Defense Bureau.

Today, our mission is one of destruction, rather than rescue, but my hope for a positive outcome feels no more realistic now than it did then.

"I don't see that we have any choice," Trigger says. "We were all in agreement about that back in the car."

"I'm still on board with the mission," I whisper. "It's the method I have reservations about." It doesn't quite seem fair that Waverly and Hennessy get to do a livecast while we're stuck sneaking into the most dangerous building in the city.

"Don't worry. I know what I'm doing," Trigger says, and that, I believe. "And your idea will hopefully make things that much safer. They should be leaving any—" He points across the lawn at the Defense Bureau, where both of the rear exits have just opened, almost simultaneously. "There they go."

Indeed, as I watch, several high-ranking Defense officials—all men and women who must be approaching the year-forty-five mandatory retirement—file out the rear doors. I lean around the corner of the Specialist Bureau, careful to stay in the shadows, and from here I can see that even more Defense officers are leaving through the front door.

"Where did you send them?" I ask.

"To a totally made-up emergency meeting at the Management Bureau. I killed their communications after I sent that ping, but Defense has protocol in place to deal with things like that. They won't wait as long as the dormitory conservators will before looking into this. So we'll have to be fast."

"But those guys are just leadership, right? There are still regular soldiers in the building?"

Trigger nods, tapping something on his stolen tablet. "They would never believe a ping asking everyone to vacate the building, no matter what excuse I used. But the soldiers who're still in there are more used to taking orders than issuing them, and that's a best-case scenario for us."

"You're sure you can get in?"

"The exits won't be locked," he says. "But if we use any scanner in the entire city, our bar codes will trigger an alarm. So we're either going to have to find someone to let us into any locked room we need access to, or bypass the scanner altogether."

We wait, my pulse swooshing rapidly in my ears, for the last of the Defense officials to disappear around the corner, headed across the manicured administration ward grounds toward the Management Bureau and the fictional meeting. Then Trigger shoves his tablet into his pocket and grabs my hand. We take off for the back of the Defense Bureau at a run and we don't slow until we're behind the building, hidden from sight.

Trigger pulls open the first door—he's right, it's unlocked—and we sneak inside, his boots silent against the white tile floor.

I've never been in the Defense Bureau headquarters; it's brighter and more sterile than I expected. There are no shadows to hide in, and all the doors seem to have scanners built into them. Which means they're all locked.

I follow Trigger down a series of identical white hallways, flinching with every squeak of my sneakers against the floor. I wish we'd found a trade laborer's uniform for me to change into. That wouldn't have helped me blend in with a bunch of soldiers, but it might have kept me from standing out so much that they look at my face and recognize me as a girl who should be dead.

Trigger stops at a hallway intersection with one finger over his lips. I go as still and quiet as I can, listening for whatever he's heard. There are no voices, but I hear the familiar squeal of chair legs against tile.

Trigger gives me a "halt" gesture, and I nod. He peeks around the corner to the right, then takes off silently in that direction.

I lean around the corner to watch. I can't help it.

Halfway down the hall, a soldier sits in a folding chair behind a small table, stationed in front of a closed door. His chair is angled away from us, and he's reading something on his Lakeview-style tablet.

He starts to turn, and Trigger lunges the last few steps. He wraps his right arm around the soldier's neck, bracing his hold with a grip on his own left forearm. The soldier claws at Trigger, but finds no purchase on the sleeve of his uniform. His feet kick against the floor and his knee slams into the underside of the table. I flinch over the noise. Then the soldier goes limp.

Trigger positions the soldier's chair behind the table again, then leans the man forward with his forehead resting on his folded arms, as if he's fallen asleep at his post. Then he grabs the gun from the soldier's holster and the standard-issue backpack from beneath the table and jogs silently back to me.

"Step one accomplished," he whispers as he tucks the gun into the back of his waistband.

We press on, and twice we have to cross hallway intersections without being seen or heard by people standing guard next to more doorways. I'm just starting to feel halfway stealthy when Trigger stops me again. He leans in until his nose brushes my ear, his breath stirring my hair, and a pleasant chill travels over me, in spite of the circumstances.

"The armory is just around this corner," he whispers. "There'll be a guard outside the door, and he won't be young or inexperienced. I'm going to need your help for this."

I'm afraid to speak and get us caught.

"I'm going to go around that next hallway and approach from the other direction. I want you to wait exactly three minutes." He pulls out the stolen tablet and taps it to bring up the clock. "Then go around this corner and distract the guard. You shouldn't have to do anything. Just get his attention. I'll take him out from behind."

I'm far from confident I can play my part.

"Three minutes." I open the clock on my own tablet. When one minute clicks over to the next on both tablets, he nods. "Starting now." Then he peeks around the corner and stealthily crosses the hall.

As I watch, he turns right at the next intersection. And I'm on my own. My heart thunders in my chest, so loud I'm not sure I'd hear any footsteps approach.

If I mess this up, we're all "screwed," to quote Waverly.

One minute passes. Then two. Every second is agony. My lungs feel like they're on fire until I realize I'm holding my breath, so I exhale slowly. Then inhale.

Two and a half minutes. I want to peek around the corner, but if I'm too early, this won't work. It might not work anyway.

The third minute ticks over. I take a deep breath. Then I step around the corner.

At the end of the hall, there's a sliding glass window next to a locked steel door. A uniformed guard is stationed in the room beyond the window. He's at least year thirty. There's a braided cord over his arm and a cluster of medals pinned to his chest.

I take another quiet step, and he looks up. "Hey." The soldier slides open the window. "You're not authorized to be in here. Who are you?"

"I . . ." The word dies on my lips. I should have spent the past three minutes coming up with something to say. *Tell him you're hurt. Tell him you're lost. Tell him there's some kind of emergency, and he's needed outside.* But my tongue refuses to cooperate. "I . . ."

"Stop where you are!" The soldier disappears from the window, then opens the steel door. His hand slides into his pocket and he pulls out a standard-issue tablet as he marches toward me. "Don't move."

I couldn't even if I wanted to. He's pulling his gun now, and I'm frozen where I stand.

Then motion over his shoulder catches my eye. Trigger rounds the corner behind him and jogs toward the soldier on silent feet. At the last second, the soldier hears him, but he's too late. Trigger presses the barrel of his stolen gun to the back of the soldier's head. "Holster your weapon," he orders softly. "And put the tablet back into your pocket."

"I—"

"Don't even try it," Trigger warns, "or I will blow your head all over this hallway."

Slowly, the soldier slides his tablet into his pocket and holsters his gun. Trigger takes the gun from him and sticks it into the back of his waistband. Then he removes the other gun from the soldier's head and smashes the butt of it into the back of his skull with a sickening thud.

The soldier's eyes roll back into his head. He collapses to the ground.

Trigger waves me forward as he kneels over the unconscious guard and removes his tablet from his pocket. He glances at the screen and exhales heavily. "He was half a second from raising the alarm." Trigger cancels the on-screen order and pockets the tablet. Then he clicks a button on the gun and hands it to me. "Hold this. The safety's on."

I take the gun because I have no choice, but holding it feels . . . wrong. Scary. I'm trained to create life—to grow food to feed people—not to take it.

Trigger squats and grips the unconscious guard beneath both arms, hefting him as close to upright as he can. "Get his arm. Open the door."

I push the soldier's sleeve back to expose the bar code on his wrist; then I hold it beneath the scanner next to the armory door. A red beam passes over it. The scanner beeps. The steel door unbolts with a heavy scraping sound.

"Open it," Trigger says.

I push the door open and hold it for him as he drags the guard inside, where his unconscious body won't be seen by anyone who walks by. The door closes behind him, and I gasp as I look around.

We're in a huge, high-ceilinged warehouse-like room, as sterile and white as the rest of the building, and blindingly lit from above by a series of fluorescent lights. Beyond the high stool stationed in front of the sliding window, racks of long black rifles and handgun stands line the walls, and rows and rows of black powder-coated shelves form a maze of aisles in the middle of the room. The shelves hold crate after crate after crate, all black and most labeled as containing ammunition for the guns on the wall. More kinds of ammunition than I even knew existed.

"This way." Trigger lays the unconscious guard on the floor in the aisle, and I follow him as he jogs toward the end of the first row of shelves. Here, the crates are a different size and are made of a sturdy green plastic.

Trigger unzips the stolen backpack, then opens one of the crates. Inside it lies a series of metal rings about two inches deep and about the diameter of my palm. At first I think they're hollow, like bracelets. Then Trigger lifts one, and I see that they're filled with a thick, clear gel.

"Here." He extends the backpack toward me. I take it

and hold it open while he carefully stacks ten of the gel-filled rings inside. "Okay. One more thing; then we're out of here."

In the next aisle, he opens another crate and removes a pen-shaped object about the diameter of my thumb, with a button on one end and a tiny screen on the side. "We probably only need one, but just to be safe . . ." He takes another pen and slides them both into the smaller front pocket of the bag. "Let's go."

We sneak out of the Defense Bureau the same way we snuck in, tiptoeing past a couple of door guards before slipping outside under the cover of darkness. The sun has finally set.

I hope Waverly and Hennessy are okay in the Workforce cafeteria.

If none of this had happened, that's where I would be right now.

"Okay, do you know where the genetics lab is?" Trigger whispers as we peek around the corner of the building.

"Yeah. My class took a tour once. It's on the other side of the Management Bureau." Where we sent all the high-ranking soldiers.

Trigger nods. "We're going to have to take a circuitous route, back around the Specialist Bureau. But the good news is that there shouldn't be anyone still working there this time of night. Unlike Defense. You ready?"

I take his hand with a nervous smile. Then we run.

We make it to the Specialist Bureau with no problem, but as we're rounding that building to come at the genetics lab from the back, we hear footsteps. Then voices.

"I want everyone on alert," a man's low-pitched voice commands, and when we peek around the corner of the building, we see that the man speaking is at the front of the returning cluster of officers.

"That's Saber 44," Trigger whispers. "The highest-ranking soldier in Lakeview."

"Call the secondary cadets out of the dorms," Saber 44 continues. "Dinner can wait. I don't know what's going on, but when the Administrator realizes that communications are down, she'll head back here immediately. In the meantime, I want everyone on patrol, but you'll have to send someone to the dorm in person while we work on restoring communications."

"Sir, there's been no reported breach from any of the gates or checkpoints," a woman's crisp, clear voice replies. "Couldn't this be a glitch? Or even a prank by one of the students? It wouldn't be the first time an ambitious Special Forces cadet has tested out his or her training here at home."

Trigger grins at me in the shadows. Clearly, he's one of those ambitious cadets.

"Until we know otherwise, we're going to assume this is real," the man's voice barks.

We're already an hour late for the wedding rehearsal.

People in Mountainside must know something is wrong by now. Including the Administrator.

"The dorms," I whisper, and Trigger pulls his tablet from his pocket.

"We'll have to warn Waverly."

THIRTY-ONE

WAVERLY

"How many stories is that?" Hennessy whispers as we stare through the tinted e-glass car window at the building we're parked in front of.

"Twenty, at least." I've tried to count the floors of the building in front of us, but I keep losing count. "And this is just the secondary dorm. There's also a primary and an intermediate."

"It's so strange that they decided to build up instead of out, when there's so much space out here."

"I think it has to do with their cluster principle. Dahlia said they're expected to spend as much time as possible with their identicals, to foster a sense of identity and purpose. That must work better when they stack everyone on top of one another." I exhale and glance at the clock on my tablet.

"This is crazy," Hennessy says with another look through the window.

"I know. You can stay here if you want. I can broadcast it myself."

He smiles and takes my hand. "This isn't how I pictured our honeymoon. But I'm with you."

"Thank you." I hand him my tablet, which is already cued up to start the livecast on my public feed. "There are already nearly a quarter of a million people signed in, waiting for the stream."

"Just tell me when you're ready."

I reach up and jab the plastic fixture overhead, and the back of the car fills with light. "One more thing." I scoot closer and pull him in for a kiss. A good, long one. Because if we get caught, it may be our last. "I love you," I whisper when I finally pull away.

"I love you too. Waverly and Hennessy forever," he says. "Even if forever ends tonight."

I can't resist a sad smile. "That's not much of a pep talk."

"You're the talker in this relationship." He lifts my tablet and points it at me. "Time's running out," he says with a smile.

I take a deep breath. "Okay. Go."

He taps the *Record* icon. The outline of an old-fashioned camera appears on the side of the tablet facing me. Through it, I can see him watching me. He gives me a wink.

I smile at him through the tablet. Then I start talking. "Hey, guys, it's Waverly Whitmore with an exclusive for you, and this can*not* be missed. So if your friends aren't tuning in yet, send them the link already! I'll wait!" I pause for a second and blow a strand of hair away from my face. "Never mind. I can't wait because I'm coming to you *live* today from inside Lakeview. In my wedding dress, because it turns out there's no official dress code for a groundbreaking exposé.

"What's that? You don't believe me because there's a network blackout in Lakeview? Well, we've punched *right* through the block, but I don't know how long it'll be before the Administrator and her thugs figure that out and cut us off, so pay attention. Tap *Record* and get ready to share this with everyone you know. I'm about to take you inside the secondary dormitory tower here in Lakeview, where *thousands* of teenage clones are gathered in nearly two dozen cafeterias having dinner. And you're not going to believe what you see.

"Ready?" I ask Hennessy through the tablet, and he nods. "What's our viewership up to?"

"Four hundred thousand and growing."

I whistle as I open the car door. "Seriously, spread the word, guys. I want one million people watching this before they cut us off." I climb out of the car, careful not to trip over my skirt, and glance around the courtyard, which Dahlia calls the "common lawn." There are a few classes of clones outside playing soccer in teams or heading toward the dorm—toward us—for dinner, and I give Hennessy a spinning gesture with my index finger. He turns to get a shot of the lawn, and I can only imagine what my viewers are thinking.

No one's seen the inside of the training ward. Hennessy's

been to Lakeview a dozen times, but he's never been past the mansion.

He turns the camera on me again as I walk backward down the sidewalk toward the building, my satin and organza skirt swishing around my legs.

"As you can see, the building at my back is huge. Like, twenty stories or more." I aim a gesture upward, and Hennessy follows it with the camera, then refocuses on me. "We're going to head through the front door to the right, where I'm told the first-floor cafeteria is currently filled with manual-labor students—clones being taught to clean, launder, and perform other 'unskilled' jobs in our homes and businesses. Think you know what you're going to see inside? I guarantee you that you're wrong."

I turn when I get to the front door and spare a second to hope that Trigger's ping worked. That the adults have all gathered elsewhere for a made-up meeting. Then I pull the door open and step into a shallow, light gray–tiled lobby, sandwiched by a bank of four elevators on each side. Straight ahead, a wide hallway leads to the left and the right, already echoing with voices from what must be the cafeteria.

"Can you hear that?" I ask the camera, and Hennessy nods at me through the tablet. "That's the sound of a couple hundred conversations going on at once. Is that what you thought you'd hear from a clone cafeteria?"

"We're at more than half a million now," my groom says as he follows me into the hallway.

"Thanks, Hennessy." I turn to the right, and see that the hallway ends in a large glass-walled room full of long tables with built-in stools. There are easily *hundreds* of kids my age sitting at the tables, eating, drinking, and talking. But at a glance, I can only see *six* different faces.

Six.

I know that clones have identicals, obviously. And I've even seen groups of up to six identicals working together. But I've never in my life seen this many people walking around with the same face, and knowing that this place exists is *nothing* like seeing it for myself.

This is *surreal*.

"Can you zoom in on that?"

Hennessy uses his thumb and forefinger to get a closer shot of the cafeteria through the glass walls, one portion of which appears to be an open glass door. "Comments are *pouring* in," he says, and when I squint, I can see them scrolling across the left side of my tablet, in print too small for me to read in reverse.

He follows me as I head slowly down the hall, watching and listening to the manual-labor students, who haven't noticed us yet.

The clones are all kind of slim and not very tall, probably from the genetic hormone deficiency, and the girls are all pretty flat-chested, just like I am. The youngest girls are shorter, with a pouf of dark hair and amber-toned skin, while the older two genomes are paler, one with brunette waves, the other with long, straight blond hair.

The youngest third of the boys are redheaded and freck-led, with pale skin. Of the other two genomes represented, one is tall with dark skin and the other has a medium skin tone with glossy, dark curls.

I can't help but stare. *So many* identical faces and heads of hair, though the girls have fixed theirs in dozens of styles. So many voices of the same pitch and timbre. So many identical uniforms.

Some of them sit in clusters while they eat from identi-cal portions on identical cafeteria trays. Some have already finished and are talking to their friends, or are drawing or playing games on sheets of actual, old-fashioned paper.

Energized and more furious than I've ever been in my life, I turn back to the camera, hyperaware that I could be no-ticed at any moment. That if the adults come back, this is all over. "Do these look like the clones you see working on the street, or in your local bakery or dry cleaner? Do they sound like the clones who cook your food or clean your room? No? That's because the clones who work for us are drugged with a substance the Administrator puts in their food, to keep them compliant and satisfied with the lives we force on them. They're not quiet and subservient by nature, no matter what you've been taught. By nature, they're just like we are. Let's go talk to them."

I can hear Hennessy's footsteps on the tile as he follows me.

My heart thuds as I step into the cafeteria, but at first, no one seems to notice us or care that we're there. Until I walk up to a group of three identical blond girls at the nearest table. Their talking ceases when they see me. One drops her spoon into a bowl of what looks like chicken soup. All three stare in awe at my poufy skirt. Then they notice my face.

Conversations at the surrounding tables fade into uneasy whispers. The only words I can make out are *dress* and *recalled*.

They recognize me. They think I should be dead, along with my identicals. They have no idea how wrong they are on both counts. And after they're done staring at me, they turn to Hennessy. He's taller and stouter than any other guy in the room, and they have no reason to recognize his face. Or the clear glass tablet he's holding.

Almost as one, they seem to realize that we do not belong here.

"Hi," I say as the localized patch of silence spreads through the room. As more and more faces turn to us. "What are your names?"

The three blond girls glance at one another. Then at Hennessy. Then one meets my gaze. "Aida 17," she says. "Who are you?"

"My name is Waverly," I tell her. "Who are the rest of you?"

"I'm Bayley, and that's Paige," the girl who dropped her spoon said. "Weren't you . . . ?"

"Weren't I what?" I motion Hennessy closer with my tablet, to make sure he can hear.

"We're at seven hundred thousand viewers," he says, reading from the counter on his side of the screen.

"Weren't you recalled?" Bayley 17 asks as more and more of the room descends into silence.

"Can you tell me what you mean by that?" I ask her while Hennessy zooms in on her face.

"I mean . . . your genome. I thought you and your identicals were all recalled last month."

"And by *recalled*, you mean . . . ?"

"Ended," Paige 17 says. "Euthanized. Because you were all flawed. Right?"

"My identicals," I repeat for the camera. "How many of us were there, do you know?"

"Five thousand," Aida 17 says as the clones at the table behind her gather closer.

I turn back to the camera. "Everyone in this room recognizes my face," I tell my audience of nearly three-quarters of a million people. "Because I am a clone, just like they are. Though my parents and I were completely unaware of it, eighteen years ago, a Lakeview geneticist designed my genome for my mother, then cloned it and put it into production as a class of trade laborers. Until last month, I had *five thousand* identicals living here in Lakeview." I pause for effect while the clones all around me stare in stunned silence. "That's right. *I am a clone.* You've known me all my life, and you had no idea I was a clone. That's because clones are just like you, until they're sold into servitude and kept drugged. Let me show you a little more."

I turn back to the table. "Aida, what's your favorite school subject?"

"History," she says, her eyes wide as she stares at my tablet. My question seems to be the only part of this she understands. "I like to read about the world, before it changed."

"Great. And you?"

"I don't like class," Paige tells me. "I like recreation. Soccer and volleyball. And sometimes relays."

"Me too," Bayley says. "Swimming relays."

"Tennis!" Someone shouts from the table behind her. Then the cafeteria breaks out in a good-natured argument over which team sport is the most fun.

"Eight hundred thousand and climbing," Hennessy tells me, a triumphant smile forming on his lips.

"Okay. Thanks," I say to the girls at the first table. "Now I have another question for you." The argument begins to quiet down, because everyone wants to hear what I'm going to ask. "What would you say if I told you that the rest of the world is nothing like Lakeview. That everyone born in my hometown, Mountainside, is an individual."

"Individual?" Bayley frowns. "No one's an individual, except the Administrator. Everyone knows that."

"Nine hundred thousand," Hennessy whispers. "And the comments are still pouring in."

"Look at my friend Hennessy," I tell them, and Hennessy obliges me by moving the camera away from his face. "Do any of you recognize him?"

Heads shake all over the cafeteria.

"That's because he's an individual. He has no identicals.

334

He's not a clone. In fact, his genome wasn't created at all. He is the product of a mother and a father who conceived him the 'archaic' way. His mother carried him in her body. She gave birth to him. And to his sister. That's how everyone in Mountainside is born."

Someone near the back of the crowd laughs.

"What's going on?" Aida 17 asks. "Is this some kind of game? A joke? What's that thing he's holding?"

"It's a tablet, like the ones you use in class, only it's made from newer technology. It's hooked up to a network that connects everyone in the world—except you guys here in Lakeview. Because the Administrator knows that if you had access, you'd know that the other cities aren't like this."

"Waverly," Hennessy says. "Time's up." He's holding his own tablet in his free hand, reading a message that has popped up on it. "Trigger says soldiers are on the way."

I turn back to the cafeteria full of clones now staring at me as if I have two heads. I don't have time to convince them that this isn't a joke or a game. But with any luck, the people I *do* need to convince around the world are still with me. And starting to believe. "Is there a back way out of this place?" I ask.

About a hundred arms point in unison to a door on the other side of the cafeteria.

"Should I stop broadcasting?" Hennessy asks as he follows me through the path that opens up in the crowd.

"No. If they're going to arrest us"—or kill us—"they're

going to do it live on camera. To be clear," I say to the tablet as I back toward the door. "The authorities here in Lakeview have no reason to let us out of here alive. We're breaking the law by showing you this. But the Administrator is breaking the laws of human decency by creating an entire population for no purpose other than to serve. A population that is designed to be sterile and to die between the ages of twenty-eight and forty-five, depending upon the class they were created for."

Gasps go up in the crowd around me, and I realize that at least some of my new friends understand what I'm saying. And they didn't know about their age cap.

But they believe me.

"Thanks, you guys!" I say to the entire room as I shove open the back door. Then Hennessy and I are outside, alone again, and the sun has fully set. "Okay," I say to the camera. "We're supposed to meet our friends Trigger 17 and Dahlia 16 at the genetics lab, but that's a bit of a hike from here, especially in this ensemble." I gesture at my dress and heels. "So we're going to drive. But I have no idea if we'll make it. We've been told soldiers are heading to the dorm, but I don't know whether or not they know we're here."

"Your mother's calling," Hennessy says, and through the glass tablet, I can see her face flashing in the bottom corner of the screen.

"Okay, my mom's calling, so they probably know," I amend. "In fact, the Administrator's probably watching our livecast right now." I stop walking and look straight at the

336

camera. "Administrator, if you're watching, know this: if you want to take us out, you're going to have to do it live, in front of nearly a million—"

"One point two," Hennessy corrects.

"In front of one point two million viewers." I turn to spot the car, then continue walking backward toward it, still addressing the camera. "Guys, if we don't make it home tonight, it's because the Administrator—Amelia Locke—sent her clone soldiers after us. If that happens, I want you to call your local police. Call all of them. Tell them what happened here tonight. Make your voices heard, like I'm making mine heard right now. I should have done this a month ago, when I first found out. Don't wait like I did. Don't be scared like I was. *Speak out.* There's no change that can't be accomplished if enough people demand it."

We're at the car, so I open the door and climb in. Hennessy comes in after me, still filming. "Take us to the administration ward, please," I tell the driver. He relays the command to the car, and it takes off along the metallic cruise strip in the middle of the lane.

On the way, Hennessy aims my tablet out the window, giving the world its first look at the greater Lakeview grounds. At the small cluster of tall buildings, separated by acres of manicured lawns, lit up at night by a series of picturesque, old-fashioned light poles.

As we pull through the small gate dividing the training ward from the administration ward, we see soldiers jogging in formation toward the dormitory we've just left. "I wonder if they're looking for us?" I say aloud for the camera. But I don't wonder enough to ask them.

What would have taken us twenty minutes to walk takes only a few to drive. "This must be it," I say when the car pulls to a stop in front of a nondescript gray brick building. It's only a single story tall—not what I expected from a building where tens of thousands of babies are made every year under factory-like conditions.

"Thanks," I say to the driver as we get out of the car. Hennessy and I run toward the west side of the building, where Trigger told us the least-used entrance is. "Okay," I tell my viewers. "With any luck, you're about to meet our friends Trigger 17 and Dahlia 16. Though truthfully, you've already met Dahlia. You just don't know it yet—"

"Waverly!" Dahlia calls out in a whisper, and I whirl around, squinting into the dark to find her. She and Trigger step out of deeper shadows around the corner of the small building. "How'd it go?" Her eyes widen when she sees Hennessy. "Are you still streaming?"

"Yes. Everyone, this is Dahlia," I whisper for the camera. "Does she look familiar?"

"Hang on." Hennessy taps something on his side of the screen, and enough light emanates from my tablet to light up our faces. "Now they can see you."

"Turn that off!" Trigger snaps.

"It's okay," I say. "They've had a good look." Hennessy

turns off the light. "And you guys, what you're seeing is real. No effects in play here. Dahlia and I are identical. And there are four thousand, nine hundred ninety-nine other girls who look just like us at a 'transition' facility in Valleybrook, waiting to be sold. But we're not going to let that happen, are we?"

"I meant, turn the whole thing off," Trigger says. "It's time to finish this."

"Oh." I turn back to the camera as he bends to examine the scanner built into the lab's entrance. "Guys, I've gotta go. But remember what I said. Share this video with everyone you know. Forward it to your local police headquarters. And if we don't make it out of here tonight, raise hell on our behalves. I love you guys! And I hope to see you again. . . ."

Hennessy ends the stream and hands my tablet back to me. "Nearly one and a half million viewers by the end," he whispers. "I can't believe the connection lasted that long."

"That's only because they don't have many people trained to cut it off. Most people here don't even know the network exists." Trigger pops the cover off the scanner and uses the knife from his pocket to cut through two of the wires. The dead bolt disengages with a raspy sliding sound. "We're in. Let's end this."

THIRTY-TWO

DAHLIA

"I'm sure the Administrator was watching," Waverly whispers as we sneak down the dark, narrow back hallway of the genetics lab. "She's probably already got soldiers on their way."

"Then we better hurry," Trigger says.

We follow him in silence, and I search for a familiar landmark, but the tour my class took didn't include this part of the building.

"Are there a bunch of underground levels or something?" Hennessy whispers, and I turn to see him holding Waverly's hand as they follow us. "This doesn't look big enough to produce all the babies that must be born here every year."

"Embryos are produced here," I explain softly. "They don't take up much space. The *babies* are produced in the nursery, across town. In a very big building." I snort. "Did you actually think we were going to blow up a building full of babies?"

Hennessy shrugs, but looks embarrassed. "So what are we looking for, exactly?"

"Cold storage. The cache of DNA. It's a room at the back of the—" Trigger stops, and I nearly run into him. "That's it. But there's another scanner." He pulls his knife from his pocket again and in seconds, he has the door open. "If they really expected anyone to try this, they would have invented a better lock," he murmurs as he pulls the door open.

I pat him on the back. "Lucky for us, the city of Lakeview trusts its soldiers."

"Not for long," Waverly whispers as she and Hennessy follow us inside. "Holy crap . . ."

I second her astonishment.

Cold storage is smaller than I expected, and a lot . . . warmer. In fact, it's not cold at all. But it's kind of amazing.

The room is round with a tall ceiling, and except for the three other doors leading out, every inch of wall space is covered by a series of glass-doored refrigerated shelving units that curve along with the shape of the room. A rope of lights around the ceiling and the floor are the only illumination, and while it's enough to see by, the glow is a soft blue in color.

In the center of the room stands a long, narrow table divided into eight microscope stations, each furnished with a bunch of equipment I've never seen before and have no idea how to use.

"I thought it'd be bigger," Waverly says as she turns a slow circle, eyeing the refrigerators. Which are probably actually freezers.

"DNA doesn't take up much space," I remind her. "There are *millions* of genetic samples in here."

"What's the plan?" Hennessy asks.

Trigger sets his backpack on the end of the table and opens it. "Everyone take two. Stick them straight to the glass doors, and try to space them evenly."

"What is this?" Waverly asks as she pulls two gel-filled rings from the bag.

"Explosives." I reach into the bag and take the next two.

"Shit!" She holds hers away from her body, as if they might spontaneously blow her to bits.

Trigger huffs. "They're very stable." He pulls the two pen-like devices from the front pocket of the bag. "That's why we have detonators."

Hennessy presses one of his rings to the door of the nearest freezer unit, and it sticks on its own. "Awesome," he breathes. Then he moves down a few feet and places the second.

I follow his lead across the room, and Waverly stakes out a spot between us.

Trigger places the remaining four rings, then presses the end of one of the pens into the last one. He pushes the button on the end, and the tiny screen lights up.

"I'm setting a three-minute timer, so we're going to need to run. Dahlia, will you set off the alarm, so anyone working knows to get out?"

"Sure." I glance around the room, but find no obvious alarm switch. "How do I do that?"

He shrugs. "You can probably just smash one of the glass doors."

I grab a stool from the nearest microscope station. "Ready?" I ask. He nods. So I swing the stool as hard as I can at the closest freezer door.

The legs smash through with a loud crash. Glass flies everywhere.

Red lights flash from the ceiling and a high-pitched alarm skewers my brain.

Trigger smiles. Then he presses the button on the end of the pen again. It glows red, and a three-minute timer appears on the small screen. Seconds begin to count down. "Let's go!"

Waverly kicks off her shoes and we race for the open door, then skid to an awkward stop when someone steps into the doorway, blocking our path. It's a soldier, a few years older than Trigger. The name Ren 22 is embroidered over her left shoulder. "Stop right there!" She shouts to be heard over the alarm. She's aiming a gun at us.

Trigger calmly steps in front of me, and I stare at the soldier over his shoulder. "I've just activated a detonator in one of ten gel-pack charges," he calls in an even, clear voice. "This building is going to blow up in less than three minutes."

The soldier glances past him to where the pen is still blinking an angry red. "Turn it off," she commands.

"I can't do that," Trigger says. "And if you don't let us out of here, we are all going to die."

"I'm prepared to die for my city," Ren 22 declares. "Are you?"

"I was until I found out my city was a lie. Show her, Waverly."

"Don't move!" the soldier shouts again, shifting her aim.

"It's just a tablet!" I call out as Waverly slowly pulls it from her pocket. She taps on the screen to wake it up, then plays a video I've never seen before. In it, she and Hennessy are kissing in a field of flowers.

"What is that? *Where* is that?" the soldier demands. "Wait, aren't you . . . ? Weren't you recalled?"

"There's more." Waverly plays a video of her mother blowing out candles on a birthday cake. The crowd around her— all individuals—claps, and Dane Whitmore pulls her close for a kiss.

"Wh-what . . . ?" the soldier stutters.

"That's the real world," I tell her. "The world the Administrator hid from all of us. A world full of individuals, and parents, and houses. The Administrator *lied* to us for our *whole lives*. Let us go," I beg her. "Come with us, and this will all be over. We can all live in that world." Or what's left of it, now that we've shown them all what they've been doing.

"Now," Trigger says. "Or we're all going to die."

The soldier blinks. Then she turns around and runs.

We take off after her, racing through the hallway toward the door still standing open. All five of us burst into the night and keep running parallel with the street. Hearts and legs pumping as fast as they can.

I have just a second to register the long parade of headlights streaming toward us from the Defense Bureau when the world explodes at my back. Trigger throws me to the cold ground and lands on top of me, pinning me to the prickly grass. He shouts something—I can feel his breath on my neck—but I can't hear him. I can't hear anything.

I'm totally deaf.

I peek beneath his shoulder to see Waverly and Hennessy lying on the ground a few feet away. Bits of burning building fall all around us. A flaming bit of insulation lands in Waverly's hair and Hennessy slaps it to put out the fire. A smoldering hunk of metal lands to his left, and he rolls toward her, screaming silently.

I stare, my heart pounding, as the rain of fire slows to a few floating embers. And when Trigger stands and pulls me to my feet, there's nothing left behind us but the smoking husk of the genetics lab.

That, and a line of trucks, from which soldier after soldier is emerging.

They aim guns at us. They're shouting something, but I can't hear anything except the roar of my own pulse in my ears and a strange, high-pitched ringing.

Trigger shouts something at me, but I can't hear him

either. He raises his hands in the air, nodding for me to mimic him, so I do.

Another line of trucks races toward us from the west, led by a long black car. The Administrator must have called in every soldier at her disposal.

Terrified, I scoot closer to Trigger. In my peripheral vision, Hennessy has his arms around Waverly, his back to the soldiers. He's shielding her with his body, and they can't hear the orders being shouted at them either. In the flickering light from the burning building, I can see that her wedding dress is covered in grass stains and dirt.

The flash of light in her hand tells me she's livecasting again.

If the Administrator is going to kill us, she's going to do it in front of a live audience.

A woman gets out of the long black car stationed at the front of the line of trucks. She's wearing a calf-length white coat and her dark hair is twisted into a severe updo. I've never seen her in person, but I would recognize the Administrator anywhere.

She motions toward us, and the soldiers start forward, shouting more orders we can't hear. Aiming rifles at us.

I'm breathing too hard. Too fast. The world is starting to look hazy.

Then the new line of troop trucks arrives. The first one stops in the middle of the street. A door in the back of it rolls up, and more soldiers pour out. They have rifles too, but they're wearing a different uniform. They point their guns at . . . the Administrator.

What? Have her troops rebelled? Did they somehow see Waverly's livecast?

A man and a woman get out of the car in front of the first truck. The woman runs toward us, and my ears pop just in time for me to hear her shout for Waverly, though her shout sounds more like a whisper.

It's Lorna Whitmore. Dane is behind her, yelling at the Administrator. Waving his fist in her face, his cheeks bright red with fury.

The new soldiers fan out around him, pointing rifle after rifle at the Administrator and her troops. They're from Mountainside. They're not here to arrest us.

They're here to save us.

Trigger pulls me into a hug. "It's over!" he shouts into my ear, holding me so tightly I can hardly breathe. "We're free, Dahlia!"

But I can't let myself believe that until I see the Mountainside soldiers force the Administrator back into her car at gunpoint. Until I see them confiscating guns from her troops. Until Lorna Whitmore begins to herd all four of us toward the safety of her car, and the shield of her stature and her credits and her influence.

Until I see that she is mad—she looks *furious*—but she understands that Waverly's livecast has tied her hands as surely as it tied the Administrator's. Lorna can't get rid of me now. She can't hide my identicals from the world. And she can no longer deny that I ever existed.

Screw Lorna Whitmore.

The world has seen me. The world knows my face and my name.

I am here to stay.

EPILOGUE

DAHLIA

"Please stop pacing," Waverly groans from her seat on the dormitory steps. "You're going to wear out the grass."

"I can't help it. He's late."

"He's not late," she insists with a glance at her tablet. "He's just not here yet."

But this doesn't mean to her what it means to me. She doesn't understand, and despite the fact that we share DNA— that we're friends now—she probably never will.

"Leave Dahlia alone," Margo says without looking up from her tablet. "She's earned a little impatience." Margo has taken the whole thing surprisingly well. Maybe because diving in to volunteer at Lakeview has brought her a ton of good press. But maybe because she's actually not a bad person.

I know. I was surprised too.

"Have either of you heard from Sofia?" I ask as I sink onto the steps next to my identical.

Waverly shakes her head. "She and Seren are still out of the country and totally off the grid. They're not answering messages. This is hard for them." She shrugs. "I mean, they lost their legacy, not to mention their home. And their mother was utterly humiliated live on camera. They might need a little quiet time."

That's understandable. And while I know they can't be held responsible for what their mother did, it's hard for me to feel very sorry for them, considering that they're still *unreasonably* wealthy. At least until the court rules on damages awarded to the hundreds of thousands of clones who haven't yet gone into organ failure at a premature age.

But Waverly says that court case could take years because first the clones have to be declared actual people, with rights, before they can sue for damages.

I find it bizarre that the fact that clones are people is something everyone in the world acknowledges now—some more readily than others—but they aren't considered *formally* real until a panel of people in white robes writes it down in some official record. But that day's coming fast, thanks to the Whitmores' lawyers. Because it turns out Waverly's marriage isn't legally binding until she's declared not just a citizen, but an actual person, and they're pushing for speed from the judiciary. They're pushing *hard*, because until someone develops a gene therapy to extend her life, she's still facing a miserable death at a young age, and her parents are not willing to let that happen without a fight.

Neither is Hennessy.

Waverly pushes up her sleeve and scratches absently at her tattoo. It's new enough that it still itches, though her skin has healed, and she's always staring at it with this oddly endearing smile. That tattoo symbolizes her bond with Hennessy, even more than her wedding rings do, because she got it a month after our broadcast. After the world found out she was a clone, and nearly half of her followers turned into vicious "trolls" determined to make her feel less than human. After she gave up her show, under pressure from the network for a civil end to their partnership. After Hennessy stood by her side, with his parents' lukewarm support.

Waverly's parents . . . They understand what we did and why, but I think they secretly blame me for most of the fallout. Not-so-secretly, in Lorna's case.

Not that it matters. Legally recognized or not, Waverly is married. She and Hennessy have a house of their own in Mountainside, and they've insisted that Julienne 20 and I stay with them. As guests. It's not a permanent solution, but I've been happy to accept so far, if for no other reason than to drive Lorna nuts.

I still hate her, but Dane is growing on me.

"Hey," Hennessy says as he comes out the front door of the dormitory. "Still not here? He's late."

"I told you," I tell Waverly, and she sticks her tongue out at me.

Hennessy glances out across the common lawn and smiles. "It's still so weird to see them all holding tablets."

I follow his gaze to the class of year-thirteen mechanics sitting in a cluster on the grass, in spite of the cold breeze, scrolling and tapping on the tablets DigiCore donated to every Lakeview resident over the age of twelve. They've learned the technology very quickly, but they still use it differently than Waverly, Margo, and their friends do. The clones laugh and talk and point to things on each other's tablets. They explore the network as if it were a team sport, instead of living in their own private tech bubbles, as most individuals do.

"What's really weird is seeing them in mismatched clothing," I say. Margo's parents donated those from one of their clothing factories, and when Network 4 heard that she was here personally distributing the garments, they offered her a contract to star in the first show ever shot on the Lakeview grounds. She'll have to live in the dorm for six weeks while it films, under the same circumstances as the clones, but she seems to be thinking of that as some kind of intrepid adventure.

I don't think she'll make it a week without her wall screen.

"Margo! Waverly! Dahlia!" A gaggle of little girls with dark pigtails spots us and comes running. Their instructor laughs while they surround us with eager little hands pulling at our clothes and a barrage of questions about when they can have tablets.

The little ones have adjusted amazingly well to the changes in Lakeview in the months since our broadcast and the Administrator's arrest. They're too young to really understand how badly they were betrayed, or what their fate would have been if none of that had happened. But many of the year sixteens and seventeens are . . . bitter. Confused. They thought they were about to graduate and start adult lives in a world that never really existed.

Instead, they're in a strange kind of limbo, waiting to hear how the world will decide to embrace and care for hundreds of thousands of orphans with unique medical needs. Their new access to the network lets them see what the world thinks of them—both the good and the bad—and that's a lot to take in for kids who didn't even know a couple of months ago that the rest of the world existed.

But watching the young ones gives me hope. They could truly be okay, especially if hormone and gene therapy find success while they're still small. Before the hormone deficiency has a chance to affect them.

Waverly answers their questions with a sad smile. She understands the same things I do—that their chances of a long, happy life are much greater than her own. And I think that's the real reason Seren and Sofia haven't come back. They can't face her, knowing that every credit in their accounts was put there by the system that robbed her of everything she should have had.

The system that made sure she will die in ten short years. Whether or not she has children to leave behind.

"Come on, girls, we're going to be late for lunch!" The instructor rounds up her charges and herds them into the building with a grateful smile for us. We've become celebrities here just like Waverly and Hennessy are everywhere else. Even if their celebrity out there feels a bit more like notoriety now that the world is changing again.

The birth of a new world order can't come without labor pains. A lot of people are angry at the loss of their servants. At the extra expense of hiring citizens for an actual salary and paying back-wages to the clones they've abused for years. But they'll adjust. Eventually.

Right?

I have to believe that human decency will prevail. That the world is better than this. That faced with the evidence of injustice, deep down they will all want to make it right.

Waverly says I'm being naive. But I like to call it hope.

"There they are." She stands, shading her eyes with one hand, and I follow her gaze to find a long line of troop transport trucks rolling down the street, following the cruise strip in the middle of the right-hand lane. They're still small from this distance, but she's right.

They're here.

My heart leaps into my throat. Adrenaline races through my veins so suddenly that I feel like I have to run to burn energy or I'll lose my mind.

So I run.

I take off down the sidewalk and veer toward the road bisecting the common lawn, heading toward the truck in the lead. I run until I'm breathing hard and I'm starting to sweat, in spite of the cold.

I run until I can see the face of the man next to the driver in that first vehicle.

The first truck pulls to a stop next to me and Trigger 17 gets out. He races around the front of the vehicle and pulls me into a hug, lifting me from the ground with the power of his greeting. "I missed you," he says into my ear. But I can't return the sentiment, because my mouth is busy kissing him.

He's only been gone a few days, but it's felt like a lifetime.

"You ready?" he asks as he finally puts me down, and I nod, my hands shaking. Trigger gives a signal to the man in the truck, and he says something to the dashboard.

A door at the back of the truck swings open. When the driver behind him sees that, he opens the back of his truck, and the message works its way down the long, long line of vehicles.

A girl climbs down from the inside of the first truck and stands in the road, blinking against the sun. She has long brown hair, pale, freckle-less skin, and brown eyes. Just like mine.

"I told you I'd bring them back to you." Trigger lets go of me and gestures toward the girl as another climbs down from the truck behind her. Then another. And another. And another.

Girls are getting out of all the trucks and there are already hundreds of them in the road, milling slowly toward the grass. Toward the common lawn they've known since they were old enough to walk. They look stunned. Confused. Relieved.

Awake.

The first girl's gaze finds me. She covers her mouth with both hands, her eyes going wide. Then she grabs the hand of the girl next to her. That girl grabs another hand, and they race toward me.

I meet them halfway, my eyes full of tears.

"Dahlia!"

Trigger made sure my roommates would be in the first truck.

I throw my arms open and nearly bowl Poppy over when I hug her. Sorrel and Violet pile onto the embrace until we're a tangle of identical arms and sobbing, laughing faces. We're stuck like that forever, saying nothing that any of us will remember in the first moments of this emotional reunion. But they're things that need to be said. Things that need to be heard.

"Okay." I wipe tears from my face when they finally let me go. "I want you to meet someone." I turn to see that Margo, Hennessy, and Waverly have joined Trigger on the lawn. They're watching us, and Waverly's eyes are huge.

Now she understands. *Now* this is real for her.

I wave her forward, and she comes slowly. Staring.

"Guys, this is Waverly Whitmore, our long-lost identical. She helped me do all this. And she's superweird because she has parents, and about a thousand pairs of shoes. But she's one of us. So say hi."

Instead, Poppy pulls her into a hug. The others pile on, and Waverly starts crying as she clings to them.

And for the first time in our lives, we are finally all together. We are finally whole.

ACKNOWLEDGMENTS

As always, I am thankful to my husband, my son, and my daughter, who put up with me during overlapping deadlines and answer all sorts of odd questions in the name of research.

Thanks to Rinda Elliott and Jennifer Lynn Barnes, for ideas at every stage of the process.

And thanks, of course, to my editor, Wendy Loggia, and to my agent, Merrilee Heifetz, who turn my passion into a career.

ABOUT THE AUTHOR

Rachel Vincent is the *New York Times* bestselling author of numerous novels for teens, including *Brave New Girl*, *100 Hours*, *The Stars Never Rise*, and *The Flame Never Dies*. She lives with her family in Oklahoma.

RachelVincent.com
Follow Rachel Vincent on ▪ ▣ ▸